Praise for

What Came Before

What Came Before is a remarkable achievement — a smart, fast-paced mystery that asks important questions about identity, family, and race. And, like the best of its genre, it's loaded with puzzles: What really happened on the day Abbie Palmer's mother killed herself? Who is the mysterious woman who shows up on Abbie's doorstep, and why would anyone want her dead? Gay Degani's prose is at all times lucid and compelling, and her exciting story will keep you glued to your chair.

~ Clifford Garstang, winner of the 2013 Library of Virginia Award for Fiction for *What the Zhang Boys Know*

A woman, who lost her Hollywood starlet mother to suicide when she was a small child, finds herself embroiled in the murder mystery of a half-sister she never knew she had. Determined to find answers and with her now motherless niece in her charge, she embarks on her own investigation and finds herself drawn ever deeper into danger. Fast-paced and sharply written, with unforgettable characters, this novel by Gay Degani will grab hold and not let go. A terrific read!

~ Kathy Fish, author of *Wild Life* and *Together We Can Bury It*

Abbie Palmer has left her husband and home, albeit temporarily, to find herself, again. And then, a piece of paper slipped under the door. A burnt house. A dead woman. A young girl who has lost her mother... Abbie Palmer's world turns upside down, inside out, and dangerous. Written like a thriller, this novel, which is one woman's emotional journey, her quest to learn the truth about herself, takes the reader swiftly through tightly bound, flash-fiction-sized chapters. Gay Degani's prose is vividly paced, something that I have come to recognise as her personal style, having read her short fiction before. The story unfolds rapidly, and yet manages to convey the sights, sounds and smells of the narrative clearly. I can't think of an afternoon spent so energetically without moving an inch from my armchair!

~ RK Biswas, author of *Culling Mynahs and Crows*

With engaging characters and a compelling mystery, Gay Degani's *What Came Before* draws you in and doesn't let go. If this had been a movie, I wouldn't have left the cinema for more popcorn. A brilliant and complex whodunit with a memorable, imperfect character at its helm.

~ Christopher Allen, author of *Conversations with S. Teri O'Type (a Satire)*

Part murder mystery, part family saga, Gay Degani's *What Came Before* is an exciting debut not to be missed!

~ Robert Swartwood, USA TODAY bestselling author of *The Serial Killer's Wife* and *Man of Wax*

Gay Degani beautifully combines suspense in her debut novel *What Came Before* with a love for language usually reserved for literary tales. Within two pages, Degani abducts the reader for a wonderful ride into Abbie Palmer's life: a stranger who can't possibly be related knocks on her front door and says, "Your mother is my mother." Soon we're racing through Hollywood, trying to track down a certain 'Palm Springs Bikini Girl' who died in the fifties, and without an extra word anywhere from this flash fiction expert, run into adultery, racial predicaments, and scheming new wives. Do not sit down to read this with only a few minutes. You won't want to put this stunner down.

~ Bonnie ZoBell, author of *What Happened Here* and *The Whack-Job Girls*

Five words scribbled on a discarded piece of paper ignite old memories for Abbie Palmer and leads to the explosive uncovering of a fifty-year-old mystery, as surely as a sizzling fuse running to a stick of dynamite. *What Came Before*, Gay Degani's debut novel rumbles along at break-neck speed. I've long enjoyed the quirky characters and tightly-written plots of Ms. Degani's short stories and her novel didn't disappoint me. The book presents great characters, including a strong older-female protagonist, and ably-managed twists and turns through the streets and people of modern-day Los Angeles, as well as the L.A. of fifty years ago. Old-school suspense at its best.

~ K.C. Ball, winner of the 2012 Speculative Fiction Foundation Older Writers Grant and author of *Lifting Up Veronica*

Like Abbie Palmer, the Twinkie-eating, Ativan-popping, bewildered protagonist, the reader is drawn into a swirling journey of unexpected deaths, unknown relatives, and old secrets. Degani's absorbing debut novel unfolds hazy memories and reveals the buried facts of a generation where society-shocking truths were kept well-hidden.

~ Stefanie Freele, author of *Feeding Strays* and *Surrounded By Water*

Hollywood movie starlets. Murder. Arson. Half-sisters and half-truths. *What Came Before* is a fast-paced murder mystery set in the heart and spirit of L.A. Though issues of class, race and politics hover in the air, the book focuses on character and story. Gay Degani is a skillful storyteller, and her character Abbie is full of enough spunk and gumption to have you rooting for her from page one. At once humorous and heartfelt, *What Came Before* also keeps you turning pages, eager to uncover more of the story.

~ Tara Laskowski, author of *Modern Manners for Your Inner Demons* and senior editor at *SmokeLong Quarterly*

WHAT CAME BEFORE

GAY DEGANI

TRUTH SERUM PRESS

Dedication

You know who you are.

Second edition published by Truth Serum Press, August 2016

ISBN: 978-1-925536-05-8

Cover photograph copyright © Hillary Degani 2011
Author photograph copyright © Rachael Wareki 2016
Cover design by Matt Potter

Also available as an eBook / ISBN: 978-1-925536-06-5

TRUTH SERUM PRESS

Truth Serum Press
4 Warburton Street
Magill SA 5072
Australia

Email: truthserumpress@live.com.au
Website: http://truthserumpress.net
Truth Serum Press catalogue: http://truthserumpress.net/catalogue/

Contents

•◇•

Author's Note
Research & Acknowledgments
About the Author

Prelude

What binds two people together? Lips? Fingertips? Ropes? Chains? Sometimes memory is the strongest tie.

The old man remembers her in patches of clarity, like catching a shimmer of an aquamarine sky behind tattered clouds. Her eyes were that color. He lifts his hand, ready to place it gently on her hair, stroke her milky skin with his thumb, but she's not there. He sighs and turns over on the chaise lounge, grips the knife-edge of the weatherproof cushion.

He remembers sitting on the bank of the little creek, feet squishing in mud, hers now as black as his. She studied the brown hills that sheltered their valley and confessed she grew up in Iowa even though her official biography put her in Minnesota.

"Why lie?" he'd asked.

She picked at the weeds under her bare legs. "Why not?"

"But no lying to me, right?" He rolled toward her, hand pressing her back, nestling against her, his skin hot as the sun.

"Not to you," she said, and kissed him. "You have no idea what it's like growing up in a small farm town, sleeping in the attic on an iron bed."

"All by yourself, baby-girl, alone in that bed?"

She put her arms round his neck, pulled him close, whispered, "Did your father drink?"

"That's something I don't know about, honey," he pulled back and looked at her. "He didn't stick around long enough for me to find out."

"Poor you." She ran her finger across his lips and into

his mouth. "Well, my father drank."

"Poor you," he said.

The old man wakes, memory warming his body. He'd heard the story a thousand times before, but her voice thrilled him then, and that voice whispers to him now, "It was my mother who betrayed me, you know? Can you believe anyone's mother would do that?"

He feels her sweet breath on his ear. He tries to answer, but she interrupts. "She told my father I was going to run away and you know what he did? He beat me. Like that was going to convince me to stay. It took two weeks for the bruises to heal and then no one could stop me. There was this boy – his name was Kenny – a scrawny little guy, but sweet, who'd always had a crush on me."

It came from her – those ragged bits of truth – at odd moments, over coffee, in the car, when she suddenly turned away from him after making love. The old man drowses again. It's his age and his medication that does this, renders him useless, keeps him in a state of suspension between the past and the present.

A desert wind caresses his skin and his eyes flick open. His backyard, his swimming pool, he has so much and yet, nothing at all. Her voice comes to him again on the breeze. "I asked Kenny to take me to Chicago, and he said yes."

"Of course he did," the old man says to the air. "I would've taken you to the moon."

The first time he'd said those words, she'd smiled at him and he smiles now, remembering how her expression softened. That boy had been her savior. He'd driven like crazy to get them to Chicago, but when she'd spied a diner off the highway, she told that fool she had to use the restroom.

The old man hears her voice again. "He asked if I didn't wanna wait till we got to the hotel because I'd shown him my wad of money and promised him clean sheets and room service and a night he'd never forget. No way did he want to stop at some greasy diner, but I just said, 'You don't want me to pee on your dad's upholstery, do you?'"

The old man says out loud, "You didn't say that."

The voice on the air answers, "I did, but when Kenny turned into the parking lot, I leaned over and gave him a big open-mouthed kiss, and told him I was hungry. That was the first time I felt bad about what I was doing. He looked so unsure of himself. I don't think he ever believed I would let him ravish me, but he wanted to keep me happy. I can still smell that diner.

"The place was busy, filled with men in plaid shirts and sunburned arms. I studied them over the top of my menu until I spied this short little guy with droopy brown eyes. I asked Kenny to order me some pancakes. My treat. He gave me this anxious look. 'Ladies' room,' I reminded him. He blushed and I felt bad, but it couldn't be helped.

"Outside, the trucker was standing on the step of his cab, kind of swinging there, waiting for me. He was going west, so I went west. When he dropped me off at a Laundromat with a roll of quarters and two weeks of dirty t-shirts in Reno, I dumped his clothes in a trashcan, stuck his coins in my purse, and hopped on a Greyhound to L.A."

The old man startles awake. Someone is calling him. Is it her? Where did she go?

Chapter 1
Stranger

Sunday, May 19, 2002

Back in 1954, reporters and camera guys were at the bungalow before the cop cars cooled down. Like radio's landmark coverage of the failed rescue of Kathy Fiscus from the bottom of a well, my mother's suicide became a media first. Images from her Hollywood lifestyle and tragic death flickered across American television screens for hours. She was the beautiful starlet who'd scandalized decent folks by appearing on the cover of *Life* magazine in a bikini, then shocked them by taking her own life while her daughter slept in the next room. Speculation was rampant. Why had she done it? How would this affect her movie star husband? And most of all, who had rescued the child?

I don't think much about my mother anymore, almost never dream about her, but when I do, she's sitting in a scratchy red chair, its textured pattern swirling into roses. I'm on her bony lap, maybe three years old, my fingers tracing the maze along the chair's upholstered arm. Her hands hang empty over the sides. Sometimes I feel a sigh riffle my hair.

It's all in my dream: the sky darkening outside the bungalow, the prickle of the chair against my arm, the smell of Maxwell House coffee on my mother's breath, the scene morphing into my front porch, a stranger in a black linen suit, a slammed door, the scrawled note, the gray floorboards beneath my feet turning to muck. I can't run. Can't breathe. Dry kernels blow through my lips.

I wake up sweating, legs tangled in sheets, eyes gritty, mouth dry, my brain jammed together like frozen broccoli. I rattle my head and the nightmare dissipates, leaving me alone in my bed at the Tiki Palms.

It was 94 degrees in our Hollywood bungalow when my mother opened the door to our O'Keefe and Merritt oven, turned on the gas, and stuck in her head. If she'd had a car, she could've driven down Sunset Boulevard through cooling hills and walked into the ocean. Maybe then she would've changed her mind. I was four.

Reporters still remember my mother's suicide, so when the stranger in the black linen suit showed up yesterday afternoon, I thought she was from *Access Hollywood* or some docudrama like *Sex Kitten Suicide*, and told her to get the hell off my porch.

Even in this morning's dim light, I can see the stranger's phone number leaching through the gasoline receipt on my nightstand, the one she left wedged between the knob and doorframe. I roll over. Give the scrap of paper my back.

If I'd only used the coin-operated washing machine here at the apartment instead of using the Maytag at my house, the woman wouldn't have found me.

Stop. Focus on today. Grocery store, essays, this afternoon's ceramics class, the feel of clay between my fingers. A shower. Get back to normal. My new normal now that I'm "on leave" from my husband to – do what? Find myself? Oh, God.

I glance at the clock – 8:15 – and flop on my back, let yesterday unreel itself against my eyelids: Phoenix was barking in the side yard. Me in sloppy sweats, grabbing wet clothes from the washer, suddenly interested in escape, not dry socks, I slammed out the front door of my house where I should be living, but don't. And then the slip of paper floated from the doorjamb onto the porch, settling, thin and persistent, at my feet.

I duck under the blanket. Shiver. Throw it off and sit up, put my feet on the floor, drop my head in my hands. Let myself remember what happened next: Stumbling upstairs to my closet, I pulled the step-stool up against my abandoned clothes. From high on a shelf, I grabbed a plastic container full of memorabilia, but it was heavier than I thought, jerking itself out of my hands, hitting the floor on its corner, breaking apart.

I tossed the junk back into the box: a broken-leather poetry book, drawings, report cards, and from my mother, a handkerchief, her crystal bracelet. Then I spied the photograph tumbled against my tennis shoes.

I reached for the stained rectangle of board, a washed-out 'Lorenzo of Hollywood' stamped on the back, and on the front, me and my mother together in that chair, just as we are in my dream.

Enough. I wrench myself out of bed, teeth aching from last night's pancakes, heavy on the maple syrup. I'll purge today, drink plenty of liquids. No coffee, just tea. Green tea. Broth. And lots of water. I won't go out. I'll write a story. Go to a museum.

The bathroom mirror reveals two crescent-shaped cuts along my hairline. I thought I was done digging into my skin at night. I grip my toothbrush, but can't resist my reflection. A brown-eyed, plainer version of my mother stares back. I have her nose, her long smooth jaw, her strawberry blond hair. But I don't have her aqua eyes, and I don't have her freckles.

In the living room, I snatch the lid from the plastic box I brought with me from home yesterday afternoon and pull out the photograph. My profile tilts toward my mother's face, but she's looking beyond me into the distance, an expectant angle to her head as if she's waiting for someone. Someone other than me.

I have to call her, that woman in the black linen suit.

In the bedroom, I smooth out the gas receipt where she'd written her name and number, then pick up the phone and dial. After the first ring, I almost hang up, but the five devastating words the stranger scrawled beneath those seven digits stop me: *Your mother is my mother.*

What can I say to her? "Your freckles don't mean a damn thing?" Because, after all, that stranger who left this note on the porch, curled between the door and the jamb, this Olita Jordan who claims to be my sister, is African-American, and I'm not.

Chapter 2
Cops

My mother is your mother. This is my mantra as I wait. The unanswered ringing of the stranger's phone finally penetrates my swampy brain. I tap the off button. Redial. Same area code as mine. So my hypothetical African-American half-sister lives nearby. How weird is that?

Forget it. She's a wily paparazzi chick angling for a story, and after years of talking to shrinks about my mother's suicide, the last thing I want to do is dredge it up.

Yet a thread of adrenaline runs through me. When I was young, all I wanted to do was track down everything I could about my mother, but eventually I buried that desire inside a tiny fold in my brain. Now this stranger shows up, dragging with her the possible answer to my one real question: Why wasn't I good enough to keep my mother alive?

Really? That's what I think?

I click off the phone, toss it on my messy bed, and hurry into the living room where I scrutinize the picture of my mother and me. Who is she looking for? And why isn't she turning toward me, her only daughter?

I type Olita Jordan's telephone number into Google and drum my fingers on the table until her name pops up and yes, her address too. 995 Marion Drive. I hit the map link, feeling a little stunned that it's so easy.

But this kind of surprise has happened before. When I was eleven, I found a *Silver Screen* magazine at a garage sale in a bin with vinyl records warping under hot sun. I thumbed through it without much hope, but there she was, my mother, Virginia Gifford, her face tucked coyly into her shoulder, light shining off her hair. Such long lashes. The article said she'd been signed by producer Jerome Tallman to shoot a motion picture, but she had to beg off at the last minute, claiming illness. I paid the lady at the garage sale a nickel and took the magazine home.

Then another memory smacks me down. My father was sleeping on the orange sectional in our Hollywood Hills house, a half-empty bottle of bourbon on the floor. I quietly closed the front door. Tiptoed toward the hallway. I was thirteen, wearing the blue-and-black plaid of Catholic school, my skirt above my knee, rolled at the waist. He must have heard me because he turned over, his eyes like hard glass, and growled, "Those sticks you call legs, don't you dare try to be like her." Then he grabbed the back of the sofa and twisted away.

I crept down the dark hall to my room. At the door, I froze. My only refuge had been torn apart. Drawers bulged from their sockets. Clothes were heaped over scattered shoes, underwear, books. The mattress tilted sideways across the bedframe, its sheets like white flags. The magazines, the photos, the scrapbook I'd pasted together by flashlight – almost everything I'd squirreled away about my mother – had been ripped apart and strewn across the floor.

I'm shivering now, my Tiki Palms apartment suddenly cold. I'd forgotten this incident. I've forgotten so much. Maybe this is why, at fifty-three, I've walked out on my husband, leaving him shocked, my daughter furious, my son unaware in Brazil, and my friends bewildered.

And where does that leave me? Thrashing around in the muck, needing an Ativan. I take one.

•◊•

This is crazy. I'm cruising Sierra Madre Boulevard still wearing my faded sweatpants and a Cal pullover – a drip of syrup smack in the middle of the 'a'. And there it is, Marion Drive, Olita Jordan's street. I slip between two cars to make the turn, an idiot thing to do, ignoring the horn blast from the guy I cut off.

Something is happening inside this neighborhood. Police cars, fire engines, and television vans cram the asphalt while uniformed officers stand behind yellow crime tape. Knots of people watch and wait. Above the jacarandas, smoke smudges the sky.

This is more than I bargained for. I shift into reverse, but there's a car behind me, and the cop who's manning the roadblock signals me to wait.

He comes toward me, clipboard in hand, and I roll down my window to the acrid smell of burnt stucco and wood, the commotion of firemen, police, and gawking neighbors.

"You live here, ma'am?" the officer asks.

"No. I —" How do I explain my unhinged impulse to track down this woman? "I came to see — a friend."

"Your friend lives on this street?"

Nerves short-circuit my brain. I can't think of anything to say, so I surrender my downloaded computer map and the gasoline receipt with its cryptic message, the one the stranger left on my porch yesterday.

He studies both, then glances up, surprise on his face. "It's signed Olita Jordan."

"Yes. That's — she's my friend."

"What does this note mean, *Your mother is my mother?*" He holds it up, as if I haven't read it a hundred times already.

"I don't know." The little half-moons of dirt under my fingernails beg for attention.

"You don't know? Your name, please."

"My name?" If I can remember it. "Abbie. Abbie Palmer."

"You have identification, Ms. Palmer?"

I rummage for my wallet, hand him my driver's license. The officer affixes it to his clipboard. Points to the curb. "Please pull over and wait."

"This is a mistake —" I say, but he's striding away,

21

pausing only to do – what? Jot down my license plate number? Shit. Shit. Shit.

I draw up to a tan Crown Victoria wearing its red strobe like a monkey's cocked hat. Ashes swirl through my open window. I sneeze and look around.

Hovering husbands and wives – some in pjs, others dressed for church – whisper in sets of twos and threes while small children race and tumble on the grass. The homes on this street are California ranch, small and tidy, their flower beds blooming with impatiens.

Except for one.

Chapter 3
Blame

The house cowers in the curve of the road, set back a little, charred, smoky, but with no visible flames, firefighters having won the siege. I glance at the address on the porch to my right, its numbers nailed vertically down a white post. I calculate. Same side of the street. Four houses up. These fragments of information shift into focus, like a clean white cloud turns into an alligator: the wreck of a house is hers. Olita Jordan's. The stranger from my porch.

Sun burns through the smoky haze. Hot and unsteady, I stumble from my car.

"Mrs. Palmer?" The voice comes from somewhere on my left. I whip around. The cop who'd taken my driver's license leads a man and a woman toward me. They're not in uniform, but I've seen enough *NYPD Blue* to understand they're cops too. I wish I'd taken my time waking up this morning. Not rushed out without thinking. Not rushed out at all. I breathe in ash.

The uniformed policeman moves away to reclaim traffic duty. The other man, obviously the one in charge, has high cheekbones, walnut skin, and intelligent eyes under bushy brows. Sweat beads his forehead; a sport coat drapes his arm. He says, "I'm Detective Warren Fuji and this is Detective Laura Tellez."

The woman next to Fuji is small with startling two-toned hair, chocolate brown with streaks of platinum blond. Her white blazer and trim black jeans, though, are pristine. I finger-comb my unwashed hair. Run my tongue along furry teeth.

I imagine myself doing laundry yesterday morning, feeding coins into the cranky old washing machine at the Tiki Palms instead of at the Woodbine house where Olita found me, or better, at my ceramics class this afternoon, my hands slick with clay —

An angry screech of brakes causes us to turn in one synchronized movement as an SUV shrieks to a stop in the middle of the street. The driver's door bursts open and a black man leaps out, racing toward the ravaged house. Without a backward glance, the two cops sprint after him.

Neighbors crowd in, advancing like zombies, necks craned. Something bumps my leg, shooting me with adrenaline. It's a dog, a mutt to be exact. He's leashed to one of two old men.

A fierce keening slices the air, slices through me. I push ahead.

At the smoldering front door, three firemen hold the man from the SUV in suspension, like a puppet, all meaningless movement. Then he collapses to his knees. Detective Fuji is there, a hand to his shoulder.

The day, unwinding until now at lightning speed, slams to a stop. Something more than a house up in flames has happened. Something far worse.

"They must be in there, don't you know?" The old man with the mutt has the popped capillary look of an alcoholic.

"They'd been warned, hadn't they, that word spray-painted on the sidewalk," says the other old guy, eyes shining with excitement. He has a dog too, a terrier as short and wiry as himself. "You can't go alienating people, even your own kind, and not pay for it. Besides I saw the car, didn't I?"

"What word?" I ask. "What car?"

"You know, racial stuff."

"The N-word." They speak at the same time, then look me up and down. One of the dogs sits on my foot, but I don't know which one.

The red-nosed guy says, "Arthur here thinks he saw the car."

"I did see the car," snaps the other man.

"You saw a car, not the car. You don't know if you saw the car."

I cover my ears. This has nothing to do with me. The swamp is sucking me down. I shove through the crowd and back to my Suburban.

I'm turning the ignition when the female detective – Tellez? – opens the car door, says, "You all right?"

"I have to go."

"Please, Mrs. Palmer. Just a few questions."

Clutching the steering wheel, I take a breath and blurt out what I don't want to know, "Is anyone hurt?"

"Come with me, Mrs. Palmer," she says, stepping aside so I can climb out of the truck. My eyes sting.

She gestures for me to follow her around the curve, past the house where firemen continue to work. The police are busy too, some in a tight group on the driveway while others canvass the crowd. The uniforms keep order.

An ambulance sits along the curb, its back doors spread like wings. Settled on the bumper is the man from the SUV, his face buried in his hands.

Detective Fuji strides toward me, says, "How're you holding up?"

"Me?"

"The patrolman told me you're Olita Jordan's sister?"

"No. I – I don't know. She came to my house yesterday and left a note. She's okay, right?"

"You saw her yesterday? When was that?" Fuji flicks a glance at Tellez. Then a voice comes on fast, so close, I jump. "It's your fault."

The black man is no longer at the ambulance. He's right here. Next to me. Jabbing a thick finger in my face. "You."

I jerk away, frightened.

Fuji steps between us. "Mr. Bethune."

Over the detective's shoulder, the man's eyes burn. "I blame you."

Me?

25

I gape at his cracked lips, a dot of white foam in one corner. I'm speechless, and yet somehow detached. His tirade, Tellez's shout, Fuji's raised voice, the approach of uniformed cops. These sounds come to me through layers of gauze. Only the word "blame" slips into my ear like a worm.

Then Bethune falters, his face going slack. He allows Fuji to escort him away.

"Mrs. Palmer?" Detective Tellez, at my elbow.

The words out of my mouth are barely audible, even to me. "Olita Jordan... she's dead, isn't she?"

Chapter 4
Detective

Detective Laura Tellez leaves me in an interrogation room straight out of *Law and Order*: metal table, metal chairs, green walls, acoustic tiles on the ceiling. And I'm still waiting for the Starbucks coffee she promised when she "invited" me downtown. I'm not under arrest. I can go home any time – they have a few questions – but they'll be disappointed because I don't have any answers.

I can't believe any of this. Most of all, I can't believe the woman who wrote the words *Your mother is my mother* is dead. Dead!

My eyes still burn from the smoke. A familiar pain settles somewhere between my neck and shoulders. I dig in with fingers, kneading hard.

Tellez strides in with a mug of coffee, steam curling off the top, and a manila folder tucked under her arm. I straighten. Shake the webs from my head.

"Sorry it took so long." Her voice isn't as friendly as her words. She sets a small black tape recorder between us. If something mechanical can look like an accusation, this is it. She reads my face. "Standard procedure. You ready?"

I nod, take a gulp of hot coffee. She presses the record button. The formal sound of my name, the date and time from the detective's lips is almost tolerable – as long as no one pries the coffee mug away from me.

"So," I manage to say, "how – how did the fire start?"

Tellez ignores my question. "I've been meaning to ask you about the scratches on your forehead. How did they happen?"

"What?" My hand flies to the three nail marks below my hairline. Night-digging. "I woke up with them. It happens sometimes when I'm upset. She – Olita – her note, what she was trying to tell me. I don't believe it's possible, what she said, but —"

Tellez stretches back. "Okay. Let's start with yesterday, your meeting with Olita Jordan."

"It wasn't a meeting. No matter what that man out there seemed to think."

"You don't know Turner Bethune? Even though he seems to know you?"

I shake my head.

"You need to speak up." Tellez nods toward the tape recorder.

"I don't know Turner Bethune. I don't know Olita Jordan, and I have no idea how they know me."

"You didn't know your mother had another child?"

"If my mother had another child, I never knew."

"Tell me exactly what happened yesterday."

I shut my eyes and picture myself folding clothes in the laundry room of my house. I tell Detective Tellez how when the doorbell rang, I was startled, thinking it might be my husband, coming in early from golf, but I knew he'd use his key. "I thought she was a Jehovah's Witness."

"Jehovah's Witness? Why'd you think that?"

"You know, she was dressed up, nice suit, heels. I was annoyed. I'd gone to the door because she could see me through the window, so I had to open it, and told her I wasn't interested in being saved. She said she didn't want to save me. She wanted to talk about Virginia Gifford."

"Virginia Gifford?"

My mouth goes dry, but I manage to say, "My mother is — was — Virginia Gifford. That's why I thought she was a reporter."

"Why would a reporter want to talk about your mother?"

"Some people are still interested in her suicide. It was a big deal back when it happened."

"When was that?"

"1954."

"And you were how old?"

"Four."

"Were you there?"

"I – I don't remember." I glance down at my hands folded on the table.

"But you have memories of your mother?"

My head whips up. "I remember she wasn't black."

She doesn't smile. "What I don't understand, Mrs. Palmer, is as tragic as your mother's suicide was for you and your family, why did you think a reporter wanted to talk about it after so many years? Who exactly was Virginia Gifford?"

I sip coffee and launch into my stock reply. "It was the first time this kind of – Hollywood tragedy was broadcast live on TV. My mother was the 'Palm Springs Bikini Girl'. She was on the cover of *Life* magazine. Both she and my father were in the movies. Some people thought we were the perfect Hollywood family, so it was a shock when my mother put her head in an oven."

The detective's eyebrow lifts. Is it because of the way my mother killed herself or my tone?

"My father refused to talk about her, and wouldn't allow me to either. Not to him. Not to anyone. When he put her in the ground, I had to bury her too."

"So when Olita Jordan mentioned your mother's name, you –"

"Told her to get the hell off my porch and slammed the door."

Tellez studies me a moment, then opens the manila folder. Inside I can see the Googled map, my driver's license, and the tattered gasoline receipt with Olita's scribbled note on the back. "These are the documents you gave Officer Williams this morning?"

"Yes."

"How did you get this note?"

"She stuck it in the door."

"The note's on the back of a Chevron station receipt near Cabazon. Have you been there?"

"I've been to the outlets. What does that have to do with anything?"

"What did you think when you read the note?"

"I thought it was crazy."

"But you were curious."

"Wouldn't you be?"

She leans toward me. "What were you doing last night, Mrs. Palmer? Say between 12:00 A.M. and five this morning?"

"I was home in my apartment."

"Did anyone see you? Visit you? Anyone who can verify your presence there?"

I've spent the last month holed up at the God-forsaken Tiki Palms, avoiding my husband, my friends and neighbors because no one ever leaves me alone. And now, wouldn't you know, just when I need someone, anyone, all I can say is, "Nobody saw me. No one came by. No one called. I was alone."

Chapter 5
Search

The Tiki Palms Apartments are as far away from my house on Woodbine Street as I can get without changing cities. Out front, an imitation Easter Island monolith spits brackish water into a lava rock fountain. Hibiscus and ice-plant fight for whatever sunlight manages to seep through untrimmed eucalyptus. Here, grape-stake fencing replaces the sedate picket of my real house. And there's no covered veranda with river rock pilasters. No porch swing. No carefully painted brown shingles. No double rows of white roses leading to the street.

Inside the sagging Tiki Palms fence are six one-story units, circa 1950 or so — three tiny houses on either side — facing a narrow center court. Curved beams jut from each roof; fake-Maori masks frown from every porch. I'm the last unit on the right where a bird-of-paradise, palm tree, and agave plant twist together like a foreboding force of nature. Had Olita come here, she might well have turned around and run the other way. And I wouldn't have known a thing about her.

It takes Tellez and another detective named Karayan maybe half an hour to go through the apartment. It's less than 700 square feet, and I don't have much more than a bed and dresser in the bedroom and in the living room a futon, three utility tables, my computer and printer. Files and books crowd a corner. Most of the furniture I bought from Ikea, and felt smug when I assembled everything myself.

Tellez asks if I used my computer last night and says any documents I opened could verify my presence at home by date and time. I feel a surge of relief before I remember I'd been too upset to work. Was it really only yesterday I came home, popped a couple of Ativans, and threw myself into bed, trying to forget that woman, her note, what it might mean?

Earlier, back in the interrogation room, when Tellez asked if I would let them search my apartment without a warrant, I questioned her again about how the fire started.

"It was a fire bomb," she told me.

"Like a Molotov cocktail?"

"Exactly. There's a strong possibility we have a hate crime on our hands. We don't know yet whether it was directed at Olita Jordan or Turner Bethune, but Bethune's received death threats in the past. We're investigating every possibility."

"And I'm one of those?"

The detective had shrugged.

Now in my apartment, when the cops' search yields no evidence of a lunatic bigot, no incendiary devices ditched behind the Bernstein's Low-Cal Vinaigrette, the tension eases from Tellez's face, and she signals to her troops it's time to leave.

As she heads out, she picks up the black and white photograph of my mother and me in the big chair and studies it. "This is Virginia Gifford?"

When I nod, she says, "You don't have her freckles."

No, I don't.

•◇•

My kitchen window looks out on Hondas and Fords, and beyond the carport, an alley and the Gold Line tracks offer less than garden views. I peek through the curtain, positive some cop's out there behind the trash cans in an inconspicuous unmarked car. I'm trying not to worry about not having an alibi by licking a spatula I've dipped into a mixture of raw Bisquick, milk, butter, and almond extract, letting the taste of cake batter calm me down. Elma's cake batter.

Elma Robinson worked for us twice a week until my mother died. Then she came every day. When my father and I moved to the Hollywood Hills, there was an extra bedroom so she could spend the night if he was gone. At first he was gone a lot, then after his movie career tanked, he began his own insurance company and was never gone. Elma called me "Miss Abbie" just like she'd called my mother "Miss Virginia." Sometimes she called me "sugar." One "sugar" would last me a week.

If a stranger knocked on my door and said she was Elma's daughter, I would've talked to her, invited her in, served her coffee and cake.

But it wasn't her. It was Olita. And now she's dead and even though it's not my fault, I feel so guilty. No! I shake my head as if I can empty it. I can't think about her or her death. What it means. Not yet.

I'll think about Elma instead. She was part of my life for so long, her face is more vivid to me than my mother's, the sharp planes of her cheeks, her dark smiling eyes, always pointing her chin at me, pretending to be mad. Would she know if my mother had had an affair with a black man? What would she have thought about that, being black herself? Had she helped my mother or betrayed her? If I could find her, maybe she would tell me.

Sucking hard on the spatula to get that almond-rubber flavor, I walk the three steps from my kitchen window to my living-dining area and plop the mixing bowl next to the computer. I'll boot up. Or maybe I should grade essays. I could journal what's happened or clean up this mess. My ceramics class must be over by now. What I want to do, what I need to do, is take a tranquilizer and go to bed early. But first, my low level "the-world-is-out-to-get-me" paranoia sends me slipping out my front door to make sure no cop surveillance van is staking me out beyond the sagging fence.

I fake a relaxed amble through the front gate. Cringe as

wood scrapes cement. Be cool. Be casual. I live here. I have every right to check my mail. Past the Easter Island monolith, I stretch and surreptitiously survey the street.

Oh, shit!

When will I ever learn to hide under the bed with the shades drawn and doors bolted? Parked at the corner and climbing out of his Boxster is my husband, Craig.

Chapter 6
Husband

Craig, the husband I recently – temporarily – left, slams the door of his Porsche and takes in the dated Hawaiian vibe of the Tiki Palms. He's a trim fifty-two with only a small rounding above the waistline of his slacks. His golf shirt tells me he's out on the course again. Taking advantage, I guess, of my absence from home.

"Hey," he says over the chirp of his car alarm. "You okay?"

"Why wouldn't I be?" It would be so easy to turn this whole thing over to him. Let him fix it. But I can't do that. It's too soon. Way too soon.

He ignores my tone, kisses my cheek. "The police called in the middle of my game, a guy named Foo-something –"

"Fuji." I turn and hurry through the gate. We don't talk until we've navigated the sidewalk, climbed up the steps, and into my little apartment.

Craig hasn't been here before so I see this place the way he must see it. Standard-issue white walls, industrial strength carpeting, all surfaces cluttered with ungraded blue-books, paint tubes, brushes, and a tablet of art paper, marked up attempts at short stories, one lopsided vase I made in ceramics class as well as discarded sweatshirts and sweaters, socks, an empty microwave popcorn bag, and last night's syrup-caked plate. And of course, the newly-added Bisquick batter bowl. Can I blame this mess on the cops?

I sit down on a folding chair, leaving the rocker I brought from home for him.

"So," he says. "Tell me about this woman who died."

"They think she's my sister."

"Is she?" he asks, leaning forward, his hands clasped in front of him, elbows on knees.

"She can't be."

"You didn't know anything about her?"

"No."

"How'd she know where we live?"

"I don't know."

"Your dad never said anything?"

"Of course not. You know we never talked about my mother."

"No mention of an affair?"

"Don't be crazy. If I knew she had an affair, you'd know. We don't have secrets from each other. Not with your third degree. You're worse than the cops." I spring out of my seat. I don't want to argue, so I say, "What did Fuji want when he called?"

"To search the house."

"Did you let him?" I start collecting coffee cups, plates, the Bisquick bowl, trash from the floor.

"The cop asked about our living arrangement. I told him you wanted 'space'." Craig looks around. "And this is really some first class space. You need to come home."

I freeze, chin coming up, my thumb sticky from the pancake plate, my body itchy from the fire this morning. "I'm not going home."

Craig stands and puts his arms around me. It's comfortable here against his chest, smelling his familiar smell. After twenty-eight years of marriage, I love this man. Will always love him, but —

"Not yet." I bite my tongue to keep from crying.

"Well, at least let me take you out for something more substantial than cake batter."

I rub my nose against his shirt. Thinking. Wanting. Resisting. "Dinner, but nowhere fancy. I'm exhausted, and I am not going back to the house."

If I do, I might never leave.

Dinner with Craig. What sense does this make? Complete sense and no sense. I lean my head against the seat of the Boxster and close my eyes, letting the day's images creep in: the fire, the cops, the angry black man. Olita. The car's low rumble supplies the soundtrack.

Craig glances over. "What's wrong?"

"I'm okay." I force myself to sit up. "Fine. Don't worry."

He yanks the car to the curb just south of the chicken place. Shuts off the motor. Pivots toward me. "I've been patient with your little adventure, but this — murder — changes things."

"I hate it when you talk to me like that. In that tone."

"So you always tell me, but let me tell you something. You're in the thick of this, and you and I have to present a united front. You need to come home."

"I don't see how one issue has anything to do with the other." I turn toward the car window, rest my forehead against the cold pane.

"The police think you're involved," he says.

"Did Fuji actually say I was the one who heaved a Molotov cocktail through Olita's window?"

"Don't be an idiot." He restarts the car.

Why did I say I'd eat with him? My brain. Swamp water. Craig in the murk, lying in wait. Forget dinner. I want out. I wrench the car handle. The door flies open just as the Boxster leaves the curb.

I start to fall, but the seat belt straps me in and before I can unlatch it, Craig slams the brakes. My head smacks hard against the door frame.

"Damn it," he says, jumping out and rushing around to my side of the car. I'm crying now. He stoops down, undoes the seat belt to pull me close, and I slump against him.

After a moment, he breaks away, rebuckles the belt, and kissing my forehead, he quietly closes the car door. I lie back against the seat, only vaguely aware of the growl of Craig's Porsche as it moves into traffic. My body feels depleted, senses numbed, except for smell. Traces of exhaust and cigarette insinuate their way through the vents from the van ahead of us. Tobacco smoke I hate, but in this moment of self-loathing, I suck it in.

I don't resist as he pulls into our garage on Woodbine Street or when he helps me up the stairs to our bedroom. As gently as a nurse, he offers me two pills and water, then lifts my t-shirt over my head, pulls off my sweatpants, stopping to take off my Nikes. When I'm undressed, he pushes me under the covers and pulls them up to my chin. His lips linger on the place where I dug in my nails last night.

Chapter 7
Woodbine

Monday, May 20, 2002

My first sensation is a long sweet pull through dark water. Then I extend again, another pull, and whoosh, I break the surface where I meet the snouts of alligators. Ash glitters on moss. It's muggy hot. But where's Olita? Hadn't she been swimming beside me, whispering that everything would be all right? Wasn't that my dream?

I'm hot, sweating, stuck in swamp mud. I toss and turn and the woman who scribbled my mother's name on a gasoline receipt is standing in the doorway of her charcoal house. She is charcoal herself and begins to crumble. I hear Turner Bethune's screech, flinch under his furious glare. The black tape recorder whirrs on the interrogation room table and the detective asks, leaning so close to me I can see the crowding of her bottom teeth, "Where exactly were you when Olita's house went up in flames?" Elma. Got to find her.

My heart thrums. Bleary-eyed, I blink at light sifting through lace. Take in the scent of my old pillow. Feel a familiar weight. Craig has an arm and a leg locked over me.

I shut my eyes, wanting to explode out of bed, get the hell gone, but there's no way I can slip gently out from under his grip. If I stay still, he'll be up soon to get ready for work. I breathe in and out, in and out, in and out.

Then he says, "You awake?"

I sneak down to the kitchen while Craig's in the shower. My head aches because of the knot lifting the right side of my forehead, courtesy of last night's conversation with the Boxster. I chase two Aleves with a tall glass of water.

It feels way too normal standing here next to my own refrigerator with its choice of ice or ice water in the door, and I realize it would be easy to slip back into my old life. Go to exercise class, guide students through the maze of research and argumentation, be a mom, a wife. Most people don't need their own apartments to release their creative side without spousal eye-rolling. Why do I?

Craig's point, exactly. "Go play with your paint," he told me when I said I'd rented a little cottage. "Have fun." But he added, "You'll get lonely. No man is an island."

I said, "That's exactly what I want to be, an island. I'm sick of being a whole continent."

I pad into the dining room. Morning gray creeps through the French doors to my left. The anemones and poppies I abandoned a month ago are withered to brown weeds, but they were like that when I left. Alligators lurk again, and I have to will myself toward the front door, shivering a little. No dark shape waits on the porch. Not today.

A tiny yelp from Phoenix, our black lab, reminds me to breathe.

In the family room, he sits straight in his kennel, riveted, waiting for me to open the gate. When I do, he leaps out with his secret weapons: wagging tail, eager tongue, and the instant rollover for a belly-rub. Fingers in fur always make me feel better.

I'm shaking the coffee grinder when Craig comes into the kitchen and pecks me on the cheek, but I don't like his grin. It's his little boy grin, the one I fell in love with. He's thinking he's won. I almost wish he had, but then I tell myself he could be the one behind all this mess, an excuse to get me home to make his breakfast, wash his socks. Hah! Ridiculous idea and not one bit fair. I'm more than a housekeeper to him. I know that, but the sudden tightness in my chest, the stiffness in my shoulders reminds me of what drove me to leave.

I was tired of the battle between my desire to be on my own, make something happen, carve a niche, and my desire to make Craig happy. And the kids. I thought it would be easier when they went off to college — first Jason, then Christie — me with plenty of time to find out who I am. I missed them, of course, miss them now, and it wasn't that easy to let go of the noise and confusion of my old life.

"You can have that girl here if you want." Craig's sitting at the breakfast table, paper open.

"What?"

"The daughter."

"You mean Christie?"

"Not our daughter. That woman's daughter. You know, the woman who died in the fire."

"What are you talking about?"

"Listen, why don't you? The woman who died in the fire has a child." Shocked, I forget I'm holding the coffee grinder and drop it. Beans and grounds scatter across the counter.

"Wait a minute." I move from kitchen to breakfast nook, sit on the edge of a chair. "Olita Jordan has a daughter? How do you know?"

"That detective told me, Fuji."

"He didn't tell me."

"What difference does that make? Maybe the issue hadn't come up while you were at the police station."

"You should've said something last night."

"You were hysterical last night."

"I was not!"

"Anyway, the detective wants to know if you'd consider keeping her here if it turns out you're the aunt."

"Why can't her father take her?"

"You mean Bethune? He's not her father."

I stand up, move around. "Why's that detective talking

41

to you about someone's child? It's not his job to be in charge of the victim's – her – daughter."

"Bethune's the target, not the woman. It won't be safe for the girl to be with him if there's another attempt. Calm down. The detective was just sounding us out."

"Sounding us out? What us? We don't even live together."

"The question is, Abbie," he says in his infinitely patient voice, "do you want to help this girl or not?"

Swamp water rising, island sinking.

Chapter 8
Daughters

Craig has made some leap here and it freaks me out. He thinks that out of the goodness of my heart – whether I'm related to this girl or not – I might be willing to take her in. But I'm supposed to be an island now. Deep waters all around, no people, not even Robinson Crusoe's Friday to distract me from figuring out what the hell I want, yet because he "knows" me, Craig thinks my island has a safe harbor for some stranger.

I glare at him. "Why should I?"

"That's who you are, who you've always been. I'm not telling you whether you should or shouldn't. I'm just saying I'm here to help."

"I'm not ready to come back here. That's what you want, isn't it?"

He shakes his head and lays the newspaper on the table, slides it over. I snatch it up. Even Phoenix's insistent nose against my knee can't distract me.

Activist's Home Firebombed
High School Vice-Principal Dies in Blaze

I sink onto the edge of my chair again and read:

A Molotov cocktail, lobbed through a window, is believed to be the cause of a blaze that swept through the east Pasadena home of African-American activist Turner Bethune. According to officials, the fire erupted at 4:30 A.M. yesterday morning, killing Olita M. Jordan, his housemate and vice-principal at Arroyo Hermoso High School. Bethune was not at home.

Witnesses, awakened by the sound of breaking glass, told police the blaze spread so quickly, no one attempted a rescue. A spokesperson for the Fire Department confirmed that accelerants are suspected to be the main cause of the heat and speed of the blaze.

Officials at the Pasadena Police Department stated the incident has been classified as a hate-crime because of previous death threats directed at Bethune and the recent appearance of racial epithets painted on the pavement in front of the house. Investigators from the FBI and Alcohol, Tobacco, and Firearms arson unit are assisting local authorities. Police are exploring every avenue, according to Detective Warren Fuji.

Bethune, outspoken on various African-American issues, focuses his attention on opposing the death penalty. His rhetoric has also angered African-Americans by calling into account the lack of commitment of black men to the nuclear family. "Our jails are filled with our young men because so many will not commit to the family values," Bethune stated in a recent television interview.

The words 'fire fighters', 'inferno', and 'death' become a blur. I wish I could go back in time, back to my front porch where I would invite Olita inside for coffee and snickerdoodles. Maybe then, she wouldn't have died.

I stalk back into the kitchen, surprised to see the mess of strewn coffee bits. I sweep off the counter and dump the grounds into the filter basket. Jam the glass pot into the coffee maker. Hit the "on" switch. My hands tremble so I brace myself against the sink. I don't want to think about Olita Jordan, her charcoal image from my dream flickering into my brain. I stare at the faucet, my face a pale smudge reflected in the chrome. She has a daughter.

What Craig manages to do to me is fill me with self-doubt and he's doing that now. He tells me I'm a good person who will do the right thing, and it's his very reasonableness that puts me in the wrong, makes me feel foolish and selfish because I want to be on my own. It makes me so angry, I can't argue with him. I always lose.

Coffee, I decide, then I'm out of here. Wait. I don't need coffee. I can walk out now, but the phone rings. It's right here on the kitchen wall next to me. If it's my daughter, I don't want her to think I've moved back because I'm marching out the door in two minutes.

Craig says, "Are you going to get that?" Irritated now.

I pick it up, walk over, and hand it to him.

Craig says "Hello," then a smile breaks over his face as he listens.

"Okay, honey. Your mom's right here." He holds the receiver out. I glower at him. Snatch the phone.

"Mom?" The delight in Christie's voice makes me wince. "I tried you at the apartment, but..." She lets her sentence trail off.

"Hi, sweetheart." Chipper me.

"So-o-o," she draws out the word. "What's up with you and Dad?"

"Nothing, Christie. Nothing. I wasn't feeling well last night."

"A-n-n-d?" she says.

"And that's it. I'm going home as soon as your dad goes to work."

"Home? You are home. Grrr. I don't get this thing you're doing. You have two bedrooms at home you could use to do your own thing –"

"Christie, did you need something from me?" I turn away from Craig, walk back into the kitchen.

"Am I disturbing you?" she asks.

"No. No. I just don't want you to think –"

"Think what? That my mother has decided to come to

45

her senses and move back home?"

"It's not like that. You don't under –"

"But I do, Mom. I understand perfectly. You had a screwed up childhood so now you want space to find yourself and you don't have time for us anymore. I get it. Look, I'm late for class so I gotta go." And she's gone.

"Christie?" I say into the disconnected line. "Bye. I love you."

Craig clears his throat. "Any coffee yet?"

I grab the coffee pot, stomp into the breakfast nook, and slam it down on the table. The glass shatters, splashing hot liquid across the newspaper and onto Craig's freshly laundered shirt, but I barely notice this as I march through the dining room and out of the house, leaving the front door wide open.

Chapter 9
Tiki Palms

I'm six blocks down Woodbine Street when I look over my shoulder, positive Craig's behind me in his stupid little Porsche, but what I hear turns out to be a yellow Corvette. As it squeals around a corner, I realized I've left my keys and purse back at the house. I feel a stinging sensation in my palm, spot a piece of coffee-pot glass stuck there. I pick it out and suck at the trickle of red. Is Craig cut too? Burned? No. It wasn't that bad, was it?

I hesitate. But I don't go back.

This losing my temper is one reason I moved out. I'm a rule-follower, a people pleaser, the smoother-over of everyone else's discomfort, and as I've grown older, I've noticed a lot of people blow through their lives breaking rules. What really bugs me is not only do they get away with it, but flourish. Me, I go five miles over the speed limit, I get a ticket.

This frustration, this bitterness, has become part of who I am and it scares me. Not long before I stumbled across the Tiki Palms, I went out to fetch the paper and lost my temper. Commuters are always speeding down our street, and on that particular day, I ran out into the street in a red haze, waving wildly at a fast-moving Lexus. I screamed, "Slow down! Slow down!" Stomping my foot, most likely.

The driver's window slid open; his morning face twisted in anger. "Mind your own fucking business."

I yelled at his sleek back bumper, "It's not a fucking freeway!"

I remained in the traffic lane, cars honking and swerving, wringing my hands. Craig raced out, took the *L.A. Times* from my hand, and dragged me back into the house.

I don't want to break rules, not really, but I don't want to be everybody's go-to person anymore. I want to be left alone. My shrink says it's okay for me to stop feeling responsible for everyone's well-being, but the universe doesn't want to let me do that. And this makes me mad.

Two miles later, breathing hard, feet aching, without any awareness of how I actually got here, I arrive at the Tiki Palms and knock on my apartment manager's door. Ben's long dark hair is tangled from sleep. He yawns, blinks, frowns.

I say, "Next door?"

"I know who you are." Now he smiles, then his eyebrows draw together. "Hey. What happened to you? You bleeding?" He gestures at the smudge of blood on my sweats.

"I'm okay. I'm locked out of my apartment." Nerves buzz along the backs of my arms. Please don't ask me anything else. Give me my key and let me go.

"You sure you're okay?"

"Really, Ben. I'm fine." Crossing my arms, kneading my biceps, I take a step back.

"Sure, sure," he says. "You got locked out. Okay, just a minute. What time is it anyway? Come in."

I don't move as he retreats into his dark apartment. Ben's a good guy; I should be nicer, but right now I am totally peopled out. If he doesn't hurry, I'm going to crawl inside my own skin to hide.

He's back at the door, holding out a spare key.

"Thanks." I take it and turn away.

"Abbie?"

I keep moving, mumbling, "Please not now."

•◊•

The first thing I do when I get into my apartment is take two Ativans. I have pills both here and on Woodbine,

48

remembering Craig's offering last night. Good. They should grow on trees.

I give myself five minutes in the kitchen with the refrigerator door open, digging through moldy blueberries, rusty lettuce, empty sugar-free Popsicle boxes, looking for anything to shove in my mouth. Settle on a tablespoon of peanut butter.

The last thing I want to do is call my boss, Elaine Chute, but I have to. I'm supposed to give an essay final later this afternoon, but there's no way I can stand in front of students, act cheery, a positive Miss Bliss. Thank God I only teach one class. Elaine's dean of the English department at the city college, and a friend. If I can get through this one phone call, I can climb into bed and disappear.

When I tell her I'm sick, she says, "Abbie? What's going on?"

"What do you mean?"

"The police called me."

Of course. "It was a misunderstanding, that's all."

"Why don't you tell me about it?"

So I give her the short version, referring to Olita as "a woman I happened to meet."

Elaine tells me the cops wanted general information about me, more along the line of a character reference. She gave me a good one.

"Thanks," I tell her, relieved.

"No problem. Email me the essay prompt for your final and I'll take care of it."

Then I call Craig. This is what marriage is: stalking off, crawling back. My keys and purse are at the house, and I can't get in. That extra key, usually hidden under a dead geranium pot in the backyard, is now here with me, either tucked in the pocket of a jacket or tossed on the utility table and subsequently buried under those yet-to-be graded research papers.

Craig says, "You ruined my favorite shirt."

"I'm sorry. Did you get cut?"

"You left the damn door wide open."

"Phoenix got out?" Of course he did. The dog's a bolter. He lies in wait for these opportunities. Unless you want him to go out, then he heads into his kennel. "How far did he get?"

"To the tracks on Fremont."

"Sorry."

"One of these days, he's gonna get run over."

"I know. I'm sorry."

Then, after a pause, he says, "I'm late for work."

"I left my purse. Can you leave the back door unlocked?"

Chapter 10
Ben

Now with all my personal terra firma sunk under swamp water, I stand in the old pink tub-and-shower combo at the Tiki Palms, hot water cranked, letting it pound my aching right shoulder. I'm sorry that my anger put the dog at risk. Phoenix can cover a mile without breaking stride. I also hate my lack of control, counterpoint to Craig's ability to stay calm. It's part of our yin and yang that's worked for years, us fitting tightly together, but we've developed fissures now, rifts threatening to open and crumble inward. Even Craig doesn't sound calm anymore. Maybe I'd better call my shrink. But I've been avoiding her too. Being alone means being alone.

I wrap myself in a bath towel and walk into the chaotic living room. Put the chain on the front door. Shut the mini-blinds. With one quick glance around, I head into the bedroom.

I flop on the bed and think about the girl, this daughter of Olita's. How old is she? At what age is it easier to lose a mother? Fourteen, seven, or four? What's going through her mind right this minute? I don't want to know.

I roll onto my side. Clutch the pillow case. I'm not up for this and besides, there's no proof she's any relation of mine, is there? Of course, I don't know, do I? I refused to talk to Olita.

Anyway, why should I be the one to take her in? Isn't it the cops' job to protect Turner Bethune and the girl from further attacks?

A loud rap at the front door makes me jump. I stiffen. Maybe whoever it is will go away. Another knock, followed by a shout. "Abbie?"

It's Ben. I've tried to keep my distance, as much as one

can from someone who collects the rent, waving when I see him, walking away fast, but he's got these two little girls, Blanca and Delia, who come over every other weekend. One Saturday, Ben asked if I'd keep an eye on them while he checked out a tenant's toilet. I showed them how to play hopscotch on the cement in the courtyard, drawing the squares with my oil pastels. So Ben and I, we're almost friends.

I lumber out of bed, exhaustion in every step, and into the living room. He knocks again and says more quietly through the door, "I spoke to the cops yesterday."

Shit. I'm dressed in my underwear. "Hold on."

Back in the bathroom, I throw on sweat pants and a sweater, then run to open the front door.

He says, "Yeah, hi. Can I come in?" His damp hair is pulled back into a pony tail; his soul-patch glistens. As always, he looks good in his faded band t-shirt, so faded I can't read who they are.

"What did the police want?" I ask, moving out of the way, catching the clean scent of soap. This embarrasses me somehow, the idea that we've taken showers at the same time. Not that I haven't been aware of Ben before. He's a musician, a drummer, and one of those men who have a natural charisma and an easy-going way about him. Of course, that's how Craig used to be. I flash on an old memory of the two of us with friends in the desert, camping and riding dirt bikes. I leave the front door open.

Hands in pockets, Ben sways a little and says, "They just wanted to ask a couple of questions."

"What kind of questions?"

"You know, the usual stuff. How long you lived here. Any suspicious behavior. Any fraternizing with felons."

Felons?

"Don't look so scared. It's all good. I saw you, you know."

"Saw me?"

"Your light was on when I got home, and I never went to bed. I was sitting on the porch most of the night, smoking and thinking, and you never left."

"You mean the night before, right?"

"Right. Last night you never came home."

So I have an alibi. Ben. Who seems to know my every move. I shiver.

"Thanks." Of course, thanks. I should hug him.

"When did the cops talk to you?" I ask, remembering the hours I spent in the interrogation room.

"I don't know. They woke me up. Maybe around noon."

"Noon!" So they must've known I had an alibi long before they finished with me. All that time in that hard, metal chair, sweating, feeling like a criminal, for what?

"You okay?" he asks. "You look beat."

"I am beat. I'm – I'm –"

"No worries," he says. His brown eyes are soft. "Anything else I can do?"

"No, but thank you."

After Ben leaves, I strip off my clothes and crawl back into bed. Spread out between cool sheets, relieved to be alone, relieved to have an alibi. Stretching my legs, my feet, I breathe in the stuffy smell of the room, and close my eyes. Maybe this thing, whatever it is, is almost over.

But of course, it's not. She's there, in my mind. The girl, whoever she is, Olita's child, a dark amorphous shape. What did Craig tell me about her? Nothing. No, I didn't let him tell me anything. I wonder if she has freckles like her mom.

This is driving me nuts. I reach into the nightstand drawer and take out my Ativan. Swallow two. Didn't I already take two? Oh, well. Take that you muck, you swamp, you.

Dead sleep. Elephants rampaging through jungles. No. That's not right, but I can't drag myself out of blackness.

53

Then echoing down a long tunnel, I recognize the sound of the phone ringing next to my bed and struggle against sleep's numbness, waking in fog, only to slip back into oblivion.

Chapter 11
Makenna

Tuesday, May 21, 2002

My swamp's been hit by a class 5 hurricane. I'm clinging to the Kon Tiki monolith in front of my building, my body pulled thin and ragged like a wind-whipped flag. The room is dark except for the numbers glowing on my nightstand: 4:30. AM or PM? I force myself to focus. AM. Early morning. I roll over in bed. Close my eyes.

But there's Olita – dead Olita. Maybe there isn't a link. Not really. Maybe Olita's just one of those people who believes in reincarnation, thinking she was once Cleopatra or Benjamin Franklin, and in some desperate fantasy, latched onto my mother. Saw her in an old movie, and thought, maybe this beautiful woman is my mother? Maybe this beautiful white woman is my mother? It happens on Jerry Springer, people living in a made-up world and making life miserable for everyone else.

Then I remember the filing cabinet in my garage at home, the one Craig brought over from my dad's apartment when he died. I've never been through it. Never once opened a single drawer. Scared of its swamp history.

Damn. I forgot to get my purse and keys. I call Craig. Yes, he'll leave the back door open again. After I hang up, I climb out of bed and dig through the ancient plastic 'Invisible Girl' Slurpee cup on the kitchen counter for the extra key to my Suburban. But I can't go yet. I have to wait until Craig's gone to work.

I make a stab at the research papers, this assignment the death penalty, Turner Bethune's personal cause. Despite a flare of interest, two essays in and the pages become a muddle, my mind bogged down by Olita's scorched house, Turner Bethune's keening, and the whir of the detective's tape recorder.

•◇•

At 8:30 AM, the traffic down Monterey is heavy, the morning bright with eastern sun. I may have an alibi, but I still feel like a fugitive. I ran away from my father. Withdrew. Avoided. Kept my mouth shut. And now I've run away from my thirty-year marriage, away from my kids, to – of all places – the Tiki Palms.

A honk blares behind me, ahead a green light. I move quickly through Fair Oaks Avenue, watching traffic as Monterey narrows.

I drive up my street. Glance at the front porch and spy, in the shadows behind one of the thick white posts, a blur of movement. Olita's ghost? No, of course not, but someone is up there, and it's too early for the mailman. I squint, not paying attention to my driving, and all of a sudden, a parked car leaps out at me. I swerve, missing the dark SUV, swinging in front of it, jumping the curb. My heart bumps into my throat. I'm an idiot. Obviously I can no longer be trusted with two tons of sheet metal on four wheels.

A man yanks open my car door. Turner Bethune – the guy who blames me for Olita's death – leans toward me, but his face registers concern as he offers a hand, saying, "You okay?"

Behind him in the street stands a young black girl with a gray camouflage backpack slung over her shoulder. Freckles again. Damn those genes. Damn the whole gene pool.

I'm more shocked to see Turner Bethune and the girl – especially the girl – than I am to realize my Suburban has one wheel over the curb. Nothing's damaged with the car – it's four-wheel drive – so I mumble, "Let me repark and I'll

56

be with you."

He nods, and they hustle back to the relative safety of the lawn.

I manage to thud off the curb and park, even though the girl distracts me. She's tall and slender, but solid too, like an athlete. Olita's daughter is real.

Coming around the car, I watch her. She meets my eye with a lift of her chin.

"I thought you two should meet," says Bethune. "This is Makenna." She holds her body like Christie does.

"Would you mind if we go inside?" asks Bethune.

We turn toward my sturdy brown house with its cream and barn red trim. River rock pilasters support a wide front porch. Iceberg roses, indecently lush, bloom along the path. Remembering that Bethune and the girl no longer have a home makes my face burn.

They follow me through the side gate into the backyard to the unlocked kitchen door. Phoenix, half black Lab and half Mexican jumping bean, wriggles his butt, his tail conducting a doggy orchestra. He sniffs and snorts at both Bethune and the girl, the girl ignoring the dog, letting him leap around her feet, lick her jeans.

The family room, like the exterior of the house, is warm and inviting, stark contrast to the modern angularity of the Hollywood Hills house my dad moved us to after my mother died. And neither place is anything like the Tiki Palms.

I invite my guests to sit. Offer them coffee or soda.

The girl flops into Craig's leather recliner and starts to gnaw her cuticles. She's about fifteen or sixteen, her long slack limbs at angles only possible for the young.

"How did you know who I was yesterday?" I ask.

"The cop, Detective Fuji. When he said you were Abbie Palmer, I lost it. I'm sorry about that." He sits on the sofa and I follow by perching on the arm rest at the other end. He says, "This whole thing with Olita. She called me in San

Antonio about you slamming the door in her face. She was upset because no one would talk to her. First her father's wife and then you —"

"Her father's wife? What father?" My heart skips a beat.

"Olita's birth father. She had his name and she found where he lives, but his wife wouldn't let her in. That's when she began to search for her mother." Then he adds in a quiet voice, "Your mother."

Chapter 12
Olita

Turner Bethune, a stranger, knows more about my mother than I do. Air vacates my lungs, and I gulp. Cough.

"I understand this is hard to comprehend," says Bethune. "It was hard for Olita."

"How did she find me? How did she find this house? How did you find this house?"

"You're in the phone book and I suppose that's how Olita did it. I left a message on your answer machine. We hoped to catch you when you got home from work."

"But you knew who I was at the fire. You knew my name because Olita told you, but how did she know?"

"I don't know. She never explained that part of it."

I glance over at the girl. She's perfectly still, eyes down, finger in her mouth, mid-chew on a hangnail. I look at Bethune. "When did this start? The whole searching-for-my-mother thing?"

"Olita went to Louisiana a couple of weeks ago because her mother died. Her sister, Tonette – she and Olita didn't get along – told her she'd been adopted."

"The bitch." A harsh whisper from the girl.

"Makenna." Bethune's voice was gentle, but firm. "Anyway, Tonette told Olita her real father lives here in California."

"He's – alive?" I ask.

"He is and Olita tracked him down, but his wife wouldn't let her see him. She was as rude to Olita as I gather you were."

I glimpse at Makenna who's refocused on her nails. "Who is he then, Olita's father?" This father, this unknown maybe-lover of my mother.

"His name is Billy Eastlake. Olita wanted to get the whole story before she said too much to Makenna or to me about her real parents. Once she learned your mother was dead, she looked for you. You were the last piece."

I rub palms on my sweatpants. Take a deep breath. "So this man said my mother — that he was — that they were together?"

"This isn't working." Makenna scrambles out of the chair, face reddening.

"Makenna." Bethune.

"What's the point? She slammed the door in my mother's face."

"Enough." Bethune is sterner this time.

I say, "I'm sorry. Your mother surprised me."

The girl folds her arms. "I want to leave."

"Please, Ken, let's see if we can figure this out."

She throws me a hard look, then slumps back into the chair. Turner Bethune may not be her father, but she treats him like one.

"The cops' theory is that Olita's death was an accident. They think the guys who did this were after me. Bottom line, Makenna may not be safe with me." Again the man glances at the girl. She gives him the barest of shrugs. He turns back to me.

"Olita wanted to find her mother. Maybe you're the sister she found instead."

Maybe I'm the sister she found instead? I clear my throat, ask the girl, "Would you like to go outside with Phoenix for a while?"

"Screw that." Her eyes flick to Bethune, but catch his nod. She exhales noisily. "Whatever."

I get up to open the door, and the dog is on the threshold, wagging his tail.

"Phoenix, stay. Makenna's coming out to you." So the dog backs up, bouncing and wriggling, gawping at the girl, excited to have company. After I close the door, I watch her droop onto the back step. Phoenix digs under her arms with his nose, forcing his head in close. She ignores him.

I turn to Bethune and say, "So there's a possibility – not proven as far as I can see – but the possibility that Makenna is my niece and you want me to take her. Is that what you're here for?"

But before the man can answer, the doorbell chimes. What now?

He says, "It's probably the cops."

"What?"

"It's okay," he says. "You can answer it." As if I need his permission.

Standing on the porch is the detective who helped Tellez search my apartment and a woman in gray slacks, sleeveless black turtleneck, and a brief case.

"Sorry to bother you, Mrs. Palmer. I'm Detective Karayan," says the cop.

"I remember you."

"We're looking for Makenna Jordan and Turner Bethune. Are they here?"

Behind me, Bethune is moving into the entry. I hold my breath, expecting – I don't know what – a confrontation? Drawn Guns? What Bethune says is, "She's fine."

The girl and a uniformed officer come through the dining room. Apparently, the cops have us circled, rounding her up in the backyard, escorting her through the house. She has her chin poked out defiantly, eyes narrowed. She folds her arms and stands next to Bethune, almost on top of him. The two of them remind me of ancient Roman gladiators, battle ready.

The officers exchange a look, and Karayan addresses the girl, "You're okay?"

"Why wouldn't I be?" Makenna's voice breaks just at the end, betraying that she's not as insolent as she's trying to put out. This too reminds me of Christie.

"Glad to hear it," says Karayan. Then, "Excuse me

while I call this in."

Again he signals to the other policeman and walks to the end of the porch.

The woman with the briefcase speaks to Makenna. "You gave us a scare, young lady." She glances toward me. "Dawn Grant with Social Services. Mrs. Palmer?"

I nod.

Bethune puts his arms around the girl. Squeezes. "We'll work it out, baby girl."

Karayan comes back. "Mr. Bethune, Detective Fuji would like to speak with you. You can come with us."

The Grant woman touches the girl's shoulder. Tears brim in Makenna's eyes, but her mouth is clenched.

"What's happening?" I ask.

Bethune shakes his head. "A misunderstanding. Not a big deal." He turns to Makenna. "You promised."

The girl turns and heads down the porch steps. Dawn Grant follows, after a slight wave in my direction.

"Where's Makenna going?" I ask.

Turner Bethune, whose dark brown eyes don't waver from mine, says, "Back to the foster home."

Chapter 13
Her Father, Her Son

My neighbor across the street waters her extravagant flower bed and gapes at the exodus of the cops. When she cocks her head in my direction, a sly curiosity in her attitude, I pivot into the house and slam the door. Retreat to the empty family room. Sink onto the sofa.

Gloom seems to grow in every corner. Chill pumps from the air conditioner. I should grab my purse and keys and split, but I can't move. Not yet.

I glare at the recliner where that girl sat ripping apart her fingers. Forget her dark skin, the face. Consider the body, the posture. It's as if —

No as ifs. The girl has nothing to do with me or my mother. My swampy brain is playing tricks.

Either way, I need to be convinced. I came over to check my dad's old filing cabinet and that's the least I can do. And this Billy Eastlake? My mother's hypothetical lover? Where is he? Who is he? His name is kind of familiar, but not really. Did my father know about him? Could he have left anything behind about this man?

In the backyard, heat rises off the grass, the late morning sun burning through the gingko. Phoenix bounces in front of me. I ignore him and head across the driveway toward the garage.

The filing cabinet is in a corner, hidden behind cardboard boxes of camping gear and the remains of Craig's dirt bike. No motor, no gas tank, just a skeleton, but I flash on hot desert trails, the dust in my eyes, my arms circling Craig's waist.

I shove at the Yamaha, but it won't budge. Irritation breaks out along my skin like hives. I heave the bike onto cases of Arrowhead water. Something spikes one of the bottles. A geyser erupts. Phoenix barks.

I seize each camping box, drop it to the side. The peeling gray face of the filing cabinet appears with its four grimy drawers. I straighten. There is a lock on the second drawer from the top. I grasp the rusty handle and tug. The drawer rolls open. I catch my breath. Peek inside.

Faded brown accordion folders jam the space. Faint black ink, scribbled on the top of each, proclaims '1995', '1996', '1997', and so forth.

I recognize them. Our taxes. Mine and Craig's.

I pull open the top drawer. More tax folders. The third drawer. It's locked. I yank on it, but it won't budge. I move onto the bottom drawer. It glides out. More tax shit. I kick the cabinet, grip the handle drawer number three, yank hard, and out it flies.

Okay, breathe. Just relax. Now look.

Of course. Taxes. Again. Why not?

I ignore the mess on the floor and tramp into the house. Phoenix tries to sneak in, but I tell him "Not now" and shut the door.

I don't want to ask Craig where he put my father's records. The only way to keep him uninvolved in this whole thing is not to involve him. So I begin to search his study.

Finally, tucked in the very back of a filing drawer, I find a thin folder labeled 'Lyle Hart'. My dad's birth and death certificates are inside along with clipped newspaper obituaries. No diaries. No references to any affair. Nothing about Billy Eastlake. And certainly no confessions on my father's part and no apologies to me.

I pick up one of the yellowed articles. The paper is dated two days after my father's death on August 27, 1971. The photograph is from the early 1950's. My mother and father head into a restaurant with another man, captioned as Lyle's agent, Dennis Ventura. Only the agent is smiling. I touch my mother's face with the tip of my finger, then read:

*Lyle Hart, dies at 45; Actor, Business Man Married
Bikini Girl Virginia Gifford*

*Lyle Hart, former motion picture actor and founder
of the now-defunct Western State Insurance
Company, died alone in his Silver Lake apartment
on August 15 of unspecified causes. He was 45.*

*Born Carlisle Francis Hartshorn in Chico,
California, Lyle Hart appeared in many westerns
including* Apache Junction, Dawn's Early Light, *and*
Siege at Fort Smith. *He received a Golden Globe
nomination for his performance as a Comanche
warrior bent on revenge in the 1949 Jerome Tallman
western* The Scout.

*Hart married starlet Virginia Gifford, famous
for wearing a bikini on the cover of* Life *magazine,
and retired from the film industry to go into the
insurance business. In 1954, Gifford committed
suicide. Hart never remarried.*

He is survived by a daughter, Abbie Hart.

The photo in *The Times* and in *Variety* is the same
headshot of my father from early in his career. I've seen it
before. He leans toward the camera in a casual open-necked
shirt, tan, handsome, pleased with himself. He looks so
young. No broken veins mapping his face, no watery eyes,
no tight mouth. My parents' marriage is like a jigsaw puzzle
without the picture on the lid of the box. A thousand pieces
and no clue as to how they fit together.

I gather the papers back into the folder. Glance around
Craig's modern office, out of step with the rest of the
craftsman-style house. Steel gray walls, sleek black cabinets,
a real Eames chair. Photos of the kids line his desk: Christie
hugging a soccer ball, accepting a writing award, with her
prom date; Jason in his cross-country uniform, laboring up a
hill, his face sleek with sweat, a smile of grim determination

on his face. Graduations, birthdays, our wedding, an anniversary.

I turn to go, but a stack of loose snapshots on the desk stops me. A brilliant green and red parrot. Dense trees streaming with light. The wide Amazon River, Jason in a boat, waving. These are pictures I've never seen. They came here to Craig, of course, because Jason has been gone long enough not to know I've left. Sadness and regret flood through me.

Chapter 14
Elma

Back at the Tiki Palms I drop my dad's folder next to the computer and rummage through the refrigerator. I'm not the least bit hungry. I decide on toast with cinnamon sugar. First two slices, then two more. I need something salty. Popcorn will do. And I pour myself a diet Coke. Take two – one – Ativan.

My mind jumps from my mother to my dad to my mother's possible lover. What was his name? Billy something, wasn't it? Elma would've known. I want to talk to someone. I want to talk to her.

Doubtful I'll find her on the computer, I still have to try. Google gives me a couple women from the mid-west, but I'm drawn to the sixth entry, an obituary. The small grainy photo makes my heart sink, Elma as I remember her.

She died this year at 86 in San Diego. Not far away. Not long ago.

Elma was dropped off at our house in the Hollywood Hills every morning , sometimes carrying a silky party dress on a wire hanger and shoes in a paper bag. She wore a uniform, but on her head was a sparkling little hat with a chiffon bow.

"Are you going dancing tonight, Elma?" I asked.

"Deed I am. You brush your teeth, Missy?"

"Will you take me dancing someday?"

"Why don't you pick a record and dance right here in the living room while I vacuum." That's what I did.

Feeling the loss of Elma all over again, I sit on the futon and stare at nothing. Use my finger to lick the popcorn bowl clean of its salt. Chew the ice in my glass. I know what it's like to feel abandoned. Where is Makenna sleeping tonight? Is she crying into her pillow? She reminds me of Christie.

They're both tough, those girls. I never was. These are the things I mull over until I'm blessed with sleep.

Sometime in the evening – I don't give a shit about time anymore – I wobble up from the futon, pee, and stand in the dark for a while.

I need to get this out of my system. Isn't that what Elma would say when I was upset? "You just get that outta you' system, girl." Then she'd send me out to the flower bed to pull weeds.

I slide into the computer chair. Boot up. Surrender. I'll let it flow, the whole thing with Olita, the cops, the girl. I'll play the keyboard like a piano. Maybe something will come, some decision, some way to bring everything into focus or push all of it away.

What I type:

We live in a bungalow. It's late at night. We're coming home. My dad is still in pictures, though my mother isn't. He won't let her. Oh. How do I know that? I don't know but I do. With certainty. He will not let her take a job. He will not let us stay home alone. If he goes to make a movie somewhere out in the desert or to Catalina Island, we go with him.

I've been sleeping on the backseat of the car. It's one of those rounded cars. Rounded fenders, rounded roof, rounded back and front like a pregnant woman. Hood ornament that gleams silver. We pull into the back of our house. Gravel crunches under the tires. The car is hazy with cigarette smoke. The crisp cold air from the opening door is a relief. My father is a shadow at the back door.

My mother gathers me into her arms. I rest my cheek on her breast. Feel her heart beating. The cardigan she's covered me with slips off. She leans over to pick it up. Stumbles, but clutches me to her. Could I be too heavy for her?

My father shouts from inside. My mother hurries, leaving the sweater on the gravel driveway. We go through the door into the kitchen. Something swoops down close to us. A quick hotness. Soft. My mother ducks. Screams. Races deeper into the house, me slipping, slipping, as my father rushes past, flailing at the air with a broom.

My mother collapses onto the sofa with me underneath, crying.

What's the matter? I ask, but she doesn't answer. Chairs tumble, a glass shatters in the kitchen, angry words spit from my father's mouth. I cover my ears at the slam of the back door.

He comes into the living room, breathing hard. I can smell his sweat. He says, "Virginia. You left your cashmere sweater on the driveway." The way he always said her name, with a period at the end, as if it were a sentence full of disappointment.

My mother says, "The bat –"

My father says, "Go get it."

My mother uncurls my arms from around her neck and pushes me onto the sofa. The loss of her heat makes me shiver. I whimper, but she doesn't hear me.

My father follows her into the kitchen. I hear the back door open. I hear him tell her, "Don't let that goddamn bat back in or you'll spend the night outside yourself."

My fingers stop, poised over the keys, my heart pounding. I was only three, maybe four. This can't be right. How could I remember this? Subconscious at work, maybe? Roiled up by the shock of what's going on? Before now, I had no memory of the bat, the cashmere sweater, the tone my father used with me directed at my mother. And now I have this memory as if it happened last night.

How amazing.

How frightening.

For the first time ever, I realize – no, I admit – my mother and father weren't happy. That my father's drinking after my mother died, his closing down, his impatience with me, might not have been about loving her too much as I'd always thought, but something else.

The earth isn't solid under my feet. But then it never was.

Chapter 15
Birth Certificate

Wednesday, May 22, 2002

I'm not worried about going to the slammer – my apartment manager, Ben, has given me an alibi – so I take a moment to study the lobby at the Pasadena City Police Station. The vaulted ceiling seems three stories high, the floor is covered with terracotta tiles, and above the wooden desk are the words 'Community Services'.

When it's my turn, I tell the receptionist I'm here to see Detective Tellez, and she asks me to wait. I wander to a bench along the wall and sit down.

Earlier this morning, while I was in bed, the words "take her in" snapped my eyes open. Maybe remembering what it was like to lose my own mother and having Elma there has softened my heart. What harm could come from taking the girl for a week or two?

The detective's office is a cubicle, more pleasant than the interrogation room. She moves behind her desk and points to the chair opposite her.

"I hear you've met Makenna?" she asks.

"It was a shock seeing her on my front lawn with Bethune. He isn't a suspect, is he?"

"Why would you think that?"

"The way the police acted. They, like, surrounded the place."

"When Bethune visited Makenna yesterday at the foster home, they left without telling the foster mother. She called us. I wasn't sure where they'd go, so I sent people to a couple of places. I was surprised you were at your house and not the Tiki Palms."

"Bethune said he's the target. Doesn't Makenna have

friends who'll take her in?"

"The case worker tried — you met Mrs. Grant at your house — but the mothers are reluctant because of possible danger to their own children."

"I think Bethune wants me to take her."

"It isn't what Bethune wants. It's what's good for the girl." Tellez leans back to consider me. "When we talked the other day, you were unsure about the relationship between you and Olita Jordan. You've had time to think about it. How do you feel now?"

"Nothing proves my mother was Olita's mother, but there's something about the girl. I mean, I'm an orphan too. That sounds silly, doesn't it? I'm an adult with my own children, but a person never gets over being left."

"It's particularly difficult when that loss is fresh. She needs a safe place, Mrs. Palmer."

"Are you saying she'll be safe with me or not safe with me?"

"You're no longer a person of interest, if that's what you're asking, and there's no apparent impediment if you want to take her in, but before you decide anything, there's something you should know. I had a copy of Olita's birth certificate faxed from Louisiana." She picks up a piece of paper from her desk and hands it to me.

The fax paper is limp, but the old-fashioned scroll work around the margins lends authority. I don't know where to focus first. Sex: female. Date of birth: December 5, 1948. Name: Olita May Riggs. Finally I read the names of the parents: Miriam and Louis Riggs. I look across the desk at Tellez. "Who are these people?"

"Supposedly Olita's parents," Tellez says. "There's no mention of a Virginia Gifford."

And no Billy Westlake or whatever his name is.

Is this the way out of this unwelcome mess? Do I want a way out? Things have changed in my world. My father is no longer a man who drank himself to death because his

71

beloved wife stuck her head in an oven.

"Just so you understand, Mrs. Palmer. In those days, people didn't always tell children they were adopted and there was a stigma attached to illegitimate children. Also the child of a mixed union, that's always a tough thing. Therefore, it wasn't uncommon for records to be altered. Proof, absolute proof, may not exist in any legal document. If your mother put her daughter up for adoption, it was done quietly, without agency involvement. She was in the movies. She wouldn't have wanted anyone to know."

"But the birth certificate's legal?"

"As far as the state of California goes, but all it tells us is a Dr. Archibald Gaines witnessed a live birth in someone's home. It doesn't prove that Olita's mother was Miriam Riggs or Virginia Gifford. Of course, DNA would be the best way to find out the truth, but I'm not sure this is the right time to do that, for Makenna's sake."

I get it. Too much is being torn away from this child. Even Bethune, the man she apparently loves and trusts, has to keep his distance. Is he a suspect? Could he have firebombed his own home to kill Olita? But why?

No. I can't accept that. He's in danger, and Makenna needs something or someone to hold onto until this whole situation is cleared up. That someone could be me. I'm a good person, idiosyncrasies notwithstanding. Finally I say, "How long?"

"There's an aunt. I'm supposed to call her when we're ready to release Olita's body to the family. There are funeral arrangements to be made. The aunt is —" Tellez looks for a bright orange file and offers it to me, "Tonette Johnson."

"Tonette?" Didn't Bethune mention a Tonette as the one who told Olita she was adopted? Didn't Makenna call her a bitch? I put down the birth certificate and take the folder. The first page contains Tonette Johnson's telephone number and address. "What if I think the birth certificate is

72

wrong? What if I want to, you know, investigate?"

"You can keep the birth certificate. It's your copy," she says, then points at the folder. "I've downloaded a list of hospitals in the area where Olita grew up. You can check their records. You can trace the doctor too."

"It would be a lot easier if Virginia's name were typed on that birth certificate, wouldn't it?"

"I'm not sure that really matters to you," the detective says. And for now, at least, she's right.

Chapter 16
Cleaning

Tellez calls me on my cell – lucky for me I remembered to bring it with me – before I'm out of the police station parking lot. She says Social Services will be at my apartment early tomorrow morning. "If you pass, you've got Makenna, for at least a week or two."

I head for the grocery store, nervous now, wondering if she'll expect home-cooked meals? Is she vegetarian or, heaven forbid, vegan? Does she like Coke or Pepsi? I troll the aisles at Vons for healthy responsible food: cranberry juice, eggs and low-sodium ham, bagged salads, broccoli, blueberries, chicken breasts, and salmon. I even buy flowers and Lysol spray to cloak the musty smell of my ugly brown carpet.

Back at the apartment, I realize my initial "lick and promise" approach to housekeeping won't be enough for Dawn Grant, that stern social worker I met yesterday, that SS agent, or whatever she's called.

I first stumbled onto the Tiki Palms by accident, driving by after a blow-out with Craig. I hadn't planned on moving, but when I spied Ben Saenz posting a 'For Rent' sign, I stopped to ask him "How much?" The tenant had died and the place wasn't clean, but I wrote him a check and moved in the same afternoon, bringing my vacuum, a spray bottle of 409, a sleeping bag, and the rocking chair from home. Next day I headed to Ikea.

Makenna can have the bedroom. The futon in the living room is fine for me. I change sheets – thank goodness I did laundry – dust, scrub, and pillow-plump. I give a half-ass nod toward organizing my papers and books, remembering suddenly there are final exam essays waiting at school. I shove away my grade book and snap up a legal pad. Jot down the things I need from Target: toilet paper, reading glasses, shampoo. I'll take the girl with me. Didn't her clothes burn up? Her iPod? Her everything?

In the kitchen I rummage through my tiny freezer, reaching around the fat-free frozen yogurt and grabbing the chocolate chip cookie dough, letting the chill from the open compartment cool down my cheeks. When the telephone rings – my landline – I let the answer machine pick up. It's Craig calling to bitch about the mess I left in the garage. I stuff another bite of dough into my mouth, savor the sugar granules, and go back to work. I put all the movable parts from the stove into hot sudsy water and attack the appliance's crusty surfaces with a vengeance. Elma again in my head. "Get your mind off you troubles, girl, and dry my dishes. No good feeling sorry for yourself."

Elma. She would've been my mother's only confidante. No friends came to my father's house to see how we were doing after my mother died, how I was doing. The steel wool cuts my fingers as I scour. Sweat trickles down my face.

I searched for Elma after my father fired her. Not right away because I was too young, but as soon as I could, I took a cab into Watts. The driver looked unsure because of the previous summer's riots. I was frightened, too, but determined. I'd been there once before to celebrate someone's birthday – Elma's it must have been – and though I vividly remembered the name of the street, I couldn't decide which house it was. They all looked so much alike. Without getting out of the taxi, I called out to a woman weeding a vegetable garden in her front yard. Asked if she knew Elma Robinson.

I wipe down the stove and remember the wary look on the woman's face. She told me Elma took her son and moved out after the riots. Son? I'd never known about a son. Or did I? The image of a little boy – younger, older? – jumping off Elma's front porch comes to me. It was his birthday, her little boy's. I've gotten in the habit of thinking that Elma was mine. But that was wrong. I told the cabbie to take me home and hurry. I was shaken by my own nerve, by her other life. And now she's gone, taking all her secrets with her.

But maybe this son of hers might know something. Maybe I could track him down. See if he remembers if she ever talked about my mother or more likely, my father, but anything at all would help me put this all together. I can't remember if the obituary listed next of kin. I fight the urge to stop what I'm doing and boot the computer. Remind myself Makenna will be here tomorrow.

When I'm done with the kitchen, I go outside to wash the front windows, folding chair in one hand, Windex and paper towel in the other, and stop on the porch to catch my breath. The dark sky boasts a quarter moon. The courtyard, dotted with yellow lights, is serene, except for the low hum of a television across the way. The smell of jasmine curls into my nose, my mouth. I savor it, allowing the hollowness in my chest to fill a little. At least Elma had been right about the therapeutic benefits of hard work. I breathe again, ready to tackle my last task of the day.

The windows are glistening when they catch a flash of headlights, and I hear a car roll into the carport. Craig? The cops? I hustle off the chair, thinking lock the door, hide under the bed.

Chapter 17
Christie

I'm struggling to get my front door open when I hear, "I told you I'd get a crew to clean your place." It's Ben, apartment manager and bestower of alibis extraordinaire.

Relief plays out on my shoulders, my neck. It shows up in my smile. "I'm done. The place is clean inside and out." I'm amazed at the sense of well-being that comes over me, then I notice that Ben shoulders droop. "No gig tonight?"

He stops at the bottom of the steps. "Nah. Just saw my girls this afternoon."

I'm looking down at him, his eyes level with my waist. I run a self-conscious hand over my damp sweat shirt. "How are they?"

He shrugs. "Doing okay. Delia's got a cold. But Blanca, she thinks she's a cat. She crawls around on all fours, you know, and meows. She wants to drink from a water bowl on the floor, so what could I do? I got out her mother's best crystal bowl, and let her."

"What about a litter box?" I ask. We laugh, me awkwardly, but it feels good.

The jasmine-scent comes back to me, then Ben sobers, shuffles his feet, and says, "Looks like my ex has a new boyfriend."

"That must be hard."

"It's been going on for a while. Here, let me help you get this stuff inside." He leaps up the steps and takes the folding chair from me, flustering me a little.

My phone rings inside, not my cell. I don't want Ben to hear a rant from Craig on my answer machine, so I say, "I've got to get that. Let's talk later if you want." I snatch the chair from him and head in, muttering a hasty "Thanks," pushing the door shut with my foot, leaving Ben on the porch.

I pick up the phone, wondering when I got so rude. Christie's "Mom?" takes me by surprise.

"Hey, sweetheart. I'm — so sorry about the last time. I've been kind of out of whack."

"That's why I'm coming down."

"What?"

"I want to see you and Dad. We need to talk about what's going on."

"What do you think is going on?"

"Dad said you have a half-sister. And she died."

"He told you?" What in the world is Craig doing? And more importantly, how do I explain I'm taking in someone else's daughter, when Christie believes I've abandoned my own?

"It affects all of us, doesn't it?"

"I don't know who the woman is. It might be nothing. Besides, don't you have classes?"

"But Dad said —"

"Sweetheart, I don't want you to worry about this. It has nothing to do with you or your dad. I'll let you know if there's any truth to it so the best thing you can do is stay in school. I'm handling this. Your dad is overprotective."

"Take a breath, Mom. Jees. I won't come, okay?" She hangs up. Damn. I start to call her back, but stop myself. It's no use. I can't give her any answers until I have some of my own.

Now that feeling of well-being is completely gone and there's nothing left to clean. I open the fridge door and slam it shut. I pick up my cell phone, but it's dead. I'll write again, let it come like before. I boot the computer, squirming in my seat while I wait. It takes forever. I shut it down before it even comes on.

Suddenly, I want out, want air, but there's no place to go. Maybe next door to cheer Ben up? Yeah, right. I'm the ideal candidate for that. Instead, I grab my car keys and hurry out to my Suburban.

I'm an automaton on auto-pilot, running on empty. Just go. See where it takes me. I back out of the carport.

On the 110 freeway going south, I exit onto the Hollywood freeway, aware on some level of what I'm doing, but keeping all thoughts at bay until I find myself on Fountain Avenue, heading toward the bungalow with its O'Keefe and Merritt oven. But I'm as lost searching for that as I was when I went to Watts to find Elma, and along this busy street no old women are out digging in their yards to ask if they know where Virginia Gifford used to live. Nothing along here but funky apartment buildings and curbs lined with unfamiliar houses.

Finally I spot a '20s style cottage and pull over. It has the requisite wide-gabled roof, a porch across the front, its entrance squarely in the middle. It's not the house I used to live in when I was little, I know that, but much the same, and very similar to my craftsman house on Woodbine.

I sit quietly for a while thinking about my mother and wonder that she could turn on the gas while her four-year-old daughter was in the next room. I consider Christie's anger and wonder how to explain Makenna. Mothers and daughters. Oh, God. The past is past and maybe it should stay that way.

Chapter 18
Old Big Ugly

Thursday, May 23, 2002

This morning, I passed Dawn Grant's inspection so I'm here to fetch the girl. "Here" is the foster home Makenna seems so desperate to leave. And there she is sitting on the front steps of the green stucco house, her gray camo backpack at her feet. Hovering in the doorway behind her is an African-American woman holding a toddler. Light shines in every window. It looks like a painting. Why would Makenna sacrifice this lovely place to be with me at the Tiki Palms?

My shoulders scrunch up around my ears, but somewhere inside me, there's a steady thump of excitement. I know why. Before I drove over, I propped the photograph of my mother and me against the computer monitor. It'll be one of the first things the girl sees.

When I woke this morning, the anxiety I felt last night had dissipated, my determination to do this "good deed" reinstated and unwavering. Elma used to tell me that a good night's sleep "lifts the burdens, sugar." One more thing she was right about.

The woman with the toddler waves as I climb out of my car and head up the sidewalk. Makenna seizes her backpack, throws a "Thanks" over her shoulder and meets me halfway. I glance at the woman and ask, "It's okay?"

"Fine by me," she says. "You take care, Makenna."

The girl keeps walking, says "You too" without turning around, and waits at the Suburban, shifting back and forth in her orange and white sneakers.

I can't leave it like that. I walk toward the woman as she steps out of the shadows to greet me.

"Good luck with that one," she says in a not-so-low voice.

"She just lost her mother."

"I know that, and I tried to help her, but she wouldn't let me near her. I don't think she's even cried."

"She's still in shock, I'm sure. Thank you for keeping her here." I turn toward Makenna and wave. She doesn't move, just stares at us.

The woman follows my look and says, "I don't mind, but be careful when she gets herself out of her shock. That one's got a mind of her own."

"Thanks again." I smile and move back down the sidewalk, my step not quite as confident as it was when I arrived.

"What were you two talking about?" asks the girl when I reach her.

"What a nice young woman you are," is my answer as I open the passenger door for her.

Makenna snorts, "Sure you were. You'd better let me drive."

"What? Why?"

"Last time I saw you drive, you went over the curb." She holds her hand out for the keys.

"You have a driver's license?" I glance quickly at the porch where the foster mom still hovers.

"Learner's."

"You have it with you?"

She holds up her book bag, then tosses it between the seats into the back. Does it contain everything she now owns in the world? Maybe this is something I can do to get us off to a better start. I hesitate, then hand her the key. She runs around the Suburban and climbs in.

"Now take it easy," I say, wary that I've given in.

"Seatbelt," says Makenna, starting the engine, but before I can buckle up, she takes off fast, my body pitching against the seat.

"Slow down. What're you doing?"

"See that car?" She hangs a sharp U-ie at the first corner.

"What car?" I crane to look down the street. "Maybe you'd better let me — slow down, Makenna!" And she slaps the brakes.

"Damn," the girl says. "It's gone."

"What's gone?" I ask. "What's going on?"

"There was a car down here when I woke up this morning. Two people in it, a man and a woman. Then when I went out to wait for you, they were gone, but now as I was driving away, I thought I saw the car again."

We're a block past the green stucco house. I point at a truck parked in a driveway. "That's not it?"

She shakes her head. "It was a car. Old. Big. Ugly."

"That narrows it down."

"Maroon, I think, or burgundy."

"Maybe it belongs to someone who lives in the neighborhood."

"Why would anyone sit in a car for most of the day if they lived in the neighborhood?"

"But you said they came and went."

"Then came and went again." She's perfectly serious. I can see that.

And she thinks it means something.

"It wasn't Turner Bethune?" I ask.

"I'd know if it was him. Besides why would he spy on me?"

"To keep you safe." Her mother is dead, possibly murdered, so when I say, "Let's keep an eye out," I mean it.

Chapter 19
In-N-Out

I order a cheeseburger and Makenna refuses anything but a diet Coke. She sits across the table, uncurling the rim of her paper cup with her thumb, not looking at me, not smiling.

I don't know where to begin. I want to ask her how Olita found me, but I need safe ground, so I start with, "I'm sorry about your mother."

Her eyes flick up at me. Her tone is cold. "You didn't even know her."

My cheeks burn. "You're right. I didn't know her. I regret that."

"Really? Then why did you slam the door in her face?"

"I can explain that."

The counter guy calls out my number.

"That's my order." I can't get out of the little plastic chair fast enough. Maybe that foster mother is right. I never should've told Tellez and Grant I'd take the girl. The birth certificate was my way out, and I didn't take it. Why do I always convince myself that something will be okay when I know right down to my unpainted toenails the whole thing will end in disaster.

"Look," I say. Food in hand, I plop down at the table, ignoring her scowl. "I didn't know who she was."

"She just wanted to find out what her mother was like, and you told her to get the fuck off your porch."

In my mind, I see Olita's Volvo parked on my street, her stiff back striding down the walk. "I said get the 'hell' off my porch."

Her eyes are dark and hard, but the top of her lip quivers.

I'm such an asshole. "I'm sorry."

"Like that'll bring her back."

"I'm sorry" is all I can come up with. She's busy unrolling the rim of the cup. I start again, "She didn't tell me who she was. She said my mother's name and that's what set me off. I thought she was a reporter."

"Why would you think that?" She turns the cup over and pinches around the bottom.

"When reporters are doing stories on starlets with troubled lives, they come knocking on my door. I've learned that if I'm not rude, they keep coming back."

Those eyes hold mine. "Did your mother's suicide scar you for life?"

"You know about that?"

"My mother told me."

"When I found her note in the door jamb, I thought it was – crazy."

"Because she's black?"

"Not because of that. It's just that there's no one left in my family. No mother. No father. No siblings, aunts, uncles. The last thing I expected was to find out I had a sister."

She glances up from her cup.

I say, "And yes, if I did find out I had a sister, I wouldn't expect her to be black."

We're quiet, me playing with my food, her ripping the paper cup into bits. A kid sitting a couple tables away starts to cry.

"What else did she tell you about my mother?" I ask.

"Not much. She wanted to get all the info before she told me anything so I wouldn't, you know, get my hopes up. All my mom said was she was in the movies and she killed herself."

"My father never talked about her. He was broken up about the whole thing." Ahhh, but was he? Old perceptions die a slow death. "He started drinking after she died. When I was little, he'd take me with him to this bar down the hill.

It had fake palm trees and palm leaves over the bar like a little roof..." I trail off, something coming to me. "Huh. Maybe that's how I ended up at the Tiki Palms. My apartment. It connects me to my childhood. You know, I don't live in that big house right now."

"The lady told me." She piles up pieces of cup, a hay stack of white and red.

"The lady? Mrs. Grant told you about the apartment?"

"She wanted me to know exactly what I was getting into."

"Yet you're still here?"

She shrugs, and we sit in awkward silence until she says, "So why'd you leave your husband?"

"It's more of a leave-of-absence so I could — it sounds silly when I say it — find myself. I've never been on my own and there are things I'd like to do. Creative things."

"Like what?"

"Paint, make jewelry, learn new things. I'm taking a ceramics class right now. And maybe write a book. I already have a good start."

She doesn't look up, but asks, "What's it about?"

"This woman goes to the dentist and he's her boyfriend too, and he hides a weapon of mass destruction in her back tooth —"

Her head comes up. "What?"

"You know, a device that can destroy the world as we know it."

"In her tooth?"

"In a molar. It's fiction."

"You can say that again. What's it called?"

"I haven't gotten that far."

She leans back in her seat, scans the room. I look too. The kid is still sniveling somewhere down the row from us, his mother wiping up soda from the checkerboard floor with napkins.

"What's the main character's name?"

"I'm thinking, maybe, Susan Valentine."

"That's a good name. When're you gonna be published?"

"Published? I have to write it first."

"When's that?"

"That's exactly why I needed time to myself so I can actually do something. Finish something. I can't focus at home."

"Why not?"

I consider telling her about the whole boggy-mire-sucking-me-into-its-depths metaphor of my life. Better not. What I say is, "The book's almost done." More fiction on my part.

Now she's patting down the stack of paper cup bits, spreading them carefully over the table in front of her. "So what was she like?"

"Who? Susan Valentine?"

"No." She hits me with that impatient gaze again. "My grandmother."

"I've got some stuff at home to show you."

"Then let's go." She's out of her seat before I notice I haven't taken one bite of my cheeseburger.

Chapter 20
Virginia

We walk into the courtyard of the Tiki Palms, and Makenna rolls her eyes at the fake Maori masks, the parrots, the drums, and when the Gold Line train streaks by behind the alley, tooting its whistle, she looks at me and says, "You know, this is the kind of place my people have been working two hundred years to get out of."

She almost smiles. "Your face?" she says. "You're white as a sheet."

I unlock the front door and watch as she takes in the living room, the futon, the rocking chair, the tidied utility table, and the grocery store flowers perched next to the computer. With the drapes open, I'm relieved to see the place has a modest coziness to it.

"I get the futon, I suppose," she says.

"You have the bedroom."

"You don't have to give me your room."

"I have work to do." I nod at the essays stacked on the table. "It's better for me to be out here."

"Where's your dog? He can sleep with me."

"I'll get him tomorrow." The words are out of my mouth before I even think about it. What's Craig going to say? Phoenix! In this apartment?

Makenna lets her backpack slip to the floor and heads straight to the picture of my mother and me in the big chair. She picks it up. "This is her?"

"Virginia Gifford."

"She's — beautiful. I've seen pictures of her on the internet, but this is different. She has freckles."

"She was supposed to be sexy. She wore make-up to hide them."

"But she had them. Like me."

"Yes."

Again with those dark eyes, this time wet. "I didn't know she had freckles."

•◊•

We sit cross-legged on the floor, the plastic box between us. It's growing dark outside and I've flipped on the orange ceramic lamp I picked up at a yard sale. The carnations and roses next to the computer give off a faint sweet smell and I feel bathed in the past. I'm both excited and reluctant to share what little I know with this girl. Her face shows an eagerness I haven't seen in her before, anger and sorrow forgotten for the moment.

There's so much I want to ask her. What was her mother like? What was her childhood like? And what about Tonette who told her she was adopted? Why did she tell her that? Did Olita believe her? And what about Bethune? Who is he that the police would consider him the possible target of a hate crime? Is he Farrakhan, Sharpton, Cosby? I've never heard of him.

Makenna reaches into the box for the broken poetry book and leafs through its pages, removing two articles my father hadn't found, skimming them one at a time, laying them on the floor, smoothing them out. When she's finished, she says, "Not much here." Should I tell her about my father and his drinking, his silence, his swat-team tactics when I was young? No. She's got enough to deal without my own lonely childhood thrown at her.

"This article says she was in a movie called *Career Girls* with someone named June Haver. What's this 'Palm Springs Bikini Girl' thing?" Makenna asks. "I've looked her up on the internet. I didn't see anything about that."

"It was her nickname, like Lana Turner was the 'Sweater Girl' and Clara Bow was the 'It Girl'."

Makenna gives me a blank look, the same one my

students give me when I mention anything that came before 1985.

"Never mind," I say. "She got that name because she was the first person in America to wear a bikini on the cover of a national magazine."

"Really? *People?* Do you have it?"

"There was no *People* then. It was *Life* magazine. And I don't have it. I never had it."

"Was it a big magazine? Would it be on-line?"

"It must be. *Life* is still around, I think, at least as a corporation."

"Or maybe on eBay." Makenna leaps up and turns on the computer. It takes ages to boot, and then, ages to connect. She raps a knuckle impatiently on the monitor. "What's wrong with this thing?"

"It's slow." I pull up the rocker to sit behind her, feeling a little shaky. When the browser loads, she types 'life magazine cover' into Google, and then clicks on the link to www.life.com. The *Life* magazine screen appears with its red and white banner. I gape at the screen. I can't figure out where to start, but Makenna clicks on the last option on the menu: *Classic Life.*

"You've never done this before?" the girl asks.

"No."

"Why not?"

"I don't know."

"What do you mean you don't know?"

Of course, I know, but I've already told her that my father wouldn't talk about my mother so what I say to Makenna is, "We didn't have computers in my day, let alone the internet. I tried in college to find out more about her, but every article said the same thing, she committed suicide. That was the main thing, or so it seemed to me. She came from Iowa or Minnesota, was discovered in a diner where she was waitressing, and gave up her career to marry my father. They all read like obituaries. After I met Craig, I got

89

busy living my own life. I – I didn't want to think about her anymore, past history and all that, until your mother..." I let the words trail off.

Makenna has something to say, I can see that, but she lets it go and turns back to the keyboard. I'm swimming naked in a swamp full of water moccasins, but learning everything we can about Virginia Gifford matters now, to this girl, and to me.

"Abbie." Makenna brings me back from deep thought. A new screen shows on the computer with *Classic Covers* as an option. Makenna points at the words in the rectangular box. *Icons, Intrigue and 'It' Girls* – they're all there.

Chapter 21
Life Magazine

Makenna clicks the link on the *Life* magazine site and my body tenses as the next page opens. From here we have two options, one by date, one by keyword. Makenna wastes no time typing 'Virginia Gifford' into the narrow rectangle, hitting 'search'. We wait. And get a 'sorry' message.

Makenna looks at me, eyebrows cocked.

"Try by date. When was your mother born? '48?"

Makenna nods.

"Try that."

She uses the pull-down menu to find the year 1948, and gradually the pictures begin to load. It occurs to me that Virginia would've been pregnant then and not wearing a bikini, but we have to go on the assumption we don't know anything. Which is true. I keep my mouth shut.

The 1948 *Life* magazine covers unfold: Pakistan's Jinnah for January 5, Laurence Olivier for March 15, through Barbara Bel Geddes, April 12, fifteen covers for the first part of the year. Makenna clicks through to page two. The cover for July 19 is called 'Beach Fun' and features a girl in a swimsuit, but the suit isn't a bikini, and the girl isn't Virginia. The rest of the year is equally disappointing.

Makenna clicks back to 1947. There's another swimsuit picture, right in the middle of January. 'Styles for San Juan'. There's one more seductive bathing suit pose in March. Neither woman is my mother.

"I didn't realize the 1940s were so sexy," I say.

"NOT." Makenna turns around.

"Funny you," I say. "Go to page 2."

June 23 is titled 'Bathing Suits'. But no Virginia.

"Can't be 1946. She hadn't been in Hollywood long

enough."

"Let's at least check the rest of the year."

"There won't be any swimsuit pictures in the fall," I say, but Makenna jumps through the next few screens anyway. It isn't until page four that we see it. The cover for December 29, the caption, 'Celebrities Romp at the Springs' and there she is, my mother, the 'Palm Springs Bikini Girl'.

We're silent for what seems to me to be a long time. Then Makenna says, "That's not a bikini."

"Yes it is."

"She's all covered up."

"But you can see her navel. See? That's what separates a bikini from a two piece," I say. "The belly button."

"Where is it?"

I point at my mother's slim torso and Makenna makes a big deal over squinting and angling her head. Then she grumbles her assent.

"Look at her," I say. Even though the bikini doesn't show what a bikini shows today, Virginia Gifford is a sexy young thing. She's on the ladder of a swimming pool coming out of the water in a what is now an iconic starlet pose – her strong slender arms gleam in the sun, her hair wet and slicked back, her mouth open, eyes sparkling.

"Wow," says Makenna. "She's got it going on."

"I guess she does."

"Let's Google her."

"Save this page first. Start a folder."

So that's what Makenna does, a folder in the favorites on the toolbar, and calls it 'Grandma'. Seeing her type that word sends an odd thrill through me, and the tickle of a guilty conscience. When do I tell her about the birth certificate? She won't believe it, I'm sure, yet my instincts tell me to keep that confusing document under wraps for now.

I say, "Put in 'Palms Springs Bikini Girl'."

"What was the deal about the bikini back then?" the girl

asks as she bangs away at the keyboard.

"Most people hadn't seen a woman's belly button on the beach before, let alone on a magazine cover."

Makenna's looking at the screen. "Only one hit. 'Pictures fem doms male strippers in San Diego'."

"I don't think that's it," I say. "Try 'bikini girl'."

She places the cursor into the search window and deletes the Palm Springs part. Clicks 'go'.

Makenna screams, "Oh my God!" Popped up on the page is a montage of leering nude and semi-nude women, not one actually wearing a bikini.

"Okay," I say. "Go back."

But she's already typing something into the search box. "You know what we forgot?"

"What?" My neck and back are hurting. I rock back and stretch.

"We didn't Google her name."

'Virginia Gifford' yields 192 hits. A state forest in Ohio is named 'Virginia Gifford', and there's a Virginia soccer player named Gifford Okatah-Boi, but my mother is there too including a couple news stories about her suicide. Makenna opens one of them:

Actress Virginia Gifford (June 3 1928 – May 15 1954) was found dead of gas poisoning in the Hollywood home she shared with actor-husband Lyle Hart and her daughter, Abbie, after an apparent suicide on Friday afternoon. Virginia Gifford's four-year-old daughter was found wandering in the backyard when police arrived after an anonymous phone call.

Her biography states that she was born in Minnesota...

There's more, but I say, "I've read those," and point to 'Movies Unlimited, Films and TV: Movie Lookup, MSV

Entertainment-Celebs: Virginia Gifford'. "Go to one of these."

Several list her name and brief filmography, each one almost identical to the previous one, plagiarism alive and well on the net. Two fan sites, however, are dedicated specifically to her, and it is from these that we learn the most. Virginia Gifford was from Minnesota, not Iowa. Her real name is either Martha Gittering or Virginia Gittering. Worked as a waitress when she first came to Hollywood.

"Do you know where she worked?" asks Makenna.

"No."

We stare at the last site. Neither one is extensive and both have photos, some of the same photos I'd saved as a kid, but no miniature versions of the *Life* magazine cover.

Makenna says, "It's kind of weird, isn't it, that the information about her is mostly about her suicide."

"Almost like her life never happened." My voice cracks.

"But it did, because here you are and here I am. Living proof." Her eyes are wide.

"Living proof." I say, scrambling up. "You ready for some frozen yogurt?"

Chapter 22
Phoenix

Friday, May 24, 2002

She looks small in my double bed, younger than sixteen, angelic because the white sheet glows behind her dark skin. I lean down and whisper, "Makenna." Her eyes fly open and for a moment, she looks as if she's going to bolt, but then her face softens, and she rolls away. I pull up the quilt and tuck it around her, my hand brushing against the damp pillow. "I'm going out for a little while. The door's locked."

"You're going to get the dog?" Her voice is muffled.

"Yep. You wanna come?"

"No."

"Okay. Don't answer the door."

From the car, I call Craig on my cell, dismissing the low battery message, and let him know I'm picking up Phoenix.

He sounds distracted. "What are you talking about? Can't this wait? I'm at work."

"Makenna wants the dog," I say.

"Makenna? Who's Makenna?"

"The girl. You know, Olita's daughter."

There's silence on the other end. Then he says, "So she's related?"

"I don't know, but I have her until an aunt comes out from Louisiana."

He's quiet again, adjusting, weighing his words.

"The girl could have Christie's room. What do you need Phoenix for? He won't like living in an apartment."

"Are you kidding? That dog has to be coaxed outside with a T-bone steak."

"Except when he bolts."

"Except when he bolts." I sigh.

"I doubt they allow pets there."

"They do." I have no idea.

"Abbie."

"I've got it under control." Hah!

•◊•

Phoenix and I make a racket arriving back at the apartment, heading into the bedroom. The butt-wagging, orgasmic dog leaps onto Makenna and smothers her with tongue. There's no smile on her face, her eyes red and puffy as she grabs the dog with both arms, and I slip out.

I leave them in the bedroom and get comfortable on the futon in the living room, my essays spread around the floor. I have to get through this batch because I have the final exam essays to pick up at school. Then the semester will be over. Thank goodness. This part of life seems detached and unimportant after everything that's happened. I glance down at Kathy Esperanza's capital punishment essay, entitled 'Stop the Slaughter!!!' in bold Times New Roman and underlined.

Turner Bethune. What had the newspaper said, that he was an active opponent of capital punishment? I'm surrounded by thirty essays pro and con on just that subject. Turner and Olita lived together. I wonder why they never got married. And then my mind drifts to my mother and Billy Eastlake.

Discipline, Abbie. Read the damn essays, get through it, now.

On the computer I type in 'Billy Eastlake' and get a variety of sites, most with arcane and disorganized information. Then I remember a password-protected biography site.

96

Biography Databank: Billy Eastlake, Also known as: William Fanfare Easley

Birth: June 12, 1924, Nationality: American, Ethnicity: African American

Occupation: Comedian, violinist, property developer

Source: Entertainment Compendium, Volume 3. Edited by Marie Becker.

BIOGRAPHICAL ESSAY: Comedian and accomplished violinist, Billy Eastlake was born William Fanfare Easley in 1924 in New Orleans, Louisiana. Eastlake won the hearts of many Americans in the early sixties with three gold record albums featuring his unique style of humor and his virtuosity on "da fiddle." Like Nipsey Russell and George Kirby, Eastlake's brand of humor transcended race lines. He looked at the human condition without regard to color, telling stories of "unrequited love, requited love, and delighted requited love." A musical "riff" often underlined the punch line to a joke.

Eastlake often told stories about his life growing up. His father, Sherman T. Easley, worked for a local bootlegger. When Billy was eight, his father left his mother, Wilma Allen Easley, with five children to support.

Billy hauled a small wagon through the city to pick up clothing for his mother to launder, bringing his beloved fiddle with him. He'd practice while waiting for dirty garments or fees he was to collect. Often the help would stand at kitchen doors listening. Sometimes the lady of the house would send a tip down to him.

He began to play street corners in New Orleans and soon learned he could get more money if he also told jokes. The fiddle music caught people's attention; the humor got them to drop a few coins into the tin he kept on the ground at his feet.

In 1937, Wilma remarried. Billy and his step-father didn't get along, so at the age of thirteen, the boy hopped a freight train and fiddled and joked his way to Los Angeles where he continued working street corners and the occasional middle-of-the-night club gig. At 18, he joined the Navy and spent World War II in the Pacific. In addition to his regular duties as a sailor, he was called on to entertain aboard ship.

After the war, Billy returned to Los Angeles and was soon traveling the country on the "chitlin' circuit," in black night clubs and juke joints, and doing bits for local radio stations. As early as 1950, he appeared on Ed Sullivan's Toast of the Town recreating one of his more acceptable night club monologues. His second album became the first of three gold albums.

Throughout the fifties, Billy appeared on television, including Red Skelton and Jack Paar. In the sixties, he was an occasional regular on Flip Wilson's show and invited to Las Vegas as an opening act. Most of his fortune came from this time when he invested in and developed property in the black part of Las Vegas. Billy Eastlake retired in 1972.

Billy Eastlake has been married twice. His first wife, Della Butler, was mother to his son. William Jr. was killed in Viet Nam. Mavis Geary became Billy's bride for three months in 1973.*

*Update: The 78-year-old comedian married singer Liv Amaral, 28, in 1999.

I'm a little blown away by this turn of events. Billy Eastlake, a regular Don Juan.

Chapter 23
Shoved

Twenty-eight! Billy Eastlake's bride is twenty-eight — or was when the article was written. I type 'Liv Amaral' into Google and click through to her website. The whole page is a black and white picture of her: her long neck arched, her lips parted. There's a brief bio at the top of the right hand column: a white California girl, San Pedro, some commercial credits, an appearance on *Late Night with Conan O'Brien*. I hear the bedroom door open, Makenna slouching into the bathroom. Phoenix waits at the door, tail flying. A few minutes later she comes out, stoops to bury her face in the dog's neck.

Long seconds pass. Poor Makenna. I consider telling her about what I've found on Billy, but decide to wait. I'm on information overload and she's been through a lot. We need time to breathe. I power down the computer and stretch. "Anybody hungry?"

Phoenix trots in.

"Hey you," I say, and scratch his head, point to his bowl of water. Makenna follows, wrapped in my t-shirt quilt.

I whip up pancakes. I make them from scratch: wheat flour, one egg, melted butter, skim milk, baking powder, salt. Usually I make a half recipe, but with a houseguest, I don't skimp.

Putting down the bowl and whisk, I reach out to her. "You feel okay?"

"Don't," she says, shrugging me off. "I don't want to talk about it."

"No problem. Are you warm enough?"

She pulls the coverlet tighter around her shoulders and glances at a yellow Sea Serpents mascot. "What are all these things?"

"T-shirts. All the ones my kids outgrew. Sea Serpents is the name of the swim team. That was Christie's and the one above that is Jason's kayak club. The turquoise one."

She twists around to look at the back of her arm and says, "Girl Scouts?"

"Yep." I go back to stirring my batter.

"So I guess you don't hate your kids if you sleep with their t-shirts."

"Why do you think I hate them?"

"You left them, didn't you?"

"They're both adults. They left me." Their absence and time on my hands is what's pushed me into asking questions about who I am and who I want to be, giving me room to remember some of those dreams I had about the future. And now here's Makenna shoving me into the past. There's something paradoxical about this, but it escapes me what.

Later we go to the college so I can collect the essay finals in my mailbox. I dread this, seeing people I know after all that's happened. A quick in and out is what I want so I suggest Makenna wait in the car, but she'll have none of it.

The English Department office is institutional, walls the same green as the interrogation room at the police station. Lurking behind the creeping Charlie plant on the counter is the department secretary. "Hey, Professor Palmer! You're feeling better?"

"I am, Nicole, thanks." I give her what I hope is an on-the-mend smile. My excuse for missing class was officially the flu. Her gaze shifts to Makenna.

"May I help you?"

"She's with me," I say.

"You need the conference room to make up the final?"

"No, no. She's not a student." I grab the essays from my mailbox and hustle Makenna toward the door.

"Wait. Dean Chute wants to see you," says Nicole. "You can go on in." Trapped. I flash Makenna a warning look and leave her in the outer office with Nicole.

Elaine Chute is tall, elegant, and has a great sense of humor. She's also straightforward, so when she hits me with, "You've decided to become a foster mother?" as soon as I walk in, I'm only mildly surprised.

"So Social Services called to check on me?" I close the door and explain Makenna's need for a place to stay, skipping over the more tantalizing details. She'll get the whole story when I'm ready, not now with the girl waiting for me.

As Makenna and I stride past the library and through the sculpture garden where the smokers hang out, I almost feel normal again. I'm doing a good deed, it's temporary, and soon, the Louisiana aunt will show up. Besides, there's Bethune. The girl loves him. All I need to do is be kind, take her shopping, get manicures.

Then Makenna turns, her cheeks tinged red. She hisses, "This isn't a stupid sit-com, you know."

Along the concrete path and across the grass, people slow down. Gawk.

"Makenna, what? What did I do wrong?"

"Why didn't you introduce me to anyone back there, not to the secretary, not to your boss? It was so — awkward."

"I didn't think —" I reach out to her and she twists away. I grab her shoulder and she shoves at me. Hard. I stumble back to get my balance. Her mouth works. Her eyes are red with tears. She whirls around and stalks toward the parking lot. I hurry after her, then slow my gait. Calm my breath.

She leans against the Suburban.

"What was that?" My voice quavers.

She doesn't look at me. Grumbles.

"I can't hear you."

"You shouldn't be driving this gas-guzzling piece of shit," she says, turning and kicking a tire. "It's environmentally unsound."

"You shoved me."

"I'm sorry."

"You're sorry?"

"I've been meaning to tell you about driving such a stupid car —"

"Is that right?"

"That's right."

"Makenna, I'm sorry if I hurt your feelings. I just wanted to get in and out as fast as possible."

"You don't recycle either. You use hair spray." She rolls her body along the car before she pushes herself away, and drags around to the passenger side.

I get in and wait for her.

She takes her time, sagging into the seat. "Where we going?"

The only ammunition I have. "Shopping."

Chapter 24
Flip-Flops

As soon as we're heading east on Colorado Boulevard, I adopt a light and cheery approach. More has happened to Makenna than just losing her mother. We have to recreate her material life from scratch, and my logic is if we start there, maybe it will help with everything else. I believe in therapeutic shopping as well as therapeutic eating. And the idea that muck doesn't stick to anything moving fast enough.

The only things she owns now are the clothes on her back and the stuff she happened to take to her friend Audrey's house the night of the firebombing, a visit that saved Makenna's life.

I have her get out the narrow notepad I keep in the glove box of my Suburban, and tick off a list. "Face wash, comb, brush, shampoo. What kind do you like?"

"Do we have to do this now?"

I have the urge to tell her about my muck/swamp theory, but decide she probably thinks I'm weird already, life at the Tiki Palms proof of that premise. So I ignore her.

"You think they have flat irons at Target?" she asks.

"Flat irons? You mean an iron for clothes?"

She gives me a disdainful look. "I mean for my hair."

Her curls do start close to her scalp, all of it pulled back neatly in a rubber band. I don't know what happened to the clip she had before.

"Your hair is darling," I say. She gives me another withering look and turns to stare out the window. I don't know why I keep offending her, but I'm sure it'll come out sooner or later, and at the most inopportune moment.

Once we get to Target, I suggest we look for clothes first. I know from experience that shopping with a teenage girl can be harrowing. A parent needs both the energy of a hummingbird and the patience of a vulture so if we wait too long to tackle this task, I'll be flying south before we buy that first pair of flip-flops.

Thank goodness summer's almost here so we can keep it simple, t-shirts, shorts, sundresses, sandals. She isn't quite out of her dark mood, not yet, even though we're slurping down one of my favorite treats: cherry Icees.

We stop at a rack of hoodies. I know that's what they're called because of my daughter Christie and her old obsession with Eminem. "He's authentic, Mom." Whatever that means.

Hangers scrape the metal rack as I look for a sweatshirt in tangerine, size small or medium, wanting to know more about Bethune, wondering how to ask. Then I hear myself say casually, "So Makenna, what's Mr. Bethune really like?"

"Turner?" She pulls turquoise running pants off another rack and holds them up.

"How long have you known him?"

"We already had this conversation."

"Is he nice to you?"

"Yeah, he is."

"Was he good to your mother?"

"What do you mean by that?"

"You know, did he bring her flowers, take her out on dates?"

"You wanna make some kind of play for him?" she asks, her jaw clenching as she jams the pants back into the rack, snapping the plastic hanger.

Red flag, red flag. I've spooked her again. Dang me. I used to be better at this.

I send her into the dressing room with a too bright "Show me everything," my attempt to get back to the somewhat neutral "whatever" mood we had before picking up my exams, but I can tell it isn't working. I sit down by the cart to wait.

My bunions ache. I've had them since I was thirty, a result of standing in high heels on cement floors in my other career. Before I became a part-time college teacher, I was a full-time mom, but before that, I worked in retail at Bradshaw's, a large southern California department store chain. What I got out of that career were rotten feet and the ability to rattle off all 44 Bradshaw locations and store numbers: Downtown was store #1, Hollywood, #2, Pasadena, #3, Crenshaw, #4, and so on, a dubious talent and one not likely to get me on "Jeopardy," but it has the ability to impress my students when they're bored and need something to give me a hard time about: "Professor Palmer, you need a life." My son Jason was born the year they built #43 in Phoenix.

We flew to Arizona, Craig and I, and after the opening, took a side trip to the bottom of the Grand Canyon on the back of mules. I've always blamed Jason's spirit of adventure on the fact that he was conceived on a sandy bend of the Colorado River. Since he's currently on a rubber raft in the Pantanal without so much as a satellite phone, I make it a policy not to think about him too much, keeping my worry-beads under the bed. I settle back in the red plastic chair with a sigh, stare at the Target bull's eye on the cart.

The dressing room attendant is buried in towering jumbles of clothes, folding pants, putting shirts back on hangers. The job seems endless. I don't know how she can ever catch up, but she's smiling to herself, humming some song I don't recognize, and I want her attitude. My life is like this waiting room, unfinished business draped over shopping carts, hangers tangled on the floor, the counter loaded with rejects. Professor Palmer, get a life.

Makenna's been in the fitting room a long time and I haven't seen one t-shirt, not one pair of jeans. Moving aside the cart, I make my way to the door. My breath catches at the sound of quiet sobbing inside. I tap-tap. When she doesn't answer, I go in, and squeeze next to her on the

105

narrow bench, take her hand. She turns her hot face into my shoulder and my heart breaks.

Chapter 25
Target

A security guard knocks on the dressing room door and comes right in, doing a double-take. Maybe it's the white and black thing, this middle-aged woman with her arms around the girl.

"You okay?" she says to Makenna, her voice pointed and sharp.

Makenna nods and I tell the security woman we're fine. She is reluctant to leave, so I ignore her in favor of Makenna, "Is there anything you want to buy?"

"I don't care," she says, sitting up, wiping her nose.

"We can go shopping again later, but we've got to get a few things now. How about this khaki skirt?"

The guard narrows her eyes at me, then backs out, closing the door behind her.

Makenna pulls away, stands up. Her voice isn't loud or even angry, yet "Don't go thinking you're all that because you're not" is what comes out of her mouth. "You aren't my mother."

I'm grateful she chooses to say this after the guard leaves. I take a deep breath and consciously lower my own voice an octave. "You're right. I'm not your mother. I never can be."

She's backed up against the smeary mirror, her body stiff with tension. The pair of short-alls she's wearing make her look incredibly young, not sixteen at all, but six.

I have to get this right. "I want to be your friend."

"You're just putting on the white lady charity act so everybody thinks you're special." She does the quotation thing around "You're special."

I take another deep breath. "I can't help what you think. I still want to help you."

This turns her face red. Her lips quiver, her voice goes shrill. "Buying me hamburgers and clothes doesn't mean you care about me. You don't even care about your own mother. You never talk about her. Well, I'm not like you. I want to talk about my mother and you haven't once asked me one question about her, your own sister, who she was, or what I love about her."

This last part staggers me. All I've wanted to do is talk about her mother. All my instincts are buried in swamp mud.

The security guard doesn't knock on the door this time. Obviously she's been lingering nearby. She comes in and says to Makenna, "You want me to call the police?"

I can't believe it. Makenna's glaring at me, like she's thinking about taking the woman's suggestion. Then she says, "This is my so-called auntie and she won't buy me these overalls."

The guard studies the girl a moment, squints at me. I'm sitting on the triangle bench in the corner. I haven't moved an eyelash. Holding my breath. Somehow I manage to say, "They're too short."

"They are not!"

The security guard folds her arms, frowns. "Next time I have to come in here, I'm bringing someone who can drag you both out of this store."

As she goes out, she tells Makenna, "You're asking for nothing but trouble in that outfit."

I get busy inspecting the discarded tags and straight pins on the floor, giving the girl space, not saying anything. I'm squirming because of the auntie stuff. I have to tell her soon about the birth certificate, but not now, not yet. And it's just a piece of paper. Not proving anything, one way or another.

Then I hear her laugh. I look up. She's bending over and wiggling her butt in the mirror. The shorts show plump round cheeks. Shaking her head, wagging her finger, she gives me a very grown-up and disapproving "Hm-m-hm-hm-m."

I laugh too and she plops down next to me on the little seat, bumping me, and we both howl until tears stream down our cheeks. When we start to calm down, and I do the "Hm-m-hm-hm-m" routine, we laugh again until the giggling finally peters out.

A few minutes pass and then I turn and ask her soberly, really wanting to know, "Makenna. Will you tell me what your mother was like?"

I wait a long time and realize with mild surprise, there's nothing else I'd rather do than wait. She says, "She was afraid of elevators."

"She was?"

"Well, she said when she was little and watching a TV game show – it had some stupid name. She said it was a town in New Mexico or Arizona."

"Truth or Consequences?"

"Yeah, that's it, 'Truth or Consequences'. I don't even know what that means. Do you?"

"I have an idea. Tell me your story first."

"Anyway, on the show some woman talked about how she couldn't squeeze onto an elevator because it was too packed up with people, so she had to take the stairs, and how the elevator crashed fifteen floors and everyone on board was killed. My mom said it was the first time she realized that something so ordinary like an elevator could kill people."

Tears sting my nose, my eyes again. Another long silence falls between us before I venture. "Well, what do you want to buy?"

"The overalls for sure."

"They're too short."

"That's why."

•◊•

When we finally leave the store, each pushing a cart, the sky is a dusky blue, the parking lot hazy in the evening light. It's funny how buying a couple hundred dollars-worth of toe-rings and tank-tops, bikini underwear, shorts, shampoo and conditioner, lip gloss, CD player and CDs, bonding over OutKast, Eminem, Pharrell, Fifty Cent — she's shocked I even know who they are — can wash the muck away.

We head across the asphalt together, but when Makenna sees a gap between two cars and a chance to reach the Suburban before me, she scoots through. I hear her laugh at the idea of stranding me, but I'm right behind. Then, as she emerges into the next aisle, her pony-tail bouncing, a car guns its engine, and, headlights blinding, heads straight for her.

Chapter 26
Bethune

I run, tackling Makenna just as the car smashes into the plastic cart, splintering it apart. Bags with red Target logos spew into the air, then clump down like so much debris onto the asphalt.

She shakes as I press her against the dusty window of a hatchback. "You okay?" I ask, gasping for breath, heart hammering.

"Your knee's pinching my thigh," she says. I back off, standing on quaking legs. Makenna uses the car for support. People gawk, the car long gone.

"Did anyone get the license plate?" I yell.

Someone says, "I think it was a Riviera, man."

"Naw, it was a Monte Carlo."

A store employee, an Asian teenager with orange hair and a lip ring who's been out collecting shopping carts, gathers up our bags and follows us toward the store. The manager along with two security guards rushes out and hurries us inside, past restrooms, down a long white hall, and into a back room. Someone must have already called 911, but I pull out my cell.

There's so much adrenaline zooming through my body I can't punch the numbers. Too much has happened. I keep thinking this has to be intentional. Makenna, like Turner Bethune, must be a target. I ask one of the security guards if she'll plug in the numbers for me. It's the nosy fitting room inspector.

She gives me a "huh" deep in her throat, meaning, I'm sure, she knew we were trouble.

Detective Tellez isn't available at the police station, so I ask for Fuji. He's out too. I tell the guy on the phone about the accident.

"She's been hit?" he asks.

"No, she's okay. He was going fast through the lot and she came out between two cars with her cart. The cart flew all over the place."

"Just stay calm. The officers are on their way," he says. "I'll have Detective Tellez call you back."

We stay in the security office where they must give shoplifters the third degree. I know my interrogation rooms by now. It looks serious enough for any *Law and Order* episode, brilliant with fluorescent light, an empty table, four metal chairs, a stack of unopened boxes labeled, 'George Foreman Lean and Mean Grills'. The kid with orange hair tries to hand Makenna a soda cup, but she's too stunned to notice. I move next to her and rest my hand on her shoulder. She doesn't push me away.

When the patrolmen arrive, we give our account. Then I ask about Detective Tellez, if she's been in touch with them.

"We can let her know," he says, but I'm not certain he actually knows who Tellez is or that he makes the connection between Makenna and the firebombing incident, but I don't enlighten him.

I'm worried about what's happened in the parking lot. It's not logical that Makenna would be a target, yet that car, that Monte Carlo or whatever, seemed to aim its fat nose right at her. I ask her if it was the same car she saw outside the foster home, but she doesn't know, the headlights blinding her. Is someone following us? Or was the car driven by joy-riding teenagers? Or distracted old men, Makenna darting into the traffic lane without looking? My brain hurts. Nothing else makes sense. But I need Detective Tellez to reassure me about this.

I glance up at the security guard from the dressing room and wonder if she's going to call channel 11 as soon as we leave. I want to offer her money to keep her quiet, but maybe it won't occur to her, and I don't want to give her the idea that this young girl is the one who escaped the firebomb that killed her mother.

Finally the officers let us climb into my Suburban. I'm nervous, glancing around the parking lot, paranoia in full swing, wanting to get home, wanting to crawl onto the futon and bury myself until morning.

Makenna seems to have recovered somewhat. The extra-large diet coke and the enthusiasm of the orange-haired kid didn't hurt. "My whole life flashed," she'd told Bleach Boy.

I start the engine and the radio sputters in and out. She's jamming buttons because she won't listen to commercials or DJ chitchat. I catch the name "Bethune" and glance at Makenna, hoping she hasn't noticed, tearing through stations until she finds something she likes. Old school. Tupac.

But eventually it's on the news. I reach toward the dial, but she stops my hand, vehemently shakes her head. So we listen.

"African-American activist Turner Bethune has been questioned for the second time in the alleged firebombing of his home and the subsequent death of Pasadena school vice-principal, Olita Jordan."

I pull over and park by a hydrant, the only available spot.

Makenna sits rigid beside me as the reporter continues in an insultingly breezy tone. "Bethune was approached by detectives outside the Pasadena Hilton this afternoon and escorted to the police station for further questioning. Two weeks before the early morning bombing, racial slurs were painted on the sidewalk of Bethune's eastside residence. Markings purportedly included stick-figure depictions of a lynching as well as an electrocution leading authorities to believe Bethune's outspoken stand against the death penalty and its racist implications was the cause for the crime. However, police are exploring alternate theories to this week's arson and death and it is unclear as to whether Bethune is being questioned as a victim of crime or as a person of interest. Authorities declined to elaborate. Meanwhile, Bethune has secured the services of high-profile attorney Darton Reglan, according to reliable sources."

All I can think to say is, "I'm so sorry," but I keep my lips pressed together.

Makenna falls back against the seat, her jaw slack, eyes unfocused.

My hands on the steering wheel are damp with sweat.

Chapter 27
Careful

W e stumble into the apartment like zombies, the phone ringing, the answering machine picking up. At the sound of Tellez's voice, I hurry in, Makenna following and stopping at the bedroom door as I snatch the receiver.

"So what happened?" the detective asks.

"What's with Bethune?"

"Let's talk about Makenna first."

"Okay. Did you get the officer's report?"

"Are you kidding? Just tell me."

So I do, including the part about Makenna being suspicious of a car parked on the street near her foster home.

"Let me talk to her," Tellez says.

I hand over the receiver and lay down across the bed, exhausted. The first thing the girl wants to know about is Bethune, her voice high and angry. Tellez must say something to relieve her alarm because Makenna begins to recite how Target-cart-pushing turned into Target-cart-bashing. The whole tale comes to me as if she's a guest on Jerry Springer, and I've forgotten to turn off the TV.

There's a silence, Makenna listening, then the girl explains about the parked car she suspected of watching her near the foster home. What an idiot I am. The two events must tie together. Someone spying on Makenna? Waiting for her to be vulnerable. But what does that have to do with Turner Bethune? If he's arrested for Olita's murder –

Makenna taps the phone against my hand. I take it, staying prone on the bed, no energy left until Tellez's strong voice brings me to my elbow. She says, "I don't want to alarm you, but there's a need for concern here. Why didn't you call me about the car near the foster home before this?"

My stomach clenches. "Random cars are parked

everywhere all the time. I didn't really believe —"

"What happened in the parking lot tonight was probably a coincidence, but I want you to be careful. The usual precautions. Don't go wandering around alone after dark. Call me if you suspect anything, anything at all, okay? You have a pencil there?"

"Just a minute." I sit up and make an air-writing movement and Makenna hands me my purse. I fumble for a pen and something to write on. I settle for a Teri & Yaki chicken receipt. "Okay. Ready."

Tellez spins off her personal cell phone number. "Use it if you need to and give it to Makenna."

"So, what about Bethune?" I ask.

"How do you guys know we had him in?"

"It was on the radio."

"The radio? Shit." I can hear her muffling the phone and shouting to someone in the background. When she comes back, she says, "Questioning family members is standard, Abbie. It's Bethune who's overreacted by getting himself an attorney. Bad move on his part because the media loves this kind of stuff."

"So it's not a big deal?" I ask.

When Tellez doesn't answer right away, I work to keep a neutral expression.

She says, "We've let him go, but we're looking beyond the hate-crime evidence for something else."

"Sure. Okay." I want to ask why, but I can't with Makenna's expectant face riveted on mine.

As if reading my mind, Tellez says, "We can talk later. How's she doing?"

"She's great."

"Good. Keep it that way. And Abbie, don't be too hard on yourself. You saved that girl's life," she says, then hangs up.

"What was that all about?" Makenna asks as soon as I replace the receiver.

"Keep our eyes open. Be careful."

"No. I mean about the arrest."

"He wasn't arrested," I say. "They just talked to him. The media jumps on any little thing that comes from the police and they make it a big to-do."

"Like *People* magazine will be here tomorrow."

"God, I hope not."

•◇•

Later, after a quick dinner of bagged lettuce and rotisserie chicken – no meat for Makenna, a vegetarian I now know – and when Makenna is finally in bed, I curl up on the futon wanting only the oblivion of sleep, but my body is still humming. I'm up to my neck in my boggy swamp, and I can't figure out how I can save myself if I have to save Makenna too. And it's obvious I've been doing a lousy job. That sudden beam of headlights flashes in my mind. I hear the jangling smash of car hitting cart. I sit up. Hug my knees. I'm never going to sleep tonight. I forgot my Ativan in the bedroom with Makenna.

Makenna. She loves Bethune like a father. Why does he think he needs a lawyer? He loved Olita. My sister? Half-sister? She stood there on the porch, her freckles sweeping like streamers across both cheeks. Like Virginia's. And Makenna's.

Once again I boot the computer. I need to start doing some investigating myself. Not about the murder. That's a job for the police, but for us, Makenna and me. To keep us busy, to distract the girl. I search for Elma's obituary again. Read through it until I find the name of her son. "She is survived by her son, Thomas V. Robinson (Louise) and her daughter, Diane Robinson Garcia (Paul), six grandchildren –"

I enter his name + Los Angeles into Google and there he is, in Baldwin Hills. There's even a phone number.

I rummage through the folder I brought from home to

see if the restaurant photo of my mom and dad mentions the agent who represented both my parents. There it is: 'Dennis Ventura'. One more person to track down. I run another search through Google. There are three likely possibilities for Dennis Ventura.

Chapter 28
Turner

Saturday, May 25, 2002

I start moving around before six, tired this morning, but dutifully reading essays. I'm far behind on all of it, the death penalty papers, the newly collected finals, but I plow on with determination, telling myself that sometime today I will call Thomas Robinson and my three Dennis Ventura possibilities.

I need to talk with Tellez too, so I can find out if there is more going on with Bethune than she told me last night, but I can't do that until I'm certain Makenna won't be waltzing out of the bedroom any minute.

I glance toward the tiny hall that opens to the bathroom and bedroom, then turn back to my paper-reading routine. I manage to do this for three more essays, my neck getting stiff, when there's a tap on the front door.

It's Craig. He's in shorts, hair slicked back, his face ruddy from his shower.

"You don't have a TV, do you?" he says.

"No, why?" I block the doorway.

"Can I come in?"

"What's happened?"

He gives me that "Who are you trying to kid" look.

"Oh, shit." I let him in. "It was on TV."

"Are you okay?"

"We're fine. Remember the accident at Farmer's Market? The old man who plowed into pedestrians? That kind of thing," I say.

"That kind of thing can leave people dead."

"I just mean these things happen. Randomly. It was just a random accident. What did they say on TV?"

"They showed the reporter in the parking lot with that big red bull's eye sign behind her. She mentioned Makenna had lost her mother in a recent fire. You didn't call me." He says this last part in a soft hurt voice, his brown eyes intense as they find mine, and I could smack him. Or better, smack myself if I only could.

"What did they say, exactly?" I ask again.

"You pushed Makenna out of harm's way. The car left the scene. Are you sure you're okay? You're very calm about all this."

"We're fine, both fine." Then I add, "We're not coming back to the house."

He looks put-out for a moment, like the idea of me and Makenna packing our bags and heading over to Woodbine Street hadn't crossed his mind. He shrugs. "A couple of reporters were out in front of the house this morning. Maybe it's a good thing you're in this dump."

"It's not a dump."

He doesn't say anything, so I have to. "Okay. Thanks for warning me. We'll stay low for a while."

"No problem. I'll come by around five and take you guys to dinner."

"Craig. We're fine. Please."

"Who's watching out for you here?"

"We've got the dog."

"Oh, that should do it. He'll lick the guy to death."

"Bye, Craig."

Once he's gone, I let the panic wash over me. First Olita dies, then Makenna is almost run down by a car. This can't really be random, can it? Things are happening faster than I can handle them. I've got to get my head on straight.

Phoenix pads into the living room, followed by Makenna. "Who was that?" she asks.

"My husband checking on us. He saw a report about last night on TV."

"Really?" She glances around for a television, raises her

brows when she can't find one.

•◊•

Out on my tiny porch, I let the early afternoon heat massage my face and shoulders. I've left a message on Thomas Robinson's phone, Elma's son, my landline number as well as my cell, so I'm hopeful about that, but not one Dennis Ventura has panned out. I don't know where else to search for him. Do entertainment agents belong to a union or something? Is there a directory of agents from the late '40s somewhere? If I can't track him down, maybe I can find one of his clients from that time. But how would I do that? What about finding Billy Eastlake? I should've looked up his address too. I am not functioning on all cylinders. I've got to get organized.

I pull myself up to do just that when Makenna, perched on the short narrow porch railing, lets out a squeal and I look first at her, then turn toward the gate as it scrapes open. Turner Bethune holds up his large hand in greeting and Makenna sprints to him, hugs, clings. No matter what happens, this girl loves this man like a dad. What will she do if he isn't who he seems to be?

He takes her by the shoulders, the two of them standing in the middle of the tiny courtyard, and though I can't hear what they're saying, I know she's telling him about what happened last night at Target.

He gives her another squeeze and meets my eyes over her dark hair, a grim smile on his lips. Makenna pulls him over to me and he says, "I don't know how to thank you."

"I just reacted. One of those things. She's doing great, huh?"

He beams at Makenna. "Yes she is."

"So what happened with the cops?" Makenna asks.

"The cops question everybody, honey. You can't blame them for that. Besides they wanted to rattle me because I took you away from the foster home."

"But they arrested you."

"They did not arrest me. I didn't do anything and they know it, you hear me?"

They stare at each other for a long moment. Then she hugs him again.

He stands there a moment, clears his throat, and says, "I did a walk-through of the house with a fire inspector. I can take you over today if you want."

Chapter 29
Neighbors

As he pulls into the driveway of the burned out house, Turner Bethune says, "Insurance is taking care of their end, but I think it's important that we know exactly what's here for ourselves."

We sit for a few minutes, the two of them in the front seat, me in the back. I can't see their faces, but Bethune's eyes catch and hold mine in the rearview mirror. He climbs out first and we follow.

Makenna asked me to go with them and I'm glad of it, though it's a sad thing, picking over what's left of the lives of three people, one of whom is no longer with us. But after the Target episode, I don't want Makenna out of my sight. No matter how she feels about Bethune, I'm not ready to blindly accept his innocence.

Although its two small panes of glass have shattered, the front door is still sturdy and locked. Turner struggles with the key, but it finally yields. Huge plywood boards have been nailed into place over the windows and one of the walls so as we go in, I expect it to be dark, but it's not.

There's a hole in one corner of the ceiling where the roof has collapsed. Shingles and charred 2x4s are scattered over the living room smothering what's left of the scorched upholstered chairs, tables, sofa. Books litter the floor, blackened from smoke, mushy from fire-hose water and already beginning to mold. And though it has been a couple of days, the heat seems to linger as well as the smell of burnt wood, fabric, exploded cans of food from the pantry, and other odors I don't let myself think about.

We stand as still as trees in a scorched forest. It's too much to take in at once. I move a little closer to Makenna and touch her hand while Turner slides the backpack he's brought from his shoulder, saying, "I want to take pictures. The insurance company came and took some, but I want to make sure we've got the same information. You never know in a case like this. I bought a couple Polaroid cameras."

He unzips the kit, and removes two blister packs. Hands one to Makenna and one to me. Then he clears his throat and picks up a lump of charcoal. What had it been before? A chair leg, a piece of a door? He drops it. Smacks his hands together. "Still feels warm to me." His voice cracks. "Probably my head playing tricks."

He turns toward the hallway, the wall almost completely burned through. Down there, I think, is where Olita was trapped in her bedroom, the house an inferno.

"You have any scissors?" I ask to cover the moment.

"Yeah," he says. "I do. The fire department shut off the utilities. At least the shell's still here. Looks as if there's as much damage from the water as from the fire. Guess we should be grateful." His voice breaks again, and Makenna puts her arms around him. I back out the front door, giving them time, taking my packaged camera with me.

On the porch, I stop for a moment and scan the quiet neighborhood. There's nothing left of the tragedy anywhere on the street, except for the house behind me.

Two girls, kids really, on bikes watch me from the other side of the street. They wave and when I wave back, they pedal over. I stride across the soft lawn to meet them.

"Makenna here?" the taller one asks, nodding toward Turner's SUV. The girls look like they're around eleven or twelve.

"She's inside," I say.

"Is she okay?" the smaller girl asks. "She's our baby sitter."

"She's doing all right."

"We live down the street. I'm Hayley. This is my little sister Kristen."

"I'll tell her you stopped by," I say.

"Is she coming back? To live, I mean?" asks Kristen. She glances at the scarred house, frowns.

"I don't know."

"Tell her we want her back."

"I will."

The girls start to move away, but I stop them. "Hey, you know the two old men with the dogs?"

Hayley answers, "You mean Mr. Cole?"

"One had a dog that looks like a mean poodle with short hair and the other had a little terrier, curls like wire."

"The curly one is Mr. Roland," says Kristen.

"The curly dog belongs to Mr. Roland, dummy. The other one is Mr. Cole. His dog is Brutus," says her sister.

"Don't call me a dummy —"

"So you know them?" I interrupt.

"They live over there." Hayley points toward a house faced in brick with a white picket fence and bright yellow gazanias in the parkway.

"Together?" I ask.

"No, Mr. Roland lives next door."

"Abbie?"

Behind me, Turner fills the doorway of his charred house and when the girls see him, they wave and yell, "Hey, Mr. Bethune," then turn to go with a "Tell Makenna we miss her" over their shoulders.

Turner waves back, nods at me, and goes inside.

Following behind, I glance down the street. I don't know what my plan is, not even sure I have one, but I know I want to pay a visit to Mr. Cole and Mr. Roland because one of them claimed to see a suspicious car. After what happened in the Target parking lot, I want to know just what kind of car it was.

I feel something inside me begin to settle. I'm doing this. Slogging into the swamp.

Chapter 30
Houston's

The clouds have shifted and Olita's house is filled with shadows. Bethune turns toward me, lifting his head expectantly, as if I might be someone else.

I ask, "How's Makenna doing?"

"She's in her bedroom, what's left of her bedroom." He shakes his head.

I want to reach out, rest my hand on his arm, but I hesitate. Standing next to him makes me feel small. The day of the fire, I'd been afraid of him, but now I'm just sad. "May I ask you something?"

"Sure," he says.

"I'm trying to piece all this together, and I have no clue as to how Olita found me. Who did she talk to?"

"That's what you want to ask me? Now? Here?" The muscles in his face twitch.

"I'm sorry." I turn toward the door, fleeing again.

"Wait."

I shift back to him. "We can talk about this later."

He glances toward the hallway. "I never heard about you until the night she died. I was traveling and when I called, she was upset because of you. I guess that's why I went off the other day, after the fire. My last conversation with her was about her frustration with you. And that's all I know."

•◇•

Turner Bethune drives us to Houston's for dinner. We've taken at least a hundred pictures between us and in the back of the SUV are boxes of recovered items including some of Makenna's clothes, smoky but not burned, books, and her mother's jewelry box. We're pretty ragged, but none of us care. A quick wash-up in the restaurant restroom will have to suffice. Houston's is Makenna's favorite place and after the last two hours, I'm happy to do anything to avoid going home to my tiny apartment and have her duck into the bedroom to cry. Today has not been easy, especially for her.

My cell phone rings. It's Craig. "Are you home?"

"Makenna and I've just left her house," I say.

"What house?"

"The house where she used to live."

"Oh. How is it?"

"Shocking. Look, I can't talk right now. Let me call you later." And I hang up without waiting for his answer.

Houston's is all sophisticated atmosphere, Murano glass fixtures, deep comfortable booths. We're seated by the window. Makenna and Bethune study the menu while I sneak peeks at the two of them. It's been an emotionally exhausting day, yet Makenna seems so comfortable with him, and he with her. Hard to imagine he had anything to do with Olita's death.

"Let's talk about school." Turner puts down the menu, folds his hands, and looks at Makenna, his eyes soft. "How soon do you think you'll be ready to go back?"

"I don't want to go back. I can't even talk to Audrey yet. It's – it's too hard." She bites her lip, and the tiniest drip of moisture appears below her nose.

"I know, darlin'. It's a tough thing, but it's something you need to get through, don't you think? Part of the healing process."

She whispers, "But I don't wanna heal."

The waitress in her crisp blouse and black pants comes to take our order. Makenna turns toward the window. Tall thin bamboo shoots grow between the building and the sidewalk. Beyond this green hedge, cars rumble through the dusk.

I consider having a glass of chardonnay, but since

Turner doesn't order anything alcoholic, I decide against it. When did I start to think of him as Turner?

Once the server hurries off, he says to me, "You're a teacher, right?"

"English 1A at City College."

"If Makenna misses the last month of school, she'd be okay? Study at home, even take the tests under your supervision?"

This man is a master of ambush. I assumed I'd have her for days, not weeks. Makenna's face is hopeful. I stumble over the words. "What – what subjects, Makenna?"

"Pre-calc, but that's easy. And biology. I'll work hard and I'll feel better adjusted by Fall."

"I know the principal. I'm sure she'll consider it," says Turner. "Makenna's a strong student, but I don't want her to sacrifice her college chances."

"I think any college would understand the circumstances," I say. "What about the aunt in Louisiana?"

"No." Makenna raises her voice.

"I was wondering about the – funeral," I say quickly.

Turner puts his hand on the girl's. "We're waiting to hear from the police about when we – we can have her, and I haven't been able to reach her aunt yet."

Tears well in Makenna's eyes. She gives Turner a slight push so she can get out of the booth, and mutters, "I gotta go to the bathroom," so he slides out, and she rushes toward the back of the restaurant.

"I did that, didn't I?" I say. "Bringing up the funeral. Should I go after her?"

"She might appreciate doing some crying on her own. A hard day today."

There's one question I want to ask while the girl is gone, so I do. "Why did you need a lawyer when Detective Tellez questioned you?"

Turner stops dumping Sweet-and-Low into his iced tea. "I'm her number one suspect."

"I don't —"

He holds up his hand. "I'm the significant other. That puts me on the top of any list, and I'm black. That's two reasons right there."

"But someone threw a pipe bomb —"

"More than one for that inferno, and I wouldn't and didn't. I know Darton Reglan personally. He's good. He's got my back."

"It makes you look guilty, even to Makenna."

"She doesn't believe that and you know it."

What can I say? She doesn't. "I don't know what she'd do if something happens to you."

"Nothing's gonna happen to me, and if you're worried about ending up with that girl, forget it, because I promise you, as soon as things get cleared up, she's back with me. No one's going to take her away."

Chapter 31
Tonette

Sunday, May 26, 2002

The next morning I get up early and take Phoenix for a quick walk around the block. Makenna's still sleeping. Christie's same habits, these two girls share so many things in common.

The crisp air, the streaks of pink and blue in the eastern sky are invigorating. I think about the possibilities of Billy Eastlake and my mother.

In the late '40s, such an affair between a white woman and a black man would have been scandalous. The Ingrid Bergman-Roberto Rossellini affair must have given my mother a sense of what her own disgrace might be like, the anger and the shame, had anyone known. Rossellini was, after all, Italian, not "colored", and yet, Bergman was still condemned as evil and ostracized to Europe. I can see it in my mind, the unfolding of the story. Almost. I am beginning to accept this as a possibility.

Back at the apartment, I make coffee while Phoenix gulps water and heads into Makenna's bedroom.

I've been checking my phone for a return call from Elma's son, Thomas, but so far he hasn't gotten back to me so I need to take a different direction in my research. The birth certificate is inside the folder Detective Tellez gave me and so is Tonette's phone number. I'm not ready to face the aunt Makenna dislikes yet, so in the Google search box, I type the doctor's name, 'Gaines', then add 'Louisiana' to narrow the field. When the page pops up, there are several doctors named 'Gaines' in the state, but no 'Archibalds'. I limit the search by typing in 'Beauport', the city where Olita grew up.

I peek into the bedroom where girl and dog snuggle together. I can't tell which is snoring. Carefully, I pull the door closed, assured I can use the phone without Makenna knowing.

There's a Dr. Anna Gaines, a dentist, and it's she I call. Beauport is small, and I figure medicine is in the DNA; fathers who are doctors beget children who become doctors. In this case, perhaps, a dentist. I get a service. Leave a message.

Still quiet from the bedroom so I get up my nerve to call Olita's sister. A child answers the phone and when I ask for "Tonette, please," I hear a female voice in the background asking, "Who is it, Dwight?"

I don't wait for the child to ask me. "Tell her this is Abbie Palmer from California, the woman who's taking care of Makenna."

The woman comes on the phone. "Who is this?"

After I repeat who I am, she says, this time with more patience, "I told that policewoman I won't be coming out. I can't do it. I got things to do and whole lot of my own responsibilities here."

The fact this woman isn't getting on an airplane anytime soon shouldn't surprise me, but it does. She goes on, "So if that's all you wanted to know, I was just walking out the door with my grandson."

"You're not coming out for the funeral?" I ask.

"Didn't I just say that?"

"Yes, you did. Sorry. Can you at least tell me why Olita thought she was adopted?"

"I told her, of course. It was my duty to tell her the truth. The two of them came down to Beauport when my mama died and I had to set Olita straight right off. Nothing of my mama's was hers."

"How did you know she was adopted?"

"My mama told me. Didn't Olita tell you all this seeing as you two are related?"

131

"We – we never talked." I glance toward the bedroom. "Just tell me what your mother said. Please."

"I don't understand why any of this is important now. Olita is dead."

"But your niece isn't."

"That's the point. She isn't my niece."

"Do you have paperwork to prove that?"

"What do I need paperwork for?"

"There is this child and she needs a family –"

"She's got you and the whole child services to help her."

"But she and I – we both want to know what your mother said to you. Or at least what you told Olita."

I hear her suck in an impatient breath, more like a snort, and I'm afraid I've lost her. I wait for the slamming down of the phone, but then she says, "She told me to tell Olita she had a father who lived in California and a mother too. And that she should look them up."

"Did she tell you who these people were?"

"She didn't know who the mother was. Just that she was white. But the father's name was William Easley."

At first the name confuses me, but I remember the Billy Eastlake's bio. Easley had been his real name.

"Are you happy now? Can I please get back to my grandson?"

"Did you give Olita any information about how to find him?"

"How would I know how to find him? I never talked to Olita again after she left. She was unpleasant about the whole thing. You know, like I was trying to cheat her out of her inheritance, which I wasn't. I was the one taking care of my mama all these years while she was out in Los Angeles living the good life."

"Okay," I say, trying to stem the tide. "Is there anything else I should know? Are you sure your mother never mentioned the woman's name?"

"I am positive she never mentioned the woman's name."

"Thank you."

She hangs up. I sit back in the metal folding chair, feeling its hard rim cut across my back.

I hear the squeals of kids and glimpse out the window. Ben's twin girls are in the courtyard wearing Barbie pajamas and playing hopscotch. Any distraction is a good distraction so I head outside.

Chapter 32
Wilma Allen

I moved to the Tiki Palms so I could be an island. Its name and the dated quality of the place convinced me I would be able to come and go as I pleased. I stayed inside avoiding human contact — and complications — as much as possible including Ben, the manager, but one Saturday he knocked on my door and asked if I would watch his two little girls because he had to repair a toilet. I taught them how to play hopscotch. That's what they're doing now.

Ben, in his ripped jeans and oversized t-shirt, slouches on his porch, smoking a cigarette, his long face telling me something is wrong.

"Hey," I say.

He shrugs. "Are you all right? I saw the Target thing on the news."

"A little rattled is all."

"I was worried." He takes a deep drag on his cigarette and blows the smoke out his nose.

The girls skip over to us, laughing, and grab my legs. "Hi, Abbie." Blanca sings her greeting.

"Daddy's a dragon," says Delia.

"Do it again, Daddy," says Blanca.

Ben draws in smoke, the tip of his cigarette glowing and crackling to the delight of the girls who wait with hands clasped in front of them, holding their breaths. This time, when the smoke curls out of his nostrils, he slowly stands up, growing bigger and bigger, spreading his arms up, up, up over his head letting out a smoky roar until the girls shriek and run back to their game.

Ben sinks down again, coughing and choking. I pat him on the back, but he pulls away.

"Don't. Makes it worse." He clears his throat. Coughs

again. We turn and watch Delia toss her 'marker'. She's using a bottle cap of some kind, most likely Heineken, and hops down the squares, splitting her legs at four and five and again at seven and eight, stepping on lines with every landing.

"My wife, Raquel? She's getting married." He looks at me, his eyes moist.

"Oh," I say.

"She's moving to Wichita and taking the girls with her. That's why they're here. Told her I need to have them as much as I can before they leave."

"I'm so sorry." We sink into a moment, me thinking how hard this is for him, and then I'm suddenly flooded with the awareness of how my family must feel. I take a deep breath to fill the hollow in my chest. I'm not moving to Wichita, but left just the same.

"You okay?" Ben asks.

"Fine," I say. "I'm fine."

"They find anybody to arrest?"

"Not yet."

"And the girl's all right, considering?"

"She's doing great. We've had some wobbly moments, but we're hanging in."

"She's the daughter of the woman who died, right?"

"Right," I say. "Can you fight it? Your wife, I mean. Take her to court?"

"I could. I might."

Again we lapse into silence. Delia and Blanca have found some creature, a pill bug or snail, traveling across their hopscotch game and have stopped to chatter back and forth, pointing chubby fingers and dipping their heads. They go down on their knees at exactly the same time to get a better look, and the action is so unconscious, so charming that Ben and I laugh. Then he says in a hoarse whisper, "I love those girls."

When Makenna rambles in, yawning, I hand her a sheet of paper. She beams at me when she sees it's the biography I found on Billy Eastlake.

"Read that," I tell her, "while I finish cooking breakfast."

She drags the rocker from the living area into the tiny dining area so we can talk and plops down. I throw her a smile. She's still wearing her new Target pajamas and her hair is wrapped in a scarf. She says, "I'm pretty sure you saved my life the other night."

Can't help myself, I walk over, she stands, and we hug. Then shaking my head, I say, "You must be starved. Eggs, scrambled or fried?"

"Egg whites scrambled, okay?"

"You got it."

Makenna reads aloud from the biography I've given her, "Comedian and accomplished violinist, Billy Eastlake was born William Fanfare Easley in 1924 in New Orleans, Louisiana. Eastlake won the hearts of many Americans in the early sixties with three gold record albums featuring his unique style of humor and virtuosity on 'da fiddle.'"

"We should look up his records on eBay, buy them!" I say. "But I don't know how to do that."

"I can figure it out." She grins, then continues reading, "Eastlake was the eldest of a large family whose father, Sherman T. Easley, worked for a local bootlegger. When Billy was eight, his father abandoned his mother, Wilma Allen Easley, with five children to support. Whoa! Wilma Allen!" She leaps from the rocker.

"What?"

She grabs me at the shoulders. I almost drop the spatula. "Wilma Allen! Wilma Allen! Billy Eastlake's mother is Wilma Allen."

"So?" I'm staring at her, my brain nothing but mud.

"My great-grandmother's name is Wilma Allen. Don't you get it? William Easley and Miriam Easley Riggs were brother and —"

"Sister!" I finally see the connection. "And Miriam is Olita's adopted mother!"

"And her aunt. My mother was raised by her aunt."

I scoop her eggs onto a plate and hand it to her along with a fork. "That makes sense. Child born out of wedlock sheltered by a family member."

"E-yew." She absently takes her eggs, reading at the same time. "Billy Eastlake married a twenty-eight-year-old woman? He's got to be forty or fifty years older than her."

"Old men with money —"

Makenna abandons her plate on the counter and heads to the computer. "If we can't find an address for him, maybe we can find one for her."

Chapter 33
Tom Robinson

Makenna at the computer taps her fingers on the table as a page slowly loads, me leaning over her shoulder. I hear a chime from the futon. My cell. I dig around. Pick it up. "Hello?"

"Is this Abbie Hart?"

I hesitate, because of my maiden name, thinking "Reporter!" and almost hang up, but say instead, "Who's calling, please?"

"Tom Robinson. Elma's —"

My heart speeds up. "Tom Robinson! Thank you for calling me back. I don't know if you remember, but my mother was Virginia Gifford, and your mother —"

Makenna sits up straight, widens her eyes.

He tells me, "I remember her."

I say, "I was sorry to hear about your mother's passing. She was very good to me." I feel the loss, an ache as painful as when my father fired her.

"It was a while ago. She's at peace now."

"Do you remember me?"

"We played tag in my front yard once a long, long time ago. Might have been my birthday. Later, after your mother died —" He hesitates, then says in a kind voice, "What can I do for you, Abbie, after all these years?"

"I'm hoping Elma might have talked to you about my mother."

"I know she loved her – and you."

"Did she say anything to you about – about —"

Makenna is standing close to me now. I can hear her breathing.

"She was all broke up about the suicide. You know, she was supposed to work that day, but Miss Virginia told her not to come. Mama always thought if she'd just gone over anyway, it wouldn't have happened."

"Oh," is all I can say.

"You were there, you know. That upset her too. You were lucky to survive."

"I don't know what happened. No one's ever told me how I got out of there."

"I don't know much. I was too young at the time," he says.

"I've always assumed my father came home."

"I don't think so. That doesn't sound right, but I don't know why."

"Did she ever say anything about her?"

"Just that Miss Virginia was a very sad lady, and I should pray for her. Sorry, Abbie, I don't know any more than that."

"If you remember anything, anything at all, will you call me?"

"If I do, I will."

"Thanks. Thank you. "

Makenna pokes me and waves the Billy Eastlake bio at me. I say, "Tom. Wait. Please." I close my eyes and say quickly, "What I'm wondering, Tom, what I need to know, is if your mother ever said anything about my mother having an affair with anyone, maybe even an African-American."

He doesn't answer right away, then, "Mama wasn't one to gossip about other people to me or to anyone else. I'm sorry."

After I hang up, I tell Makenna who Tom is and who Elma was and everything he said. She nods, a little disappointed, then returns to the computer to find out what she can about Billy Eastlake's young bride. Surfing the web with lightening fingers, it doesn't take her long to discover Billy Eastlake has set up housekeeping in Palm Springs with Liv Amaral.

"Palm Springs?" I ask.

"Palm Springs," says Makenna. She tries to find an address, but her search comes up empty. "What now?"

I start to explain to Makenna my method of "standing over the evidence," something I share with my students who are working on research papers, how it helps you see the big picture. I have an analogy I use in class, but with Makenna, I don't have to tell her about it, I can show her. As if on cue, Phoenix pads out from the bedroom, nudges my leg.

I say, "Let's get out of here for a while."

I let Makenna drive, Phoenix in the backseat, his nose smearing the window glass, his tail thumping. We park on the street next to a path into the Arroyo. Makenna grabs the dog's leash and we trek down. A warm breeze stirs the smell of grass. I take a deep breath, glad I remembered this.

We walk for a while, busy with our own thoughts, Makenna patient with the dog and his desire to sniff every weedy clump.

My mind wanders back to the premise we're trying to prove, that Olita is my sister and Makenna, my niece, and although I have the birth certificate as counterargument, I'll be more willing to face the truth — whatever it is — if I approach this as an argument with a premise and evidence. That's a lie. I do want to know the truth, regardless, ready to get to the bottom. The swamp surrounds me and I'm in a boat for a change. A leaky boat maybe, but the gators are sleeping.

My conversation with Tom Robinson bothers me. I believe that Elma wouldn't gossip about my mother, but he seemed on the verge of telling me something, something he saw or overheard. This might be wishful thinking on my part because he was just a little kid when everything happened.

After our hike, we tromp back up to the car, but before we leave, I ask Makenna to pull over by the San Rafael Bridge. We walk out to the halfway point and look north.

Below us lies the flood channel, the twin trails on either side, two young girls on horseback, dog walkers, a runner, vegetation sloping down on either side of the dry river bed, the La Loma bridge a short distance away, the mountains beyond, and a wedge of blue sky. We stand there side by side.

"It looks different from here, doesn't it?" I say.

Makenna leans against the cement railing. "Different from what?"

"From how it looked when we were down there in the middle of it."

She turns her head and squints at me. "Why do I get the feeling you mean something else?"

I grin. "Because I do."

Chapter 34
Standing Over

B ack in the apartment I pull out the evidence I've collected, including my dad's obit, my junk box, the few downloads on Virginia Gifford, notes on Elma and her son Tom Robinson, the photo of my mother and me.

"What we need to do," I say, "is lay everything out, everything we know about the past, and then stand-over-it."

"Like on the bridge," says Makenna.

"Like on the bridge." I must look smug because she rolls her eyes.

I grab some plain white paper and a pen and write a name on each piece: Virginia, Billy Eastlake, my father Lyle, Liv Amaral and try to line them up on the brown carpet, but Phoenix is everywhere, sniffing and stepping on everything.

"All right, you! Bedroom," Makenna says, disappearing with him into the other room, adding, "I've got some stuff, too."

Under 'Virginia', I place the ancient articles from my junk box, the photo of the two of us in the red chair, then her wedding ring and crystal bracelet.

Makenna comes back a few minutes later with her mother's scorched jewelry chest as well as printed online articles about the firebombing and the police investigation. She asks, "Shouldn't we have a column for my mother?"

I snatch another piece of paper and scribble *Olita*.

Nothing in her mother's box has retained its original form. Everything is warped.

She picks up a gold and diamond ring and studies it, that line between her brows creasing. "I never saw this before."

I take it from her and hold it up to the light from the window. "It must have been very pretty." I pause a minute, then pull out my mother's simple wedding band, place it next to the misshapen one on my palm. "They're both yellow gold. They could almost be a match."

We exchange a glance, and I say, "But they're not. This is the one my father gave her when they got married."

She shrugs and takes the diamond ring. She tries to slip it on her finger, but it's small and misshapen and won't go beyond her knuckle.

"Maybe the diamond is from your father?" I say.

"He gave her a different ring. A sapphire. She always wore it. She would have had it on when – when she died."

This doesn't seem to get any easier. It's only been a couple of days and these moments hit like earthquakes. She shakes her head and says, "I used to play in her jewelry box when I was little. I would've remembered a diamond ring."

"Did you know your father?" I ask.

She leans back against the futon. "I don't remember much. Like with you and your mom, I was too young. He died in the Gulf War. I'm not really sure how. In some kind of ambush, my mom said. We have – had a couple photo albums from that time. Actually we had photo albums from way back too, with pictures of my grandmother or who I thought was my grandmother and my mom and Aunt Tonette, but they were in my mother's bedroom."

Sharing a wall with the living room and with a window toward the street, Olita's bedroom had taken the brunt of the blaze. "I'm sorry, Makenna."

"It was hard on her, you know, losing my dad. She loved him." She's still holding the ring, turning it over and over with her fingers. "That's one of the reasons I love Turner. He made my mom happy."

"That's what matters, isn't it, wanting our loved ones to be loved?"

143

By the time we finish putting everything into columns on the floor, we can barely see the apartment's brown carpeting, and I ask Makenna to stand next to me and look at what we've created.

"Okay," she says. "Now what?"

"Well, if this were a research paper, we'd study the evidence supporting our premise and decide if it's convincing, and if it isn't, we'd do more research."

"Abbie, all this standing-over-it stuff isn't getting us anywhere. Why don't we just track down Billy and ask him?"

She's like Alexander the Great and the Gordian Knot, cutting right to the heart of the matter. I nod my approval. "Turning to a primary source. Yep, that works too."

"Then let's go to Palm Springs."

"We don't have his address."

The telephone rings in my bedroom. Makenna follows me in. Hovers at the door.

Detective Tellez says, "Abbie. Where's Makenna?"

"Here." I glance at the girl.

"Don't say anything to her. I have bad news. We've gotten back the coroner's report and the results are disturbing." The detective's voice is matter-of-fact, like a recording.

I glance toward the door. Makenna leans against the jamb, arms crossed in front of her, lips tight, watching me. Waiting.

Detective Tellez says through the receiver, "Usually with crimes involving firebombs, perps don't go inside. They don't want or need to take that chance. Murder isn't usually a fire-bomber's goal. Intimidation and terror are."

"Okay. Go on."

"Olita had a contusion to the left side of the skull consistent with a severe blow. Someone was in the house with her, made sure she couldn't leave. The M.E. found evidence that accelerants were used near and/or on her body."

"So what are you trying to tell me, exactly?" I ask.

"It looks as if Olita was targeted."

Chapter 35
Arrest

"Targeted? By whom?" I didn't mean to repeat that word. The bed shifts under me as Makenna sits down, so close I can hear her breathing. I reach out and grab her hand.

The detective sighs on the other end of the line. "We've arrested Bethune."

"No. Not possible." I flash on him arriving at the fire, leaping out of his car, the keening noise he made as he was held back from the door.

"There are possibilities and probabilities and then there is most likely. A good percentage of victims in California are killed by their spouses or significant others."

The receiver goes damp in my hand. "But —"

"There's a clincher," she interrupts.

"And what is that?"

"Bethune wasn't in Austin the night of the firebombing. He was here, in Los Angeles."

Makenna can see the shock on my face. I should have made her leave the room, told her this was personal, but I had no idea what Detective Tellez meant by "bad news."

"How do you know about that last part?" I ask. "The where."

"Airlines keep accurate records. He flew back early."

"Did you ask about it? What did he tell you?"

Makenna, huddled next to me on the edge of the bed, lets out a small noise. She's a smart girl. She knows. She clutches my arm.

Tellez says, "He claims he spent the night with a woman."

"What?" It takes me a moment to sort this out. "Wait. Doesn't that give him an alibi?"

"It might if we could find her."

"What does that mean?"

"It means we're not sure she exists."

Shit. Shit. Shit. If he has a girlfriend, it looks bad. If he doesn't have one, it looks bad. When I hang up, my head is spinning.

Makenna says, "They arrested him, didn't they?"

I try to put my arms around her, but she leaps to her feet. "If they arrested Turner, it means they think my mother was killed on purpose. Who would want to kill my mother?"

"I can't imagine."

She starts to pace. "They have no reason to arrest him. What do they base it on? He would never hurt her."

She wants answers, and I don't want to give them to her. I don't even want to be around when someone else tells her. But who is there, but me? Maybe it's better to get it out there. She has to understand they have reasons for suspecting him, so finally I say, "There's evidence that points to Turner."

I choose my words carefully, keeping each syllable even and in a tone that seems to me to be quite reasonable, telling her about the arrest and the reasons behind it, including the autopsy, Bethune's lie about being in Los Angeles on the night of the firebombing, his supposed "alibi woman," now missing, the implications of what this might mean.

She stares at me in disbelief and when I'm done, she says, "There's another explanation. They – they came into the house to spread the gasoline and didn't know she was there. When they found her, they panicked and knocked her out. They meant to scare Turner. They didn't want to actually hurt anyone. It's some racist thing."

I can see her trying to put it all together. To find answers that will satisfy her.

"And he was in Austin," she goes on. "Mama talked to him. She told me when she called me at Audrey's to say

147

good-night. Besides, Abbie, think about it, he's a smart man. Wouldn't he do it a different way? Why call so much attention to yourself by firebombing your own house and destroying everything you've ever worked for? That's stupid. And the woman? He's always counseling people who have husbands and sons in jail. That's part of what he does."

Is this something he would fly home from Texas and then spend the night doing? Coincidentally the night Olita is murdered?

Then she turns to me and rubbing her hands together, says, "We have to prove he's innocent. We need to go on-line and research hate groups, skinheads, radicals, extremists, Nazis." She ticks the names off with her fingers, then adds, "They all have chat rooms."

Nazis. The thought drains me and I'm pretty sure I don't have the hacking skills to make much progress along these lines. "Don't you think the police have already done all this?"

"Maybe, but they won't try anymore. Don't you see? They think they have their murderer. Somebody is after Turner, one way or another. He has a history, Abbie. When he was young, he was a Black Panther. You know who those guys were?"

I remember the names. Huey P. Newton, Eldridge Cleaver, Bobby Seale. Turner must have been in college too. "I know who they were," I say soberly, remembering angry black fists. "Did he really believe in all that?"

"Of course he did. It was the times and he wasn't involved that long, but people remember the bad things about the Panthers and it makes them think he's somebody he's not."

"Okay," I say. "I get it, but I'm not about to start tracking down hate-groups. I can't see us going to meetings, shaving our heads, wearing camo, pretending to be haters."
Did I say "we?" What am I thinking? Makenna couldn't go.

Those Nazis would take one look at us, and we'd be digging our own graves. Literally. It would have to be me, by myself. Unless Craig came with me bringing his litigation skills and maybe a purloined Smith and Wesson. It's ludicrous, but I'm going to have to do something.

Chapter 36
Date Shake

Monday, May 27, 2002

Early the next day I let her drive to Palm Springs. It's only two hours away and tracking down Billy Eastlake is a lot safer than going all swat-team on some skinhead bake sale. Plus I have no idea how to circumvent the cops to prove Turner Bethune's innocence. For Makenna's sake, I called Detective Tellez this morning to ask when we could visit Turner. She said she'd get back to me, so this trip is the perfect distraction.

Although we don't know Billy Eastlake's exact address, I'm hoping when we get there, we'll find someone who does. After all, celebrities have flocked to Palm Springs for decades and anyone living there can tell you Bob Hope's house is on the side of the mountain.

After a while I say, "The visitor center should have a pamphlet about Palm Springs' history: pictures, records, that sort of thing. Maybe Virginia will be mentioned since she was the 'Palm Springs Bikini Girl', don't you think?"

"They should be selling posters of her," Makenna answers.

Finding Billy Eastlake will go a long way to blunt what may be ahead for Turner Bethune, and by extension, Makenna. I keep an eye out for Olita's gas station, the one from the receipt where she scribbled the words, *My mother is your mother.* Was that only a week ago?

As green hills turn to sand and billboards, I call Craig. If he finds the dog in the backyard of the Woodbine house, he might raise an alarm.

I punch in his cell number. Notice my phone is low on juice. Again. He doesn't answer so I leave a message. As soon as I hang up, the phone rings. Craig? No.

"Ben? Hi. Is something wrong?" As manager of the Tiki Palms, he has my number, but he's never called me before.

"No. Just wondering if you and Makenna want to hear my band play tonight."

"Would they let her in?"

"It's not at a club. We're playing a Memorial Day benefit at Plaza de la Raza, Mission Road. Kids invited."

A week ago, I would have said an emphatic "no," keeping my distance, but with Makenna and not knowing what's going to happen today, I say, "Sounds like fun and we should be able to make it, but we're heading for Palm Springs this morning. We'll try." If today is a bust, it will be good to have this secondary diversion.

"We won't go on until around eight," he says. "You know how to get there?"

"I do. See you then."

I explain to Makenna who was on the phone and the reason I want to go — that his wife is taking their two daughters to another state and he might need some moral support.

She says, "Tonight we can be his family."

A billboard for the Cabazon outlets reminds me of Olita. I ask Makenna, "You and your mom ever shop here?"

She glances at the outlet signs along the road, Mikasa, Levi, Adidas, and says, "Are we stopping?"

"If you want, but you've never been here before, school-shopping or anything?"

"Nope. Why?"

"Just wondering. They have good stuff." Of course her mother stopped somewhere along here and filled her gas tank. Did she find Billy Eastlake on that trip? Didn't Turner say that Billy's wife wouldn't let her in? Or did I dream that? I turn to Makenna. "You want to stop? You could use more clothes."

"No," she says. "I want to get going on what we're doing. I'm excited."

"How about a date shake, at least?" Hadley's is ahead, a desert orchard ranch famous for nuts and dried fruit.

"A what?"

"A date shake. You know, a milk shake with ice cream and dates."

"Gross. I hate dates."

"You won't hate these dates. Get off at the next exit."

•◇•

My shake — I buy a large for both of us — tastes delicious, so I look over at Makenna. She curls her lip in an exaggerated way and slowly puts her mouth on the straw.

"Well?"

"I haven't had any yet," she says.

"Go ahead."

So she does. I watch her face change, from snarl to delight. My work is done.

I'm driving now and pull into the gas station just down the road from Hadley's. It's large and impersonal, but I'm pretty sure it's the same one that supplied Olita with the receipt she left in my doorjamb.

"We still have three-quarters of a tank," says Makenna, a line of purply-white ice cream on the side of her lip. I gesture with my tongue and she licks it off.

"Gas is cheaper here," I say and climb out of the car. When she starts to follow, I hand her my credit card. "Can you pump while I go to the bathroom?" She frowns, the typical teenage knee-jerk reaction I remember from my own kids, so I say, "Drivers pump their own gas." And she does that eye-roll thing.

Inside the gleaming mini-market, I don't go to the restroom, but straight up to the clerk and ask her if she remembers an attractive African-American woman sometime within the last couple weeks.

The woman behind the counter, her black hair a tribute to 1980's metal bands, gives me a you-gotta-be-kidding-me look. "Do you have any idea how many people go through here?"

"She was driving a red Volvo," I say. "She was tall, pretty, very classy."

The woman is chewing gum and takes a few minutes to turn the wad in her mouth over a couple of times.

"Nope," she says. "With the mall next door, there's a lot of them rich folks coming out here these days."

"Thank you anyway," I say. Then I stop and ask a question I hadn't planned to ask. "You ever hear of Billy Eastlake?"

"Billy who?"

Chapter 37
Twinkies

"Billy Eastlake," I say again. "He was a comedian, back in the fifties?"

"Oh him." The cashier nods her head. "Sure I know him. Not personally, but yeah, he lives right here in the Coachella Valley."

I can't believe we're following clues and getting somewhere. I'm a regular Kinsey Milhone from those alphabet mystery books. Maybe I'll throw out my whole wardrobe, don a little black dress, and start running two miles every morning just like the Sue Grafton character. "Do you know where?"

"Don't think he's in the Springs. Every once in a while his name gets in the local paper. It's either Indian Wells or Rancho Mirage. He used to hang out with Sonny Bono, Cher's ex, before he skied into a tree. Sonny, I mean."

"Indian Wells?"

"Palm Springs isn't what it used to be. The rich keep moving east."

"Do you think anyone around here knows which it is?" I survey the rows of potato chips and magazines, the counters lined with coffee urns and bubbles of lemonade and cherry punch, to see if there might be another font of information, maybe a geezer hunting for a Michelob Lite.

The cashier takes money from a guy who's muscled in front of me. He's pierced in places I don't want to even think about. I wait for her to divvy up his change, which she takes her time doing, then she gives me a blank, gum-popping stare.

"Billy Eastlake?" I remind her. "Any idea where I could find out where he lives?"

"You could try a phone book or you could check at the

casino in downtown PS. All those old guys gamble there now. Some still come out to Morongo, but why bother with one right there at the Springs? Although Indian Wells, I guess, either one would be a drive for Billy Eastlake."

More nuggets. Sherlock, watch out.

"Thanks," I say again, then grab a handful of Hostess Twinkie packages and throw them on the counter. I have no intention of eating them, but I give her a twenty and leave before she figures out change.

I've managed to inhale three Twinkies before we hit the 111 Highway exit south into downtown Palm Springs. All on top of a large date shake.

"Throw the rest of those sugar torpedoes into the back," I say to Makenna. In between spongy chews, I've been telling her what the woman in the mini-market said. Makenna has a map of the Coachella Valley spread over her lap and a travel guide flipped open. Like the good detectives we want to become, we stopped at the AAA to pick up supplies before we left on our expedition.

"Let's go to the casino first thing," she says.

"They won't let you in."

"We're not gambling, you know, and I can walk through with an adult. Besides, I look old for my age." She draws down the corners of her mouth and sticks her nose up in the air.

"Okay, okay, we'll see. So you've been to the casino with your mom?"

"No, but we went to Las Vegas once, Turner, me, and my mom. How can they have casinos here anyway?"

"Native Americans own most of Palm Springs and just lease it to the city. At least I think that's the deal. But they're allowed to do whatever they want on the land they don't lease."

"I don't get it."

"They're an independent nation," I say.

She gives me a frown. "I didn't think the U.S. government would allow that. Let a group of people go off and be their own country."

"They were here first. This is all reservation and that was the deal. We give them a tiny bit of land in the middle of nowhere and we'll let them do whatever they want. I think if the guys who made that deal had known what was going to happen out here, they never would have agreed."

"I wonder if Malcolm X knew about this."

The city of Palm Springs blooms slowly between the mountains on the right and the desert everywhere else, but it doesn't really feel like desert, the kind you see people crawling through on their hands and knees with full beards and lobster skin. This is desert that uses water as if it was located at the confluence of the Nile, the Amazon, and the Mississippi.

T-shirts seem the major item for sale in many of the shops along Palm Canyon Drive. I begin to understand what the big haired woman at the gas station meant. Even to me, a stranger, it looks as if progress has moved on. I feel a surge of disappointment, wonder what my mother saw when she first came to Palm Springs, because this is, of course, the weird feeling that descends on me next. Like the closeness in my dream, I can feel her around me in this place.

I park the car down from North Indian Canyon Drive, and we get out. It's only May, but it's already hot. I break a sweat just walking the short distance to the large complex that is the renovated Spa Resort Casino. It covers a lot of area in the middle of downtown Palm Springs. The entrance is pink and turquoise with boulders and water and lots of agaves, palms, and other vegetation I can't identify.

The lobby is cool. Huge potted plants and deeply cushioned furniture, gleaming marble floors. The water around my swamp boat seems calm today. Makenna is prancing around, checking everything out. She asks, "Can we stay here tonight?"

"We're going to Ben's show."

"Next time then," she says.

We search for the casino and walk in. Makenna immediately changes her demeanor. She is consciously trying to appear older. None of her usual teenage slouch as she puts on a catwalk gait, almost as if she's about to lift a cigarette to her mouth. I can tell she's gonna be trouble.

Chapter 38
Cascades

Now that we're inside the casino, I'm not sure what to do. The place is loud with gongs and bells, shrill conversations and flashing lights. Slot machines blink and clang, and each gaming table – blackjack, I think – is surrounded by persons young and old, well-dressed and not, some dizzy with the adrenaline-rush gambling brings, some hanging on by their fingernails.

I turn to Makenna and ask, "What now?" but she's not here. She's standing at a far door, talking to a uniformed guard, a heavy-set Native-American guy, while she anxiously scans the room, rising up on her tiptoes. Makenna appears to be upset, gesturing toward the crowded rotunda, yammering at him, and I'm tempted to walk over and demand to know what's going on, but I don't. Whatever it is she is trying to achieve, my sudden appearance will mess it up.

I'm afraid to lose sight of the girl, so I dig in my purse for change to pop into the slot machine next to me, then realize the machine doesn't take coins. By the time I figure out the slot for my credit card, I'm dizzy with the possibility of charging my game play instantly, but Makenna is back at my side.

"I got it," she says, her face beaming.

"What have you got?"

"Cascades," she says. "In Indian Wells. That's where he lives."

"How'd you find that out?"

"I told the truth, kind of. I'm his granddaughter and I've been sent to bring him home."

"And the security guard told you where Billy lives?"

"He asked if I wanted him to call a cab to take me back

158

to Cascades since my grandfather isn't here."

"Wow. That's pretty lucky."

"Not luck, Abbie. Skill."

"Okay, skill," I say, laughing. "So Billy Eastlake does come here?"

"Not any more. That was the tricky part. The guard thought I should know he wouldn't be here because his wife doesn't allow him to come anymore."

"Really?"

"The guard mentioned he'd been sick, but I couldn't really ask how sick. That's something I should already know."

"Right. Well, let's go find this place."

The desert heat hits us like a furnace blast after the chilled air of the casino.

As we climb into the car, Makenna's forehead wrinkles with worry. "You think he's okay, don't you? He won't die?"

"No," I say. "He's fine. He's just getting old. We all are."

Cascades is a gated community at the end of Indian Peak Road. An odd name for a place in the middle of a desert, but then nothing out here is like the desert unless you happen to stumble across a sandy vacant lot dimpled with sagebrush. The area from Palms Springs to Indio is a giant oasis flanked by dusty mountains. And here, there are waterfalls galore right in front of us. The landscaper has dumped mountains of boulders on each side of the entrance and sure enough, silvery water is cascading over them.

We are at the entrance to this exclusive neighborhood in Indian Wells where Billy Eastlake and his wife are supposed to live. There's a massive gate connecting the two sides of the eight-foot wall surrounding the homes; and, on either side of the driveway, columns rise up behind the tumbling waterfalls two stories high, then a façade spans the four lane entrance road into the development like a freeway on-ramp.

"There's one of those little booths," Makenna says. "With a guard and he's looking at us."

I drive to the kiosk and the uniformed man puts on his cap and steps up to the car.

"Good afternoon. Can I help you?" He's got a broad smile, a gold tooth, his gray hair thick under his cap.

"Good afternoon. We're here to see Billy Eastlake?"

He steps inside to consult a clipboard, then brings it out with him. "Your names, please?"

"Abbie Palmer and Makenna Jordan."

He scans the list looking for something we already know isn't there. Then he shakes his head. "Are the Eastlakes expecting you?"

"Not really, but could you call them and ask if it's okay? Tell them we're here about Virginia Gifford."

The guard moves like a turtle, extending his neck toward us and as solemnly as if he's imparting a recent bit of distressing news, he says, "Virginia Gifford is dead. Has been for almost fifty years."

"You remember her?" Makenna asks excitedly from her side of the car.

"Yes, ma'am. She was in *A Tangle of Clowns*. Small part, but you knew she was there. I had a crush on her. I was maybe, I don't know, fifteen, at the time. Yeah, Virginia Gifford, perky all over. Hmmmm. What does Mr. Eastlake have to do with her?"

"Actually, that's what we want to find out. So will you call and ask if they'll see us?"

"No, ma'am. You don't ring up Mrs. Eastlake and ask if she's willing to see just anybody. Especially not reporters."

"We're not reporters."

"The people who live here, they consider me calling and asking them if I can let someone in, they consider that

160

harassment on my part."

"But this is important," I say.

"Yeah, well, that's the problem, you see? They all say that, don't they? Nope, you gotta have an appointment. Your names gotta be on the list."

"We would've made an appointment, but we couldn't find their phone number."

"That's the kind of security measures we take around here. You can't be too careful."

"How else do you get to see these people?"

"You don't."

"What if I just floor it?" I put on what used to be my charming smile, but he frowns.

"We've got our own security force and then there's the city police, ma'am. You wouldn't make to the end of the block."

Chapter 39
Stake Out

What can I say to get the Cascades guard to change his mind and give us access to Billy Eastlake? It's on the tip of my tongue to tell him I'm Virginia Gifford's daughter, he's so smitten with her, but I don't. He likes his job and he wants to keep it. No point in telling him something he doesn't need to know. There's got to be another way, but I don't know what it is. Still I give my name again and phone number and tell him we'll be back.

I drive down the street lined with "normal" houses outside the gates that probably sell for only a million or so, instead of the ten mil ones in Billy's community. We go up and down and around the block, and I pull over across from the Cascades entrance.

"We can sit here and wait awhile," I say.

"A stakeout?" asks Makenna.

"Surveillance."

"They have to come out sometime, right?"

"And we know what they look like." When I say this, Makenna digs around the folders at her feet, and pulls out pictures we've printed up from the net. One of Billy and one of Liv. They're not great photos. My printer cost $49 without the coupon, but the photos are in color and up close. I reach into the back seat and snatch two Twinkie packages, hand one to Makenna.

"We may be here a while."

We sit outside the development on Indian Peak Road and watch the Benzes, the Rolls Royces, Ferraris go in and out. We eat Big Macs from McDonalds down on the highway. We took a chance and headed over, then rushed right back.

I down the patties. Makenna the buns. We split the veg

and secret sauce. The car reeks of French fries.

"We're like the cops," Makenna says.

"Detectives," I say. "Fuzz."

"Pigs," she says.

"Oh," I say. "No. Not Detective Tellez."

"She arrested Turner. It's like he's always said. 'If you're black, the man's on your back.'"

"I don't think he was officially arrested." I want to tell her how the detective was concerned about her well-being from the beginning, but then it occurs to me that perhaps that concern arose out of Tellez's initial suspicions about Turner. So today, this meeting with her grandfather might go a long way toward helping Makenna cope. And of course, I'm anxious to meet my mother's hypothetical secret lover for my own reasons.

It's hot in the car, even with the windows rolled down. I can't imagine being a cop out here doing a stakeout in August. Makenna climbs into the back seat with her CD player, and she's got it turned up so loud I can hear the bass. I start to say something about her inevitable hearing loss, but stop myself. Things are fine. I don't want any trouble. I'm not her mother. I'm an aunt. Maybe. No matter. We're friends.

I doze off and when there's a tap on the driver's door, I jerk awake. A cop leans into my open window. "Ma'am? You okay?"

In the rearview mirror, I see Makenna glaring at the cop from the back seat. I say quickly, "We're fine."

"And you're out here in the heat because – why?"

I hesitate long enough that he says, "May I see your license and registration?"

I shuffle through my purse, through the glove compartment, and hand them to him.

He looks them over. "The guard in the kiosk wants to know what the heck you two think you're doing."

"It's really very simple, Officer," I say. "Makenna, my

niece, has a school report due on the chitlin' circuit."

"What's that?"

Our recent research on Billy Eastlake has given me this excuse so I explain how African-American singers, dancers, comedians performed at various nightclubs all over the United States primarily for African-American audiences back in the day.

"The Apollo in Harlem was the Carnegie Hall of the chitlin' circuit," I say, but obviously this doesn't help. "White people started to show up there, too. You've heard of the Cotton Club, haven't you?"

"Tie this all up for me. Why are you here?"

"We're waiting to see Billy Eastlake."

"You're fans of Billy? The comedian?"

"She wants a chance to talk to him so we're waiting for his wife to come out."

The officer scratches his head and peers into the back seat at Makenna who's slumped down again.

"Where do you go to school, Miss?"

Makenna mutters, "Arroyo Verde High School."

He glances down at the license and registration in his hand and says, "Wait right here, please." Makenna is up and watching out the back window as policeman checks something on his radio. My eyes are glued to the rearview mirror.

"You called me your niece," she says. "Here he comes." The girl flops back into her sprawl.

The cop hands me my license and registration and says, "You need to move on."

"But this is a public street, isn't it? What is the parking limit here? We're just resting."

"Loitering," he says.

"Okay, okay," I say, thinking, shit. But lucky us, as I start the engine, Makenna whispers in my ear, "Look! Over there." And there she is: Liv, or at least it looks like her behind the wheel of a silver Jaguar.

To the police officer, I say, "You're right, sir. We'll move along, maybe she can do her report on Redd Foxx." I smile, roll up my window, and ease away from the curb.

Chapter 40
Yoga

We've hit the timing jackpot, Billy's wife leaving Cascades just as we're being told to move along. Makenna shouts, "She went down there."

And as soon as the officer turns the corner, I hang a U-ie.

The Jag glides through a yellow light. I speed up, the old Suburban growling, but the light changes before we get to the intersection. Makenna extends her tall body through her open window in the backseat. There's a slight rise in the street, and she calls out, "She went left!"

The light flashes green. I take off. Makenna is still out the window and says, "Here! Here! Here!" and we turn, and our prey is only a couple of cars ahead. She climbs inside and into the front seat, laughing and panting.

Finally the Jaguar turns into a parking lot and pulls behind a grouping of date and sego palms. The low building is like a Roman villa, tile roof, arched entry framed in tiny mosaics, tall soldier-like cedars stationed on either side. Above the heavy door a sign, 'Bikram Yoga and Mediterranean Spa'. Below that, 'Open Memorial Day'.

We watch Liv Amaral Eastlake waltz through the coppery glass doors. "What do we do now?" asks Makenna.

"I guess we go in."

This place is like a new-age salad for the senses: nothing is missing, cushy softness underfoot, sage-colored walls with planters of lush ferns, sandalwood incense, sitar music, lemons floating in large Italian blown-glass jugs.

Down the hall, several women in spandex chatter in front of a closed door, but none of them are Billy's young bride. A woman at the counter smiles. "Welcome. My name is Terri. Are you here to try the yoga class or a glycolic peel?"

"Yoga?"

"Have you ever done Bikram before?"

"No." I spot Makenna moving down the hall. She's doing the same thing here that she did at the casino, and I've got to go with it, keep this woman distracted while she searches for Liv.

"Don't be nervous," says Terri. "Everyone's new the first time." She takes me gently by the arm.

We pass a glass door and I scan the room. Among several men in shorts and tanks, women in shorts and sports bras, all stretching in various directions, is Liv.

"What's in there?" I ask.

"That's where you'll do your yoga. It's 105-106 in the practice room so you'll want to take off your sweats."

"105? Degrees?"

"Here's the dressing room." The receptionist opens a white canvas curtain.

Okay, I've always wanted to try yoga so I strip down to my underwear, black, looking somewhat passable for sports gear, but no way. I put my sweats back on.

I pull back the canvas to find Terri waiting with a rolled up rubber mat and a small white towel. She looks me over. "You're gonna be hot."

The studio is like Dante's Inferno, the outside weather frigid compared to this. The yoga acolytes stand in three alternating rows, making snoring noises like a bunch of old men rocking on a front porch. Terri helps me lay out the mat, then waving, disappears through the door. Lucky her. It's a luxurious 72 degrees where she's headed.

Settling in, I look into the mirror and straight into the eyes of Liv Amaral in the front row. Lustrous brown hair in a messy bun, Liv stretches gracefully, oblivious to my presence, but I vow to myself that when this is over – if I don't collapse with heatstroke first – she'll invite us for green tea and edamame with Billy.

The yoga leader is tall and slim, a colorful tattoo

covering her left shoulder, a fat goldfish in coral. She smiles, waiting for me to hold my arms out straight in front, legs slightly apart, and lower myself into a squat. Obviously she has no idea what it's like to be middle-aged.

She comes over and presses my shoulders down, away from my ears. My thighs are burning. When she says "Release," my legs turn to rubber.

Next comes something she calls the eagle and there's no way I can do that with my leg. Wrap it where? The instructor lifts my chin, pushes her palm against my back, but I'm not an eagle. More like an albatross.

Liv nods reassuringly at me in the mirror. Maybe all I have to do is smile and we'll be best buddies for life, but then a car alarm shrills, and I stumble out of my half-baked bird position.

A minute later, Makenna bursts through the door and yanks me out of the room, man-handling me down the hall toward the front door. I'm yelling "My purse," but she's hollering, "I got it!" and I see the bag swinging from her arm. The women pile out of the exercise room, the hot air whooshing along the corridor. Liv is waving, coming after us, but Makenna is dragging me out, my heart bumping against my rib cage.

Outside, the warm desert air chills after Bikram's prescribed 106. Makenna paws through my purse as she runs, clicks the doors open on the Suburban, and climbs into the driver's seat. "Come on. Hurry. Go around. Go around!"

I have no idea what's going on, but I clamber into the passenger seat while Makenna throws the truck into reverse and slams the accelerator. We haul out of the lot backward just as Liv rushes from the spa. She glances at her Jag, alarm screeching and the passenger window smashed to bits, glittering like a hundred diamonds in the sun, and then she turns and watches us drive away.

"Stop this car right now," I say, but we're jouncing over a dip in the street, making our getaway, and I can't believe it.

Makenna is grinning. She says, "I got their address."

Chapter 41
Retreat

"I didn't think about a car alarm," she says as she squeals the Suburban around the first corner.

"Slow down!" My heart has bumped into my throat. She punches the brake, 40 to 30 mph. The car lurches, jerking her back.

"All that noise, I thought the police would come. I just wanted a look at the registration, wanted their address."

"What good is an address if you're in jail?"

"I panicked is all."

I press my palms hard against my eyes. "Shh, give me a chance to think."

"You should be thanking me. I almost left you behind."

"We need to go back," I say. "Right now."

"We can't. Not yet. She needs to cool down. It's just a car window and nothing's taken. It'll be okay once we explain what happened. Billy won't care about the window once he meets us."

"She's his wife, Makenna. She's going to be pissed." I'm angry, but I force myself to breathe, count to ten, give into the sway of the car. Makenna slows to a stop. I look up. The traffic light is red. I peek over my shoulder. I don't know what I expect. Liv coming after us in her Jaguar to make a citizen's arrest? That's crazy.

"So that's your plan?" I ask.

"Plan? Plan. Okay. We go to Cascades tomorrow and apologize. Give them the name and number of your insurance. I bet they'll tell the guard to let us in this time."

"We should go back now," I say, not wanting to, not now, my brain darting here and there, like there's a bee caught in my frontal lobe.

"Tomorrow's better," she says with confidence. "Liv

will calm down by then and besides, what about Ben's gig tonight? We promised him."

"I think he'll understand when we tell him we're in jail."

"I didn't mean to break the window. I was prying it open and it broke and the alarm went off and I freaked. Tomorrow we drive back when everyone's calmed down, pay for the damage, and meet Billy."

I stare at the desert. I do not want to face an angry woman and cops. But was Liv angry? There was something about her as she watched us drive away. She was unruffled now that I think of it, arms folded over her chest, nodding her head. No better word than that. Like none of this surprised her.

"Okay." I don't want to be hard on Makenna, really, but I have to remind her in some way that this isn't a game. "We'll go home now, but you're going to pay for the window. We'll figure out how and you're going to apologize to Liv and you're going to listen to me from now on."

She expels a long slow leak of air as if she's actually been holding her breath all this time. I don't say anything else.

By the time we get to the Tiki Palms it's already 6:30. There are messages on my answering phone from Christie, Craig, and my boss, Elaine Chute, as well as one from Detective Tellez. Christie wants to talk, Craig wants to know when I'm going to get the dog, and Elaine wants to know how I'm doing – and oh, by the way, will I have my grades in on time? All this does is remind me that my real life is slipping into the sludge because the only phone call that I return is the one I assume is about Turner Bethune. I dial Tellez back, but get voice mail. I leave a message to call me on my cell.

Makenna and I take turns showering and are ready to go in about forty-five minutes. She's got me rattled by breaking into that car and all my fears of what happens when you let people into your life have resurfaced like the eyes of swamp gators.

When we get to Lincoln Park and the Plaza de la Raza Cultural Center, the place is packed with people and music. The row of food trucks entice with the smells of tortillas, corn bread, chicken stew, spices. A sign hangs above the center announcing that tonight's benefit is for children's art programs, and this lightens my mood.

Makenna sniffs the air. "Can we eat? Aren't you starving?" She's trying to smooth things out. She seems to sense I'm still uncomfortable about coming home instead of driving back to Cascades to talk to Liv about her car. I'm also worried we may have ruined any chance of meeting Billy. Everything depends on Liv, and it's hard for me to believe she won't sic the police on us as well as ban us from ever meeting her husband.

I buy us taquitos so we can walk around and search for Ben. We head toward the music and soon find a crowd surrounding a platform stage. Strings of multicolored Christmas lights wink in the canopy of trees. There are six musicians on the stage, lead guitar, two bass guitars, a keyboard, trumpet, and Ben behind the drums, their band name emblazoned on the skin of the bigger drum: Mission Street Band. They are rocking it with a little mariachi influence, and to my surprise, some rap thrown in. The singer has a resonant voice that suits the song, but the lyrics, both Spanish and English, are lost in the speakers.

Standing among strangers at night in a public park is a welcome salve after the day's craziness. Laughter and chatter around us, lovers holding hands, toddlers piggybacking on dads' shoulders, big kids playing tag on the grass, it feels good. Makenna's moving her body next to me so I know she's enjoying it. She turns her head, sees me looking at her, gives me a hug and whispers, "Sorry about the car."

I hug her back.

Chapter 42
Watermelon Candy

When another band moves on stage, Ben finds us waiting next to a palm tree wrapped in twinkling bulbs.

"Thanks for coming." His face is flushed, and his unhappiness about his girls leaving California seems temporarily eased.

"You guys are pretty good," I say and Makenna chimes in with enthusiasm.

We stroll through the balmy night toward the main building to look at a display of student art. Ben guides us over to a large white canvas with black animals painted across it, the kind you make with a flashlight and your hand. 'Delia Saenz' is painted in capital letters along the bottom.

"Delia did this?" I ask.

Ben grins. "She did. It's something we do, the girls and I, and they've gotten pretty good, your basic dog, rabbit, wolf, goose. You see them?"

We study the painting which is almost like a piece of patterned fabric, each animal equidistant from one another.

"There's a goose. Dog. Anteater," says Makenna.

"Elephant," Ben corrects. "She's just a kid."

"And she couldn't come tonight?" I ask.

"They went back to Wichita to look at houses."

"Sorry, Ben. She's very talented. Like her dad."

"Can I treat you to something to eat? Some cotton candy? A watermelon lollipop?"

"Watermelon lollipop? Real watermelon?" Makenna asks.

"It's candy."

"I think maybe we should go." Suddenly I'm drained, both physically and mentally. "We drove out to Palm

Springs today and have to go back tomorrow," I add.

"A little vacation? Glad to hear it," says Ben.

"Detecting," says Makenna.

Ben frowns and glances at me. I shake my head. I don't want to get into this right now.

He says, "Sit down on this bench and let me get a watermelon lollipop for you, Makenna, and I'll walk you guys to your car. I have one more number – a group thing, or I would follow you home."

We do as he says, both extending our legs, me stretching my hands over my head. I watch the crowd around us, feel a cool breeze on my cheek, surprised to find myself here in this public park. So much has happened, my life turned upside down, but I feel detached. No, just calm. Not thinking about running away any more, not pulling inward for a change, but looking outward.

Makenna lays a hand on my shoulder and says, "Abbie, thank you." I look over and she's smiling at me. I nod and smile back.

•◊•

On North Broadway, I unlock the Suburban and climb in, Makenna going to the other side. Ben leans over and quietly asks, "Everything okay? You're not trying to help out Bethune, are you?"

"I wouldn't know where to begin. This is something else."

"You don't know what's going on, so be careful. That Target thing might not have been random."

For a moment I want to tell him we broke into a car and fled the scene, but I just smile. "Will do."

"Okay. Let me know if there's anything you need from me." He squeezes my hand. His eyes meet mine and there's concern there. For a moment, something in me opens to his kindness and his sadness.

174

"Thanks," and my voice cracks a little.

•◇•

The red light is blinking again on the answer machine when we get back to the Tiki Palms and I almost don't check it, thinking Craig or even Christie again, neither of whom I can handle tonight. But it might be Tellez and since Makenna is in the bathroom, I pick up to listen to the message.

The female voice, self-assured and cool, is unfamiliar. She says, "I'd like to see you and Makenna. Give me a call back. And don't worry about the car window. It's insured." She reels off a number and I'm too surprised to jot it down. I know who it is, and I can't believe it. Liv Amaral!

I'm guessing she was able to track me down because someone in the parking lot got our license plate number, but how could she make the connection so fast? Of course, I left my number with the guard at Cascades. She was able to put two and two together when she got Makenna's name. Did I leave her name? And does Makenna's name mean something to her? She must know the girl is Olita's daughter. But Olita said Liv wouldn't let her see Billy. What's changed? Why now? My head aches with questions. I'm tired. Really tired. I can think about this tomorrow.

I take an Ativan, go out to the futon, and lay down. I'm asleep before Makenna finishes in the bathroom.

Chapter 43
Charged

Tuesday, May 28, 2002

Light cuts a thin line between the shade and the window sash of the living room. In the gray of morning, I remember Ben's hand on mine. He made me feel safe. And I drift off again, caught somewhere between a mosaic of dreams and the splashing of cars through rain outside the window.

"Abbie."

I shake myself awake, my head a wad of swamp moss.

"That detective called. She wants you to call her back." Makenna sits in the rocker. "Hot chocolate?"

"We have hot chocolate?" I push against the wall to sit up, and she hands me a mug.

"When did she call?"

"A few minutes ago. We're going back to Indian Wells today, aren't we?"

Then I remember. "Oh, Liv called."

"She did? When? Did you talk to her? Is she furious?"

I take a sip of the hot drink and say, "No, actually, she wasn't."

"How did she get your phone number?"

"The guard at the gate, I guess." I glance around the apartment.

Something's different. "You tidied up."

"I'm not the slob."

This time it's me who does the eye-rolling. "Thanks for not being the slob. I appreciate it. Why don't you take your shower while I finish drinking this and then, I'll take mine." I've learned that Makenna-in-the-bathroom gives me the most amount of time, and I call the detective back.

"We're going to see Billy? She'll let us in now, won't she?"

"Most likely."

She breaks into a grin as she holds up two thumbs and disappears into the bathroom.

As soon as she closes the door, I move to the bedroom.

First words out of the detective's mouth are "Is Makenna around?"

I sit down, heart pumping, thinking now what. "She's in the shower."

"The district attorney has charged Bethune with murder."

"We knew that."

"No. You knew he was arrested. Arrested means there is suspicion. Charged means the district attorney believes there's enough evidence to convict."

"What evidence? What about his alibi? That woman?"

"Still in the wind – if she ever existed. We've gone to the apartment in San Dimas where Bethune claims he met her, but the tenant there never heard of her. The guy's got a sheet, petty theft, drug possession, but there's nothing connecting him to Bethune or Olita."

"Makenna says Turner helps people who have friends or relatives in prison. Couldn't that be it?"

"Abbie, we've got enough to make a case."

"Except for motive," I say. "And if it was him, he picked the stupidest way to do it."

"Maybe he didn't think it through."

"They didn't think it through. They got into the house to knock her on the head and spread the gasoline, then they went out, got in a car, and threw Molotov cocktails through the window? It's a stupid plan, and he's too smart for that."

I look up and Makenna's at the door, her face stricken. I say, "She'll want to see him."

"That's not such a good idea."

"She's going to insist."

"I'll call the D.A., but no promises."

I hang up and look at Makenna. "How much did you hear?"

She sits down on the bed. "I heard your side. What's her side?"

Again I dread telling her what's going on, but I have to. I explain about the difference between arresting and charging. She takes it calmly, more calmly than I did.

She asks, "What about bail?"

"He has that lawyer, Darton Reglan. If he can get him out, he will." I'm starting to understand why Turner involved him from the beginning. He's been playing the statistical odds. Or because he's guilty.

Makenna says, "Thanks for defending him and asking for me to see him."

"She's going to try, but no promises."

"They have to let him have visitors. I'm his family."

We sit, me thinking that if Bethune is the guy behind all this, was it he who ordered an accomplice to run down Makenna? The thought makes me shiver. What could have triggered this behavior? What could his motive be? Swamp creatures loom.

"What?" asks Makenna.

"I'm slogging through the swamp again, yet I've never been in a swamp. I mean literally. How do I know what it's like?"

"Everyone knows what a swamp is."

"Do you know what a swamp is?"

"What are you talking about?"

How do I explain my doubts? "It's just — the cops are so certain. In the last few months, did your mother and Turner ever argue? Or maybe they, I don't know, were growing apart? What could've happened to cause stress between —"

"You want to know what happened?" She raises her voice. "You happened. The only stress my mom ever felt was this search for her real parents. And they never fought about it. He asked if maybe she should just let it go, but she couldn't. Everything bad happened after my mother found you."

"But that has to be a coincidence."

"Does it?"

That stops me for a moment. "How can meeting me have anything to do with your mother's death? I didn't even know she existed —"

"I don't know that it does," she says, quieter now, "but it's something to think about, isn't it? My mother meets you and she dies?"

I don't answer her because my mind is whirring along. She has a point. I have no idea how that could be, but —

"Are we still going to Indian Wells today?" she asks. I can see she's trying to calm down.

"We have to, don't we? The broken car window? Billy?"

"We should stay here, call that lawyer, do something about proving Turner's innocence."

"Seriously, what can we do, and I don't want to hear about Nazis and the KKK." This is my best strategy. My only strategy. Let her try to figure out what exactly we can do and when she sees there's nothing, the idea of meeting Billy — something we can do — will distract her.

Chapter 44
Chuck

When I come out of the bathroom, Makenna greets me with "Turner will tell us who the woman is so we can find her."

Makenna won't let go of the idea that she and I can prove that Turner Bethune is innocent of murdering her mother. I follow her into the living room. "If the police can't find her —"

"Your detective doesn't believe she exists —"

"She's not my detective —"

"And besides," Makenna interrupts, "your detective thinks she's got the killer so she doesn't care." She starts pacing. "He'll give us details he won't give the cops because he's protecting her. If we can find her and convince her to step forward —"

She thinks this makes sense, that Turner Bethune expects her, and by extension me, to locate this mystery woman. "What if it turns out that she's not who you think she is?"

"What do you mean?"

"What if — and I'm not saying I believe this — but what if it turns out she's more to Turner than just a woman who needs help?"

"You mean a girlfriend." She's standing still in the middle of the room, glaring at me.

"It's possible," I say.

"I don't believe it."

"But it's possible," I repeat.

"Then we'll deal with it. The point is someone has to get Turner out of this mess."

"Whoever did this thing is dangerous. Turner doesn't want you to play detective."

"He can't stop me."

"But I will. Please don't add to his problems by letting him think you're in danger."

I wait for her to defy me, to tell me I can't stop her, but that's not what she does. She flops down on the futon, slumps forward, nibbles on her fingers. When she looks up, her eyes are wet. "I lost my mom. I don't want to lose Turner, too."

I sit next to her, but before I can think, my words spill out. "Maybe we can get a lead on the car, the one that tried to run you down."

"How?"

"I was there the morning of the fire, on your street – remember, I told you that – in the crowd, and I talked to the two old guys with the dogs?"

She nods, alert. "Mr. Cole? You said he saw a car that morning."

"I don't remember which one saw the car, but we could go over there, have him describe it. Maybe it's the same one from the Target parking lot." Why hadn't this occurred to me before? Or did it and I dismissed it as improbable?

"Let's go." She's up, heading for the door.

"I'm not even dressed yet."

"Then get dressed."

"What about Indian Wells?" I still haven't called Liv Amaral back.

That should be the first thing I do. But the girl is already outside.

•◊•

It seems a lifetime ago that we came to salvage what we could from her burned-out house, though it's only been a couple of days. There it is. Two newspapers on the lawn, yellow and abandoned, the structure looking sadder than ever. I glance at Makenna. Her face is a mask.

I park the Suburban. While I fetch the papers and toss them into the backseat to be thrown away later, she stands on the sidewalk not saying a word. I wait. Then she shrugs, turns, and points toward the side by side houses of the two neighbors. She is incredibly tough.

When the old man with the shock of white hair answers the door, his dog, the shepherd-poodle-whatever mix, leaps to put both paws on my legs.

"Brutus," admonishes the man.

The dog glances back and reluctantly obeys his master who eyes me over his glasses, brows like storm clouds above his reddened nose, then he spies the girl. "Makenna! I am so sorry about your mother. I can't believe what happened. Come on in. Brutus, heel."

"Thank you, Mr. Cole." Makenna slips in and the dog attaches himself to her, sniffing for a head pat.

I follow. "Hello, Mr. Cole. My name is Abbie Palmer."

"Chuck. Please, call me Chuck. Mr. Cole was my father." He moves his face close to mine, and I smell a whiff of whisky. "You look familiar."

"We came the other day with Turner Bethune. Makenna's staying with me now and —"

"I heard about Turner, but it don't make any sense. Why would any man burn down his own house?"

"That's why we're here," says Makenna. "We want to know more about that car you saw early that morning."

"I didn't see a thing. It was Art, next door. He's got insomnia these days. He's up to go to the bathroom and can't go back to sleep unless —"

"So he was awake," I ask, "when the firebombing happened, you mean? Maybe at the window, looking out at the street?"

"He was in his front yard, but don't go telling anyone. He's not supposed to talk about it. The cops, you know, they want to control everything they can, but now they got their arrest, I guess it don't matter."

"Do you know if he's home?" asks Makenna. "I want to talk to him."

"Well, come on back."

We follow him through the musty house, him keeping up a steady stream of talk. "I got Folgers's crystals so I can whip you up a cup of coffee. I don't drink the stuff myself anymore. Just lost the taste for it."

Mauve apples and slate blue grapes curl above the dark wood cabinets in the kitchen and along the breakfast nook walls. Sunlight spills from a greenhouse window. Makenna and I pull out chairs with cushions that match the wallpaper exactly. I wonder if Mrs. Cole, who no longer seems to be around, approved of the half empty bottle of Wild Turkey on the kitchen counter.

Chuck picks up the receiver to the wall phone and shakes his head. "I'll call Art, but personally, I think he made the car up. You know, for the attention."

Chapter 45
Arthur

They come into the kitchen through the back door, Arthur Roland and his dog, without knocking. "You got water heating, Chuck?"

Chuck heaves himself up to pour hot water into four cups. "These are the people I told you about, Makenna from across the street and her step-mother – I forgot your name."

"Abbie," I say. "I'm not Makenna's step-mother, more of a temporary guardian. Nice to meet you, Mr. Roland."

"Call him Art," says Chuck as he brings two coffees to the table with shaky hands.

"Call me 'Arthur', if you don't mind." The second old man sits next to Makenna, his dog curling at his feet.

"Arthur," I say. "We wondered if you might tell us a little more about the car you saw the morning of the bombing. Did you see the driver?"

"The police told me to be careful who I talk to." Arthur throws a look of annoyance at Chuck who puts two more cups on the table and sits down. I suspect he's poured whisky into his.

Chuck says, "It's not like Makenna isn't our neighbor, and this woman," he nods toward me, "isn't she the woman who came by to see Olita and knocked on your door by mistake?"

"No, it isn't. That woman was younger." Arthur smiles at me. "No offense."

I shrug.

"But I recognized her the minute I saw her on my doorstep," says Chuck.

"She's not that woman and you never saw her anyway."

"I saw her leave."

The two old guys grimace at each other, but then, they

bickered when I first met them on the street too. I ask, "What woman was that? When did she knock on your door, Arthur?"

"A week before the fire. I think she was a lawyer. I pointed her toward Olita's house, she thanked me and went on over."

"Did she give her name?" I ask.

"She didn't say."

"And she was looking for Olita, not Turner?" Could this be the woman Turner was helping the night of the bombing?

"She asked for Olita Jordan, said she was sorry to bother me, and left."

"They're here to talk about the car from the bombing," says Chuck.

"You really saw a car?" I ask.

"I saw the car."

"Wait," said Makenna. "What did the woman look like?"

I throw her a grateful look, glad she has the wits to ask.

"About your size," Arthur looks at me, "but dark hair, lots of it, brown, pretty too. Of course she was wearing sunglasses."

"Was Olita home? Did you see this woman go inside?" I ask. Makenna leans forward in her chair, chewing a fingernail again.

"She went inside, but not sure if it was Olita or Turner who let her in."

"What kind of car did she have?" asks Makenna.

"Ford," says Arthur.

"One of them foreign cars," says Chuck. They glower at each other.

"What color?" I ask.

"White," says Chuck.

"Beige," says Arthur.

Then together, they say, "Looked like a rental."

"Why a rental?" I ask.

"Had an Avis license plate frame," says Chuck.

"It did not."

"So," I say, "what about the other car, the one from the morning of the bombing?"

Arthur sips his coffee, the only one of us who has, and says, "I take Taffy out a couple of times during the night. She has a petite bladder."

The dog's tail thumps at the sound of her name.

"We were standing in the corner of my yard, just breathing in the air, when this car came around the corner. Shady-looking car. Old, moving slow. I stepped behind my camellias. I thought this could be one of those drive-by shootings you're always seeing on the news. I don't know why. The car slowed down in front of Olita's house, sped up when it got by."

"They threw something out the window?" I ask.

"No. I didn't see that. This happened maybe an hour or so before the house went up. Taffy barked a couple of times, but that was it. The car turned the corner, she did her business, and we went inside."

"How do you know the car had anything to do with the firebombing?"

"I don't," he says, "but I spend a lot of time out there in my yard in the middle of the night, and cars never come down the street. Or almost never."

"What did the car look like?" asks Makenna.

"Big American car. Maybe a Chevy, a Monte Carlo. Not sure of the color. Maroon or Moroccan burgundy comes to mind."

"Oh." I catch Makenna's eye. "Did you see who was in the car?"

"No. My eyes aren't as good as they used to be."

"White men? Black men?" I ask.

"One man, not two, but I don't know the color."

"How could one man throw a firebomb and drive a car

at the same time?" Makenna again.

"Easy-peasy," says Chuck. "He parked down the street and hoofed it."

"That's what you figure. I'm not so sure," says Arthur. "Could've been someone laying low in the backseat the first time around, sat up the second time. I heard glass breaking, but that was later."

I stand up, the maple chair almost tipping. "Thank you so much."

"Not much help," says Chuck.

"Alas, it's all I know," answers Arthur.

They follow us out, the dogs, too. I walk through the front door and the cool breeze on my forehead feels like freedom.

Makenna and I cross the street, the girl leaning into me, whispering, "The car in the Target parking lot was maroon."

"A Riviera or a Monte Carlo. It can't be a coincidence."

"You think she's the woman who was with Turner that night?"

"Maybe, maybe not. But if she is, what does it mean?"

Chapter 46
Doubts

By the time we get to the Tiki Palms, I need a nap. Not because I want to hide, not this time, but more to let my subconscious work on the supposition that the car cruising down Olita's street the night of the firebombing is the same car that tried to run down Makenna in the Target parking lot. How can I protect her and from whom? Turner?

Makenna ambles toward the bedroom. "At least now we know that the car is the same car."

"Most likely the car is the same."

"Blinking lights in here. Maybe that detective called about my seeing Turner." She peeks around the door. "You want me to listen to the messages?"

"No. Wait for me. I have to pee."

In the bathroom I fetch my bottle of Ativan from the top drawer. It will calm me down and I need to calm down because my mind is going places I don't want it to go. Just how innocent can Turner be? That woman, the one the old guys said went to see Olita, is she the same woman Turner claimed to see the night of the firebombing? Did she visit Olita so she could fling her affair with Turner in Olita's face? Did Olita confront Turner and he then decided to get rid of her? Maybe instead of giving him an alibi, this woman could be the district attorney's star witness, and that's why she's disappeared or was murdered? Could he have... ? I shake my head hard. Dumb idea. Or is it?

I wish I could talk over these possibilities with Makenna, but they're inconceivable to her. There isn't anyone except for Craig, and he'd put his arms around me and tell me to come home, he'd take care of everything. Isn't that why we seek out partners, so when difficult times come, we're not alone?

I'm losing ground. Water rising, boat sinking. My private island is quickly disappearing. I'm no longer in charge of my life and I'm ready to bolt. But I won't. I can't.

There's a loud knock on the bathroom door. "Hey Abbie, you okay?"

"I'm coming."

I stare at the pills for a moment before putting them back in the drawer without opening the bottle. Splash my face with cold water, then peek into the living room. She's sitting at the computer munching lettuce out of a bagged salad.

"You know there's dressing and tortilla strips inside that bag. You could make it into a real salad," I say.

She shrugs. "I don't want to bug you, but could you check the messages so we can find out when Turner's out on bail. If not today, we can go to Indian Wells."

Makenna traipses into the bedroom behind me. I should send her away, but I punch the answering machine without saying a word. Craig's deliberate voice fills the room. "You know Bethune's been charged? What did you find out in Palm Springs? Where are you? Call me."

Second call, Craig again, now agitated. "Goddammit, Abbie, why don't you answer your cell phone? I've left six messages. Are you in trouble? Is that girl – " I click the skip button. Don't even look at Makenna.

The third is from Tellez asking me to call her. Elaine Chute, my dean, Tom Robinson, Elma's son, both want me to call. I give Makenna a thumbs-up after listening to this last one, and jot down his number. I call the detective first.

"Tellez."

"Hi, this is Abbie Palmer. You left me a message?"

"Hi, how's Makenna doing?"

"As well as expected. Did Turner make bail?"

"Bail isn't usually granted for capital murder cases in California."

"But he has Darton Reglan."

"I'm trying to get you two in to see him, but nothing yet, so tell Makenna she'll have to wait."

"But it's a possibility." I glance at the girl. This is getting way too familiar to me, her hovering while I discuss Turner Bethune's fate.

"Don't count on bail, but the visit can happen. Meantime, everything okay?"

"We have some information," and I tell her about our visit to the two old men, the coincidence of the cars, and about the woman in an Avis rental who came to see Olita and knocked on Arthur Roland's door by mistake. I don't convey the story very well because she keeps asking if the woman was in a maroon Monte Carlo. Finally, we straighten it out and she says she'll check the rental records at Avis. She's careful not to mention the woman's name. Not that I have any idea what I could do with it. Then she asks about our search for Billy Eastlake.

"He lives in Indian Wells," I say. "Actually, his wife contacted us." I don't mention anything about staking her out, skulking after her, or breaking into her Jaguar.

Tellez thanks me for the information and we hang up. I tell Makenna that his lawyer is working on getting Turner out on bail, but I don't tell her it's unlikely.

"What about a visit?"

"She's working on that too. Maybe she figures if he makes bail, she won't need to set up a visit." This isn't exactly what she said, not even close, but it could be true, couldn't it?

"Good," she says. "I still think we can track that woman down if he tells us her name."

"That's not going to happen," I say.

"You don't have to sound mad."

"I'm not mad."

"You sound mad."

"I'm just tired."

"I'll drive," says Makenna.

190

"Drive?"

"To Indian Wells."

"No. Wait. It's too late to go today." I have zero energy to trek all the way to Indian Wells. I feel battered around the head and thinking about that nap again. Hard not to, since Makenna's counting on me to save her from her own personal hurricane. Facing Liv, meeting Billy? I don't think I can take it. Not now. Maybe never.

Chapter 47
Aunt Neenie

"**A**bbie. We can't quit now. We're getting close. Or is that what you're afraid of?"

"I'm not afraid. I'm tired." I don't move, don't say anything, just let myself float on the surface of the bed. I didn't take an Ativan, did I?

She says, "You don't have time to be tired. Turner's locked up in jail for something he didn't do and there's a grandfather I've never met out in Indian Wells."

I don't want to fight with Makenna about this. We can go to Indian Wells as easily tomorrow as today. If I wait a moment, ignore her, maybe she'll go away.

"Abbie!" She plops down next to me.

I mutter, "Maybe we should stick close to home in case Turner makes bail."

"You think he might?"

"It's a possibility."

"That's what Tellez told you?"

"Possible, maybe he will."

"Okay, so what do you want to do?"

I sit up on my elbows. "Honestly, I just want to take a nap. Let me do that, and then I'll call both Liv and Tom Robinson."

"What's wrong with you?"

"What is it about exhausted you don't get?"

"I get it, but what am I supposed to do?"

"Go read those death penalty papers out there."

"I can't do that. How can I read college papers?"

"You'd be surprised. Anyway, you don't grade them, just highlight thesis statements and the topic sentences. You know about theses and topic sentences, right?"

She gets off the bed and stomps away. Waves her hand

over her head. "Okay."

"There's a pad of large stickies if you have comments —"
BAM! She slams the door behind her. I don't care.

•◇•

When I drag myself awake about an hour later, Tom
Robinson comes to mind and I wonder why he's called me
back. Is it something he remembered about my mother?
About her relationship with Billy? Or maybe he just wants
his mother's recipe for crumb cake.

I roll over in bed and stare at the phone. Am I afraid? Is
this why I feel so physically exhausted? My fear of finding
out why, after all this time, my mother was so unhappy?
Maybe, just maybe, she wanted Olita and couldn't have her.
Maybe she never wanted me because Billy was her true love,
not my father, and that reality was the undercurrent, the
tension, whatever it was, that gave my whole childhood its
swamp-water feel.

This thought makes me feel better because it means
something bigger than me caused my parents' misery. The
miasma around my swamp lifts a little, and I am beginning
to see the outline of what came before.

Sitting up, I dial Tom Robinson's number.

"Mr. Robinson's office." The voice is female.

"Hi. Mr. Robinson left a message on my machine to
call."

"Your name, please?"

"Abbie Palmer."

"Just a minute."

Almost at once I hear, "Abbie, it's Tom. How're you
doing?"

"Hi, Tom. I'm fine. You called?"

"After I talked to you, I phoned my mother's sister in
San Diego."

"I didn't know Elma had a sister."

193

"She has – had six sisters. Auntie Neenie's the closest to her in age. They were best friends. Mama was living with her when she passed. Anyway, I told her you were doing research on Virginia Gifford and asked her if she knew her, and she said yes, she remembers her quite well."

He pauses and I take a breath.

"Anyway, she used to pick Mama up and one time your mother invited her in and gave her an autograph. Aunt Neenie said she was really, really sweet."

"Oh, thanks, Tom." While this is nice to hear, it doesn't really tell me anything. "Nothing else?"

"I have the names of a couple gentlemen who knew your mother quite well. They're pretty old by now – older than Aunt Neenie – but they might still be around."

"Okay." I brighten a little, but can't help thinking, a couple of gentlemen? Did my mother have more than one affair?

"Apparently, she worked for them. She was a waitress. They had a place in Hollywood, a diner called The Ranchhouse or maybe it was The Range? I don't think it's there anymore, but I have their names, Ambie Lipscomb and Jack Holmes."

"Oh, that's great. I'll try to track them down."

"You don't have to. I know where they are."

"You do? How?"

"Apparently, my auntie knows them. My mama knew them. That's how she got her job working for your mother, through them. Auntie Neenie says they're up here in L.A. at an old folks home for movie people. That's what she called it. She's seventy-seven herself, but thinks she's thirty-seven. Anyway, I don't know the name, but you could find out. They worked in the movie industry, I guess, before the diner. Or maybe during. I don't know any more than that."

"Thank you so much. I've never talked to anyone who actually knew her, my mother, I mean, except for your mother, and my dad." I'm a little breathless.

194

After I hang up, I go out into the living room and tell Makenna what Tom Robinson's found out.

"Did you call Liv?" she asks.

"Not yet, but I will. Can you do your computer wizardry and see if you can find that old folks home?"

She does and soon, I'm on the phone with the Motion Picture and Television Country House and Hospital in the San Fernando Valley asking someone to find out if either Ambie Lipscomb or Jack Holmes, both residents, is willing to talk to us about Virginia Gifford. I rattle off a thank you and my phone number and hang up.

"Now what?" asks Makenna.

"We wait."

Makenna looks up from the computer. "Now can you call Liv?"

"I don't want to tie up the phone."

"Use your cell."

I wonder where I put it. That's the problem with wanting to be an island. Phones are the enemy.

Chapter 48
Death Valley

The windows are down as we drive out the 101 Freeway to Woodland Hills. Traffic, for once, isn't too heavy. We haven't said much to each other, though Makenna seems reconciled to the fact that we're seeing Jack Holmes and not Billy Eastlake. We both hope this visit will give us a clearer picture of Virginia's life before she became the 'Palm Springs Bikini Girl', but disappointed we won't meet Ambie Lipscomb who's in the hospital for cancer tests.

Jack Holmes, the other man Tom Robinson mentioned, worries me because when he called me back, he said, "So you want to come see me out here in Death Valley?" He was making a joke. He didn't mean the real Death Valley, but the San Fernando Valley as in "I wouldn't be caught dead there." His humor, my humor, not the same. Or maybe I'm just not myself.

"You have your cell phone on? Did you charge it?" Makenna asks.

"Can you check for me?"

She rummages through my purse. "It's not in here. You forgot it again. I'm sure Turner will call as soon as he's out and now we'll miss him."

"He'll call again or come over." I wish now I'd been straight with her about how unlikely his getting out on bail is. I should've been straight about everything. What else, though, have I concealed from her? Just the birth certificate, and we should know about that soon enough.

"I can't wait to see Turner," she says, watching the flat valley landscape of post-war tract homes flash by.

I try to steady my thoughts. Think about something else. This freeway reminds me of the days when my job took me out to Bradshaw's store #14. Since my father made my mother quit the movies, I always felt like I was living out her career fantasy, albeit humbler by far. How full of self-importance my attempt to emulate my mother seems now.

"He'll be thrilled to see you. You're his only family and he yours," I say, remembering them back to back in my entryway on Woodbine Street when the cops came to take Makenna back to the foster home.

Makenna swings her head around, her voice snapping. "You're my family too."

"I just meant you two have each other. Count on each. Your bond is important."

"You mean it's important to you. You want to dump me as soon as you can."

"I don't want to dump you. Makenna, don't make this into a big thing, please." She thinks I still have doubts. Well, I do. I've seen the birth certificate. Only Billy Eastlake can tell us whether Virginia was Olita's mother. And yet, here I am, not heading to Indian Wells, not accepting Liv's invitation to see Billy. I haven't even called her back.

Things are still tense between us when we arrive at the Motion Picture and Television Country Home with its many buildings, swaths of grass, and flora my nosy neighbor on Woodbine would covet, but it isn't really the "country," not any more. L.A. County consumes almost 5000 square miles of Southern California "from the desert to the sea," as Jerry Dunphy used to say on the TV news when I was a kid, and now, the city is everywhere.

We enter the air-conditioned lobby and check in at the desk. A toothy administrator leads us down a sunny hallway into the cafeteria. Seated at a large rectangular table, a heavy-set man, sunglasses perched on his shiny dome, dominates the room. He's surrounded by laughing octogenarians and a couple of scrub-clad aides, and when the man spies us, his face lights up and he lets out a loud

"Ho-ho!"

Pointing a finger at me, he says, "Wow, did anybody ever tell you how much you look like Virginia Gifford?" This must be Jack Holmes.

Heads nod, all of them obviously suffering from cataracts since I bear only the mildest resemblance to my mother. Still I beam.

Someone brings over two more chairs. The man says, "Sit down, sit down. You hungry? Go make up a tray, anything you want. It's on me. They have pork chops today, no gravy, but better for your acid reflux. Sit down. You're still standing. Who's this young lady?"

"This is Makenna Jordan, my — a very dear friend." The girl glares and opens her mouth to say something, and I glare back. Our personal business isn't something to discuss with strangers, but I can't say that out loud. I pat the chair next to me for her to sit down.

Jack makes a sweeping gesture around the dining room. "Welcome to what I like to call the 'Final Curtain'. It's a nice place to visit, but you wouldn't wanna live here, unless you're old enough to remember vaudeville, and if you don't, they stick it to you — with a hypodermic. And they stick it right up your ass —"

"Mr. Holmes." The administrator clears her throat.

"Just a joke, just a joke." The dinner crowd laughs their agreement, except for one old lady who looks up from her creamed spinach to say, "Get over yourself, Jack." More laughter ripples around the table.

I smile, though I feel uncomfortable in this crowd. "I'm excited to find out what you can tell me — and Makenna — about my mother?"

His face sobers. "I always thought you'd show up one day. Ambie said I was a fool, but here you are. I am so sorry about your loss."

"My loss?" At first I think about Olita and wonder if he knows everything, then realize he means my mother, her death. "It was a long time ago." Almost fifty years.

"But you're curious, aren't you?"

I can feel Makenna leaning in to listen, her warmth on my arm. "We are. Can you tell me how you knew her?"

Chapter 49
Jack and Martha

Jack Holmes lowers his voice. "Ambie's my life partner."

"You can speak up, Jack. We're familiar with your proclivities." Again the lady with the spinach.

"You're right, Martha, but back then, if we broadcast that fact, we'd end up in jail. Anyway, I wanted to call the diner Holmes on the Range, but Ambie said no, considering the implications, so it became The Range. The name on the sign was written with a rope, like a lasso. We already had too many waitresses in cowgirl hats, but Virginia comes in one afternoon — we called her Gin — and Ambie hires her on the spot. After a while I saw she had something. I didn't know if it was a big something, but she had a shot."

"What was she like, her personality?" Makenna scoots her chair closer.

"When she was on, you didn't need to have the sun shine. She brought it with her. Customers loved her. She was good for business. Ambie, he brought it out in her. He does that."

"Worked miracles with you," Martha pipes up. Heads nod.

I remember Ambie's in the hospital, ask, "How's he doing, health-wise?"

Jack waves a dismissive hand. "He's fine. He's tough. He's too stubborn to give an inch."

"Stubborn's good. We'd like to meet him sometime."

"What about the movies? How'd she get discovered?" asks Makenna.

"Ambie and I, we had a hand in it. I'm not saying she wouldn't or couldn't have done it on her own, but we were in the biz and that always greases the movie reels. Ambie was a damn good cook, but before that, he was an entertainer on the chitlin' circuit. You know what that was, young lady?"

"It's where black people could go to see other blacks perform. Do you know who Billy Eastlake is?" She's excited now.

"Do I know Billy Eastlake? Of course I do. We all know Billy."

"Who's that?" Martha asks and again, everybody laughs.

"Billy and Ambie knew each other from the circuit. Ambie could make you roar with laughter, then break your heart with a song. But he wanted to settle down and thought he might like running a diner. We went in together because no one would rent space to a black man back then, not in the middle of Hollywood, so I signed the lease. Other than that, I was just window dressing."

"Ambie's African-American?" In this web of possible connections, I glimpse a thread, Virginia to Ambie to Billy.

"Black and proud of it." He glances at Makenna who shrugs, then he adds, "I like your freckles, young lady. Today you don't have to hide freckles with make-up." Then he squints at me. Yep, no freckles scattered there.

"Your mother's timing was always good. Ambie was getting bored flipping Buffalo burgers and frying Teepee poles – I named the French fries 'Teepee poles'." He winks. "Gin got a kick out of that."

"Move on, Jack," Martha says.

"If you'd stop interrupting, Martha. Now, Ambie taught your mother a little soft shoe and how to pick the right songs for her voice, and how to stand just so." He straightens his shoulders, elongates his neck. "Tummy in, chin up, looking confident, expectant, and be very, very still, and wait – wait – wait for the heads to turn."

"Makes me think of the bikini picture," Makenna whispers in my ear.

I whisper back, "Me too."

201

Jack's still talking, "I took charge of clothing and make-up. She had freckles, which nobody liked back then, but I worked my magic. Found her a good agent, too. Dennis — Dennis — " He snaps his fingers.

"Ventura," I say. "Is he still around?"

"Right. Dennis Ventura. I heard he died. He had a reputation for getting pretty young girls noticed in a land of pretty young girls. He was always trying to make the big splash and his best idea was to put Gin into that bikini. Cover of *Life* magazine. You ever see that?"

"We looked it up," says Makenna. "On the computer."

"What else you find about her on the computer?" asks Jack.

"Not much," I say. "Every bio's the same, brief and contradictory. She's from Iowa, from Minnesota, Ohio. She ran away from home. She didn't run away from home. Her father gave her money to go to California. Her jilted boyfriend gave her the money."

"All made up. She never said a thing about her past, not one word, not even to Ambie."

"So is that how she met Billy Eastlake?" I ask. "At the diner?"

Jack's eyes catch Martha's, then he glances at the aides along the wall. The taller one comes over and whispers in his ear. Jack slaps his hands on the table. Hits a fork that clangs like a bell. "Time for my shot."

"I thought you didn't get shots," I say, remembering his joke.

He shrugs, "My age, what're you gonna do? Doctors. You can't live with them and you can't live without them. Excuse me, ladies. Keep in touch. It's been a riot." He stands up, wobbles a bit, addresses the table. "Thank you for inviting me. It's been an honor." And with his rolling gait, he lumbers out of the cafeteria.

Chairs scrape. Everyone gets up and wanders away, except for Martha, who pushes her plate aside and looks at us. "Did you find out everything you wanted to know?"

"Not everything."

"I worked for the producer Jerome Tallman back then, and there was plenty of talk about your mother. You might not want to find out everything."

"What kind of talk? What did they say? That's why we came, to find out the whole story."

She signals the aide. He strides over and pulls her wheelchair from the table, then she holds up her hand for him to pause. Studies Makenna, then turns to me. "This isn't my story to tell, and it certainly isn't Jack's. Go find Billy Eastlake if you can. Ask him about your mother."

Chapter 50
Tension

Back on the freeway, a refrain plays in my head: Ask Billy Eastlake. Ask Billy Eastlake. We trekked all this way to determine what we already knew. The key to everything is Billy.

Makenna taps her feet, fiddles with the radio, chews her hangnails. She says, "You know, my phone burned up in the fire."

"You didn't have it with you at your friend's house?"

"Mom took it away. We had a fight."

"I'm sorry. Are you okay about having a fight and then..." my voice trails off.

"We made up. It was okay, but she took the phone away for a week."

"We could've gotten you one at Target."

"I didn't care then. I didn't want to talk to anybody."

She rubs at her eyes, then punches the scan button on the radio. Blips and blurts of songs, then a trumpet. I say, "Let's listen to that. Do you mind?" It's Louis Armstrong's *Wrap Your Troubles In Dreams*. Then Billie Holiday comes on with *You've Changed* followed by Lena Horne singing *Stormy Weather*.

These songs remind me of my father. He'd come home from work and I'd be in my bedroom, Elma having fed me earlier, leaving his dinner in the oven. His car would rumble into the garage, the garage door cranked down, the side door slammed. A few minutes later, he'd put on a record, Lena or Billie, and others I didn't know the names of. I rarely ventured out of my room. I've spent my whole life hiding.

Back at the Tiki Palms, the answering machine is empty and my cell is dead.

"I guess he didn't make bail," says Makenna. "Call the detective. Ask her what's going on." She paces around the small apartment, jittery, frowning, all the serenity of the car ride home evaporated.

I use the house phone, but it goes to voice mail, so I leave a message for Tellez.

"What now?" I ask.

"Find your cell and plug it in."

"We should buy you one."

"Or just give me yours since you don't use it."

"We'll get you one."

She sits down at the computer, doesn't turn it on, thrums on the keyboard anyway. She stops and swivels to look at me, "Maybe we should just go see Billy now."

"Tomorrow."

"I can't stand doing nothing."

"I'll call Liv and set it up."

"You haven't called her? You know, Abbie, you say you're not afraid to find out the truth about your mother, but that's a lie."

"There hasn't been time," I say.

"No. You had to take a nap."

"Look what's happened in — what — a little more than a week, Bethune's arrest or charges or whatever they're calling it now, and wanting to help him, and then searching for info about my mother and your grandfather. All this takes a toll and Makenna, you've lost your mother. You need some time to grieve —"

"I don't want to grieve." She growls at me, her hands tight fists. I reach out to touch her shoulder, but she waves me off. "I am so frustrated. I wanted to see Billy today. I wanted to see Turner today. And I can't do anything. It's driving me crazy."

"Bethune will be out by tomorrow and we can —"

"Why don't you call him Turner? You were all Turner this and Turner that before the cops started questioning him and now, you talk about him like he's a criminal. I don't even know what I'm doing here anymore."

Again I reach for her, and she yells, "Don't!" Her body quivers with anger as she stalks into the bedroom and bangs the door.

•◇•

I decide to let her stew because she's right. I do have doubts. I want to believe in Turner Bethune, trust him, yet letting down my guard might end in disaster. If he isn't who we think he is, it will crush her. If it turns out he had any part in hurting her mother, it will ruin her. I do my own stewing, but must drift off to sleep because I wake up to the ringing of my cell phone. I lean over to where it's charging on the floor and answer it.

"Hello?"

"Mrs. Palmer. Abbie, can I call you Abbie?" She sounds weary. "This is Detective Tellez. Call me Laura, please. I wanted to let you know the district attorney has asked the judge to deny Bethune's bail."

"Why?"

"First, it wasn't likely in the first place and second, there's concern about Makenna's safety. Not that he would hurt her necessarily, but rather he might leave the country and take her with him."

"He wouldn't do that."

"You don't know that. You just met him."

"Makenna loves —"

"If he skips, he might take her with him."

"Wait. If he's guilty, wouldn't he be the one behind the car coming after Makenna in the Target lot?"

"That's the other argument for not releasing him."

After we hang up, I tap on the bedroom door. There's no answer, so I tiptoe in.

The room is dark and the closed blinds clack against the window frame. I tiptoe over and reel them up. Cool air breezes in. The window is wide open.

"Makenna?" I turn toward the bed to wake her, but she's not there.

I run to the bathroom. It's empty. Back to the window, I peer into late afternoon gloom, at the grape-stake fence, straight ahead four feet away, to my right toward front, then left. The gate to the alley yawns open.

Chapter 51
Complications

The living room blurs as I head into the courtyard, calling her name in a low urgent voice. My throat tightens as I race to the carport. The Suburban is gone. She's taken the car. No one stole her away. She's vanished, but to where?

I race into the apartment, leaving the door open, and into the bedroom. Reach for the house phone, but still holding my cell. Dial 911. The dispatcher sounds annoyed when I blurt out my teenage niece has left the apartment at six in the evening without telling me.

"This," she says, "is common for teenagers, ma'am. She probably snuck out to be with some boy. File a report with your local police if she's not back in twenty-four hours."

I call Tellez. Laura.

"Makenna's missing. She took my car. She wasn't snatched, right, if she took my car?"

"Wait a minute."

I can hear her talking to someone, then she says, "Abbie, is this you? What's happened?"

"We had a disagreement and she went out the bedroom window while I was in the living room. I don't know what to do."

"Did you tell her Bethune wouldn't be released? Maybe she went to county to try and see him?"

"I didn't tell her. She was already gone. He's still locked up, isn't he?"

"If she doesn't know bail was denied, she might've gone to wait for him. Or at least to visit him. Let me see if she's shown up over there. I'll call you right back."

I'm numb, my brain pickled. Where would she go? It has to be the jail. She's avoiding her friends. Where else?

When Laura Tellez phones back, she tells me that Makenna hasn't tried to see Bethune, but they'll be on the look-out for her.

"I can't just sit here," I say.

"She may have gone to her house," Tellez says. "Does she have a key?"

I quickly survey the bedroom, but don't see her green camouflage backpack anywhere. "I think so. She's taken her school bag. Her key would be in there."

"I'll send a patrolman over to look for her."

"That might scare her."

A loud rap sounds in the living room. My heart pumps. "Wait. I think she's back."

But it isn't Makenna. A man, dark head, dark jacket, dark jeans, hovers in the door.

I squint. "Ben?"

"Your door's wide open. You okay?"

Tellez hollers into my ear, "Is it Makenna?"

I say to Ben, "Hold on a minute," and speak into the phone, "Laura, it's my neighbor. I'll check over at her house and let you know."

"Good. And Abbie, there's something else you should know."

Every time she says this, it's bad news. "What now?"

"Remember the guy who lives in the apartment where Bethune supposedly met the woman the night of the firebombing? The tenant?"

"Yes." I'm feeling a little impatient. I want to get moving.

"He's the one who claimed she couldn't have met Turner over there because he'd never heard of either one of them?"

"I remember." I hold up a finger to Ben, glance around for my purse.

In my ear, "He's dead."

This snaps me back to the detective. "What?"

"Looks like he OD'ed, but we won't know for sure until they do an autopsy. The Sheriff's department is handling it. It probably doesn't have anything to do with this case."

"Then why are you telling me about it?"

She doesn't answer right away, then says, "Something doesn't feel quite right. The case is getting too complicated. Maybe this guy really did overdose. A coincidence, but I want you to be careful and call me immediately when you find Makenna."

This revelation, this incident – a murder? – tangential to what's going on with Olita's murder, shakes me. After I hang up, I look at Ben and ask, "How much do you believe in coincidences?"

●◇●

Ben drives. We're almost to Olita's house, my body bristling all over. This is where she's come. It has to be.

"There." I point to the house. Anyone can see it's been in a serious fire, windows boarded up, dark scars radiating from windows, the roof caved in. "She isn't here. My car would be parked in front."

"Maybe it's in the back or around the corner. I mean, she wouldn't want the neighbors bothering her. We'll find her," says Ben.

He parks his Honda at the curb and we hurry out, me trotting straight for the front door. I don't have a key, but I'm sure she'll open it by the time I get there. And if she doesn't? I don't want to think about it.

The door is locked. I knock. "Makenna?"

Ben comes up the walk, checking out the neighborhood, his hands tucked into his pockets. The sun lurks behind the trees.

I knock again. Rattle the handle.

"Locked?" he asks. When I nod, he strides across the grass toward the back of the house. I follow. There's a gate here, the backyard is fenced, but no lock. He reaches over and pulls the latch. When we came to do the insurance photos, I only glimpsed this area through the sliding glass doors. I'm struck now at how intact it looks, how little the police and the fire department have disturbed this part of the lot.

Ben tests windows. I peer through the slider. The glass is warm from the afternoon sun. I rap on it and call Makenna's name.

"I don't think she's here," I say.

Ben opens the side door into the detached garage. "There's a car here. A Volvo."

"That's Olita's. Anything in the alley?"

He peeks over the fence. "Nope."

I cover my face with my hands. I can't believe this. I run our conversation over in my head, and our voices were raised and she was frustrated, yes, but to run away? No. I can't figure out what she's thinking, where she'd go on her own.

Chapter 52
Gone

As the sun drops behind the trees in Olita's back yard, I begin to shiver. I shouldn't have given Makenna such a hard time.

"Hey."

I look up. Ben's standing on the roof. How he got there so fast, I don't know.

"I'll let you in," he says and he drops out of sight and in a few minutes, he appears inside the house, sliding the glass door open.

A cold silence has settled on the house. The minute I step inside I know she hasn't been here.

•◊•

I ask Ben if we can wait in the car for a while, in case she shows up. "Sure. I'm not working tonight."

"The only other thing I can think of is Billy. She wanted to see Turner and she wanted to see Billy. Either that or she's been snatched —"

He puts his hand on mine. "She took your car. That means she left because she wanted to leave. We'll find her."

He has a pale blue tattoo on his forearm I never noticed before. It says 'Delia'. The other arm must say 'Blanca'. He says gently, "I know who Turner Bethune is, it's on the news, but who's this Billy, her boyfriend?"

"Her grandfather. We've been trying to piece her history together. It's a long story."

"This is for her mother's funeral?"

"I wish it was that simple."

"Nothing is ever that simple."

The street glows with porch lights and street lights.

Hard to imagine anyone turning onto this street to spray-paint graffiti on the sidewalk or throw an incendiary device into a house.

"You want to wait a little longer? No pressure," Ben asks.

I shake my head. "I should call Billy's wife and find out if Makenna's shown up there. We need to go back to the apartment."

"Let's do it."

On the way, he asks, "You told me about Makenna's relationship to Billy Eastlake, but if you don't mind me asking, what's Makenna to you? You treat her like a daughter. You don't have to tell me, though. It's okay."

"Hypothetically, my mother had an affair with Billy Eastlake and they had a daughter, Makenna's mother. That's Olita, the woman who was killed in the fire."

"So you and Olita, you'd be half-sisters?"

"That's the theory, but I have a birth certificate that shows it isn't true."

"Huh. So how did this whole thing get started? I mean, the part that involves you?"

I tell him about Olita's visit to my house on Woodbine and how, after I chased her away, I found a note in my door that said, *Your mother is my mother.* "The next day, I looked her up on the computer and drove over only to find her house burned down and her — well, you know."

"That must've really played with your head."

"You're the first person who gets that."

"Now I understand why you needed the alibi," he adds.

"I don't know if they seriously considered me a suspect, but I'm glad you were home to vouch for me."

"Actually," he says. "I wasn't home."

I look at him. "You lied?"

He shrugs.

Well.

•◇•

The Suburban isn't parked in its spot at the Tiki Palms. As Ben pulls the Honda in, he says, "I was hoping she'd be here too." He reads minds. Then he says, "I'll stick around if you want."

"Would you? I may have to go out there. I'd pay you to take me."

"I can do that. You don't need to pay. You'd help me if something happened to one of my girls."

I flinch at the thought of those two little girls in danger, squeeze his arm. "Thank you."

He follows me into my apartment.

"There's soda in the fridge. Not much else. Liv's number's on my answering machine."

If it was dark in the bedroom earlier, it's black now. I flick on the overhead and notice Makenna's lined up pictures of Billy and my mother along the top of the dresser. None, of course, are of the two of them together, but seeing them like this, photo edges touching, it's like they are together.

"You okay?" Ben's in the doorway.

"I'm looking at these pictures of Billy and my mother."

When he hesitates, I say, "Come see."

"I wonder how they managed it?" he asks.

"Managed it?"

"I mean how they were able to be together enough back then to fall in love. Were they ever in the same movie?"

"I don't think so. I couldn't find any that listed both their names. We did find a connection, Makenna and I, how they probably met. At this diner in Hollywood called The Range."

"Never heard of it."

"It's long gone, but she was a waitress and the owner of the diner knew Billy Eastlake. I don't know if Billy came in as a customer or maybe they went to see his act. He was a comedian. This is what we're trying to piece together."

214

"It must've been hard for them if she had a baby."

"I'm sure it was. They used to hang black men for even looking at white women."

"That didn't happen in their day, did it?"

"It did. One name, Emmett Till."

"Okay. I want to hear more about this, but why don't you make your phone call, and then we can talk when we get on the road."

"Sounds like a plan."

He heads back into the living room while I search the room for some paper to copy down Liv's number from the answering machine. The piece I grab already has the digits scribbled on it in Makenna's handwriting. She must've called Liv. What did Liv say to persuade Makenna to drive out there tonight? Or was it Makenna's idea?

I call Liv, too, and standing there, listening to the phone ring and ring and ring, I'm reminded of the morning just a while ago when I called Olita and she, too, didn't answer.

Chapter 53
Bribes

By the time we arrive at Cascades where Billy Eastlake lives, the desert is cool and dark. The same guard who blocked our entry last time, blocks it again. His smile is friendly enough until he spies me in the passenger seat. "You were here the other day. Had to have the police out then too."

"You had the police out here again?" I lean toward the driver's window to ask.

Ben gives me a shake of his head, a silent request to let him talk.

"Hey man," he says. "We're looking for a girl, Afro-American in a Suburban. You see her?"

The guard puffs himself up. "She's the one who caused the commotion. The police came and everything."

I fumble with the door handle, scramble out of the car, and hurry around to face him. "What happened? Is she okay?"

Ben climbs out too. The guard steps back, putting a couple of feet between him and us. He says, "Oh, she's fine, I guess. Better than fine."

"What does that mean?" I ask. "Where is she?"

"I don't have to tell you anything."

I steady my voice. "We're not trying to put anything over on you. Mr. Eastlake is the girl's grandfather. We were invited back by Mrs. Eastlake, and I thought it was too late to come, but Makenna didn't want to wait. She's been through a lot and she was anxious to see him." A part of me is furious I have to tell him anything. Another part urges me to do whatever is necessary. "I just want to make sure she's okay."

"I guess it's all right." The guard shifts his feet. "Mrs.

216

Eastlake took care of the police."

"How?"

"Yeah, the girl tripped the alarm around the perimeter when she climbed over the wall. The police came rolling in, but when they got to the Eastlake house, everything got squared away."

"So she's up at their house?" I ask.

"She's with them," he says.

"Then open the gate," says Ben as he turns back toward the Honda.

I sprint around to the passenger side, but before I can open the door, the guard says, "Won't do you any good. They left in a limousine about two hours ago."

"Who left?"

"They all did."

"Billy too?"

"He's with them, so you two have to move on so I can get back to work." He retreats into his kiosk.

I bite my lip and throw myself into the Honda. Ben pulls out of the driveway and onto the street without a word.

My brain is drained. Finally I say, "The detective. I could call her."

"Does she know about Billy Eastlake?"

"She does. I'll ask her to check to see if Billy has another house somewhere." I make the phone call, but it goes to voice mail.

Ben asks, "Now what?"

"What if I offer him a bribe to tell us where they went?"

He grins. "Let's do it."

The guard sees us coming and stands in the middle of the road, his hand up. Ben stops the car and I scramble out, gripping the little bit of money we have between us.

"What if I were to give you some money, would you tell us where they went?"

"How much money?"

"Fifty-two dollars."

"That's not very much."

"That's all we have. It's a good cause."

"Yeah. Yeah. Give it to me."

I hand it over. He stuffs it in his pocket.

"So where did they go?"

"I told you I don't know."

"You just said —" I want to smack him.

"I didn't say I knew, but Ramona might know something."

"Who's Ramona?"

"Ex-housekeeper."

"Ex?"

"Mrs. Eastlake fired her."

"How can we reach this Ramona?"

"She's up the street working for someone else. She's a live-in. I'll see if she'll come down."

It doesn't take long for Ramona to drive her Dodge Neon through the gate and park it on the street. We move behind her and get out so she doesn't have to, but she meets us halfway.

She starts spewing Spanish, pointing at the guard, looking angry.

"Shit," I say.

I catch a few words: "gato," cat, and "val verde," green valley, "chica negro," black girl. Ben intercedes in her language, but she looks confused. He slows down and soon they are having a conversation.

Finally Ben jogs back to his car, opens the trunk, and pulls something out of a box. When he gets back to us, I can see it's a CD. Ramona doesn't smile, but takes the offering, nods at me, says something to Ben, and climbs into her car. The guard who knows nothing gets $52 and the woman who knows something gets a CD of Ben's band. I smile, thinking, she's getting the better bargain.

"So what was that all about?"

"Ramona doesn't like your friend Liv," he says as we

get into the Honda and he starts the engine. "I couldn't make out much of what she was saying, you know, but I got that part."

"And did you find out where they went?"

"Billy has a house up near Magic Mountain, in a place called Val Verde."

"I read about that place when Makenna and I were Googling. It used to be called the 'black Palm Springs'. Is there a phone? What did she say about Makenna?"

"Actually, Abbie, I don't speak Spanish very well, just what I learned in high school. And no phone. And no address either. They never took Ramona up there with them."

"No address?" I feel defeated. "Then we're stuck, but I can't just sit here." He puts the engine in drive and pulls into the street.

I sit back in my seat and close my eyes. I can't think straight. I grumble, "Where are we going now?"

"We're going to buy a map."

"Good. And go? To the green valley?"

"To the green valley."

Chapter 54
The Green Valley

According to the map we bought at the gas station – along with Twinkies and diet Coke – Val Verde is near Magic Mountain just north of where the 126 Freeway heads to the coast. As we travel up the 5, I keep an eye out for Hasley Canyon Road. Since my daughter Christie moved to Berkeley, I've driven by here several times, but never thought there might be a tiny hidden-away Shangri-La beyond the hills. Now, late at night, speeding by gas stations and the occasional McDonalds, I begin to doubt.

Val Verde used to be a vacation spot for African-Americans. In those days, people of color were not allowed in "white" Palm Springs except to change sheets or whip up appetizers and martinis. What was it like for Billy Eastlake back then, a respected member of the entertainment industry, but barred from most places?

The exit comes up suddenly, jolting me from my trance.

"Here," I say, glancing down at the map, and Ben takes the turn. Soon street lights reveal houses on the right and rolling countryside on the left. The next road is the one we want and all we can see are thick spring grasses in the flash of our headlights as we curve through hills heading west.

The windows of a solitary old house glint from behind a giant oak, standing guard against the real world dropping by, causing trouble. We are arriving in the dark and the odds are not in our favor. How am I going to find Makenna way out here?

The road veers around the base of a knoll, and we drive by a couple of porch lights.

"The mini-suburbs," I say as we pass by. Soon we're heading up a steep rise. At the top, Ben stops the car to survey the small town nestled between dark hills, its scattered lights like constellations, its houses and secrets as invisible as black holes.

We roll down the hill and into the quiet town.

"What do we do now?" I ask. "It's the middle of the night."

"We have to wait until people wake up."

"You think that's okay? Makenna's safe?" I can't keep the worry out of my voice.

"We could call the local cops, but we don't even know what's going on. If she came up here to visit and everyone's all sacked out in their beds and happy, I don't know. Is there any reason to think she's not safe?" he asks.

I give him the best reason I have, "She's not with me." Then I remember the dressing room at Target and how the security guard assumed something bad was happening. It wasn't, but later in the parking lot, when that car came out of nowhere, something bad almost did happen. It's hard to recognize what's dangerous and what's not.

"Let's drive around," I say. "Maybe we'll spot the limo."

A rich man's automobile in this town shouldn't be hard to find, and we travel up and down several roads, all of them undulating and narrow, with small houses on both sides. We cross over a bridge and onto what seems to be a main road, but there's no apparent commercial center. When we find a large county park, Ben turns into the lot. "I don't know about you, but I need a rest room."

We locate the facilities and after, while I wait at a picnic table, Ben retrieves what's left of our stash of Twinkies and Coke. We eat across from each other, thankful to be out of the car for a while.

The spongy sugar melts on my tongue, insubstantial, but satisfying in the same way the Bisquick cake batter I crave is. But it's not comfort enough. I feel a flood of sadness. I miss Makenna in a way I could never miss my mother. I know this girl.

Ben's eyes rest on my face. "It's going to be okay, you know."

"I hope so." In the quiet night, my mind shifts to my last conversation with Laura Tellez. How she said "the case" is getting too complicated. What did she mean? Aren't most murders complicated?

"Abbie," he says. "What are you thinking so hard about?"

"How odd this case, Olita's murder, is."

"You want to talk about it?"

"Yeah. I do." A bit of moonlight allows me to see his face. What a nice man. I say, "Here goes. The detective said it was a coincidence that he happened to overdose and it had nothing to do with the case, but how could that be? He's the man who denies knowing the woman who met with Turner Bethune in his own apartment and he turns up dead? And the woman herself has disappeared?"

Ben's face is all scrunched up. "You've completely lost me."

I glance at the sky, the glimmering moon. "Can we move back to the car? It's getting cold."

He gets up and waits for me, then puts his arm around my shoulder, squeezes it.

It's not any warmer in the car. Ben turns on the heater and puts his arm around me, and I tell him everything I know about Olita Jordan, my mother and Billy, and the case the detective is building against Turner Bethune.

When I'm done, we sit in silence awhile and then he says, "You told me when you moved in you'd probably be leaving the Tiki Palms at the end of the summer. Still the plan?"

"I don't know. I can't think about that now. So much depends on what happens to Makenna, and that depends on what happens to Turner Bethune."

"What about your husband?" he asks.

I shift to look at him. His eyes meet mine. Even in the

dark car, I can feel them pulling me in. He leans in close, and I let him because I never thought I'd ever again feel the thrill of a first kiss.

Chapter 55
The Grocer

Wednesday, May 29, 2002

In the morning, I wake up with my cheek pressed against the foggy window, remembering the surprise and pleasure of Ben's kiss. I kissed him back and pulled away, but now, I hold onto the memory of it, feeling young and a little giddy. Then I sit up, thinking of Makenna and whatever danger she might be in.

Ben isn't in the car. I open the door, and chilly air rushes in. He's standing on the grass, a rumpled statue, watching a coyote trot across the street and disappear into a yard. He glances at the car, waves, and ambles over.

I do that finger thing with my hair, taste my sour breath.

He says, "What do you want to do?" His eyes meet mine, and I look away.

"Find Makenna."

"Did the detective call you back?"

I check. My cell is dead. "You have a phone?"

Ben shakes his head. "At home. We left so fast."

"Someone around here must know where Billy Eastlake lives."

We retrace last night's route through the town, looking for a phone and people. It's still early. No one's around. In daylight, I can see the streets are reminiscent of the 1920s and 1930s, houses made of wood, some of stucco. Purple rosemary, wild roses, or other plant life edge property lines. Narrow asphalt roads, few sidewalks. We haven't seen a gas station, a grocery store, or the limousine. Children in pajamas play outside the largest house we find. Ben slows, says, "Good place for a rich guy."

I climb out of the car, holler over the fence. "Hi, there.

Do you know Billy Eastlake, where he lives?"

A man walks out onto the porch. "You kids, come over here." Both race up the steps without looking back and huddle behind the man. "What do you want?"

"Billy Eastlake?"

"Don't know him."

"Could we borrow a telephone ?"

But he's disappeared into the house, kids in tow, slamming the door behind him. We move on, up and down a few more streets before Ben drives back toward the park. I'm ready to suggest nearby Castaic to find a telephone when I spot a small market. We must have gone by it before, but didn't notice because the word 'Market' is on a piece of tagboard in the window.

Ben parks across the street. Two boys, about eight or ten, come out the front door eating powdered sugar donuts.

The place has a slapdash country feeling; two ancient refrigerator cases sit in front of the counter while low shelves on cement blocks contain a smattering of canned goods, household cleaners, and a couple racks of junk food. A large, dark-haired man with granny glasses halfway down his nose reads a tabloid behind the counter, narrow boxes of Hostess donuts at his elbow.

"Hey," Ben says.

"Yes?" The man straightens up, puts down his paper.

"We're looking for Billy Eastlake? Do you know him?"

He frowns. "Are you reporters?"

"No, friends," I say.

"And I'm the one who lost the address," says Ben, jumping in, surprising me with his quick thinking. "You'd get me out of trouble if you tell us how to get there."

The grocer takes in our disheveled appearance. "They came up?"

"Last night," I say. "I'm supposed to talk to Billy about some legal stuff."

The guy shakes his head. "I do not think you'll be

talking much to him."

"Why not?" I ask.

His brow wrinkles. "I thought you were friends. You should know if he was sick."

"We know he's ill. We're worried we won't make it in time." Ben's words surprise me. The guard at the casino in Palm Springs told Makenna that Billy was ill and that's why Liv didn't want him there anymore.

"I haven't heard it's that bad," says the man, reaching over the counter in a gesture of kindness. "He has the Parkinson's, like Michael J. Fox, on TV, and he's not well, but it is something else now?"

Parkinson's. Is it mild or severe? We have to find him. We have to find Makenna. I ask, "Have you heard about a teenager with him? A girl? Maybe she walked to the store to pick up milk or something?"

The man shakes his head. "I did not know they were here so I don't know about this girl."

"She's the reason Mrs. Eastlake called us," says Ben.

"So what is it you need? To bring papers, to see Mr. Billy, or to find some strange girl?"

I say, "All of that. It's complicated."

"I don't want Mrs. Eastlake to be upset if she's expecting you, but I don't want her angry with me if you show up and she's never heard of you." He considers a moment, looking from me to Ben, then says, "I will take you there. Make sure you are welcome. My name is Luis. You have a car?"

"Yes! Could you? That would be terrific. This is Ben. I'm Abbie."

"Just let me close up."

It takes him forever to lock the cash register, bolt the doors, and tape a yellow piece of paper to the front door saying "back shortly" in a surprisingly artistic handwriting. I wonder about the tagboard sign. I wonder who wrote it? Maybe he's forgotten it's there.

It only takes a couple of minutes in the car to turn onto a

dusty, winding canyon road and a couple more for the road to end.

"This is it," says Luis. So close to where we'd been driving, yet I never noticed this street.

Behind a six-foot hurricane fence, the driveway is hard-packed dirt, no cars here, a plain brown house, looking much as it must have when it was built. Between the driveway and the cabin is a dry streambed, a wooden bridge connecting the two sides. Trees rustle overhead. And there she is, Makenna, coming out onto the front step in a sundress I've never seen before, drinking something from a mug.

Chapter 56
Billy's Porch

Makenna sits on the steps of a 1930s wooden house and before I can roll down the window and shout, a woman follows her outside. A kind of dizziness hits me because I think it's my mother or the ghost of my mother, but this woman — my brain pounds at me — despite her strawberry blond hair, is, of course, not Virginia, but Liv. I dig fingernails into my palms to yank me back to reality.

Ben pulls the car along the weedy shoulder, and we climb out, slamming doors. The girl lets out a whoop, jumps up, and snatches Liv's hand. The older woman's resemblance to my mother, I see, is more of a suggestion, similar to a picture I've seen. Her shorts and a halter are vintage 1940s. Her hair drapes over one eye, fat curls brush her shoulders. Wasn't Liv a brunette in Indian Wells?

They laugh as they come across the little bridge toward Ben and me where we wait on the other side of the rusty chain-link fence.

An elderly African-American man moves clumsily out of the house, pushing a metal walker. It must be Billy. Again my heart speeds up.

Makenna waves at us. Yells, "Come on up," then turns to run and help him. Liv, too, does an about-face and strides toward the porch. She says something to Makenna I don't catch, and the girl laughs.

They seem like a family, the three of them, the family that should have been. It's as if someone's whispering a secret in my ear. I am the person who never should have been, the poser, the fake, the unwanted child from an unwanted man. This thought stuns and chills me. I take a step back and bump into Ben. He's grinning. He sees them as a family too, and it makes him happy. He opens the gate and leads us through and up to the porch.

"You guys found me. And I found my grandfather." Makenna glows. She's already forgotten she's run away, taken my car, given me cardiac arrest. And she's wearing a sundress I've never seen before. She looks so pretty. It must be one of Liv's.

"Are you okay?" I ask. Relief and anger seem to be taking turns in my chest. Finding her safe, seeing Billy for the first time, meeting Liv face to face, all of this puts me back in the swamp, not dragged down, but floating unsteadily along the surface, an eye out for alligators.

Makenna says, "You weren't worried, were you? Liv called and left a message telling you I was okay, that I was coming up here with them. That's how you found us, right?"

"Not exactly. I've been so worried about you." Tears make my voice break. "I'm still worried." Ben's hand squeezes my shoulder.

"You didn't get the message? You let your phone die again?" asks the girl, on the defensive. "Because she left you a message."

Liv slips an arm around Makenna's waist, trying to contain the girl's emotions in the same way that Ben is trying to contain mine. She says, "So happy to meet you, Abbie Palmer."

I force a smile. "Nice to meet you too."

I look beyond her at Billy who's now sitting in an old wooden rocker. He has one of those faces that remain sharp and unlined even with age. Makenna says gently to him, "Grandfather, this is Abbie Palmer. Abbie Hart. She's Virginia Gifford's daughter."

As soon as she says my mother's name, I get the body-buzz. Is this how I'm going to learn the truth, suddenly, and in bright sunshine?

He turns his ear to Makenna, and says, "What's that you say?"

229

"This is Abbie Hart. Virginia Gifford's daughter."

He squints at me. With no recognition registering in his face, he says, "Can you get me some lemonade?" I knew Billy wouldn't know me — why would he — but the mention of Virginia brought nothing to his eyes. I feel swamp waters rising.

Liv leans over and pats his skinny knee. "How about orange juice, Billy?"

His mouth frets. "That'll do."

"Mrs. Eastlake?" Luis, the forgotten storekeeper, walks up the uneven path toward us. It was Luis who said Billy has Parkinson's. Maybe he's waiting for a tip, and I wish I had some cash so I could run down and hand it to him, flee from Billy's befuddled state.

"Is everything okay?" Luis asks. "I wouldn't have brought them up, Mrs. Eastlake, but they said they have legal papers."

"Legal papers?" Liv looks alarmed.

"That was me," I say. "I made it up so he'd give us your address. Sorry. No legal papers here."

Liv gives me a thin smile, turns to the grocer. "It's okay, Luis. Thank you. You did the right thing."

He retraces his steps, goes out the gate, and heads down the canyon road. Ben hollers after him, "Wait. You want a lift?" The man doesn't turn around. Just raises his right arm in the air as a perfunctory wave and keeps on walking. I have to fight the urge to go with him, back to his store, and eat a box of those powdered sugar donuts.

Chapter 57
Vanilla Wafers

Makenna is talking to me, but I've missed part of it. "...she said she wanted me to meet Billy, but they had to come up here —"

Liv cuts her off. "It's all right, Makenna. Mrs. Palmer understands."

Again the woman gives me that smile, her red lipstick becoming a pout as she turns her attention on Ben. "And I don't know who you are. Not Abbie's husband?" Her pale hand with its scarlet-tipped fingers lightly touches Ben's larger one on the palm.

A memory surfaces. My father saying something about a woman tickling the palm of a man's hand? He was angry because it means something. Sex? Was he saying it about my mother? To my mother? Or to me? I let the thought slip away, try to pay attention to the conversation around me.

Ben is chatting with Liv. "...I remember seeing you on *Late Night with Conan O'Brien*."

"You remember that?" she laughs. "I was surprised to be invited —"

"Lemonade?" Billy interrupts, and Liv leans over to Makenna and asks, "Would you mind getting a glass of orange juice for your grandfather?"

"Sure." The girl leaps up and whispers to Billy. He nods and grins as if they've been together the last sixteen years of her life, then she scurries off into the house.

Ben's talking. "You had a blond Marilyn Monroe thing going on."

"Now, I'm just myself and almost finished with my EP."

Billy stares at the road. I follow his gaze, down the broken concrete walkway grouted with grass. An empty beer bottle leans against the fence, weeds flourish along the verge, ramshackle houses perch on scrubby hills, the morning coming on too bright, too harsh. I'm tired and uncomfortable sitting on a folding chair and realize how much I want to go home, but no longer sure where home is.

Makenna returns carrying a tray, five glasses of orange juice and a plate of Vanilla Wafers. First she offers these to Billy. His hand jiggles as he struggles to get his fingers around the glass, but Makenna has become a patient person overnight. She waits, letting him do it even though juice splashes out of the glass. Once he has the glass, she gives him two cookies. He smiles up at her. "Thank you, sugar."

Both Liv and Ben take a juice and forego cookies. I don't want any of it. When Makenna sits down on the step, I lean over and say, "So, Makenna, where's my car?"

"I left it at McDonalds, the same one we went to in Indian Wells. I have the keys inside the house. You want me to get them?"

"When we're ready to go, yes, thanks. We do need to go soon."

"I was hoping you'd stay a while."

"You make it sound like you're not coming with us."

"I'm not."

Billy tries to put his glass on the table next to him, and Liv reaches over and gently takes it from him, turns and says to me, "I want Makenna to spend a day or two with us. I want her and Billy to have a chance to get to know each other. I'll bring her back to your apartment when I go into L.A. You won't have to come back out."

She wants? She wants? Since when does that count? I must be frowning because Ben interrupts, "It's really nice that Makenna found her grandfather, you know, and for you to offer your hospitality."

"Billy seems more himself out here, and I try and bring him at least once a month, and Makenna is so good for him."

Ben stands and stretches. "Mind if I look around? This place is so cool."

Liv nods, and he saunters away, heading up the little creek bed. Being thoughtful again, giving us time to talk.

"I'm happy she's found Billy," I say, the words stiff even to my ears. "But we can come back here or go to Indian Wells to visit another time. Makenna, don't forget about Turner. He's going to want to see you." He's not getting out any time soon, but I don't let that stop me.

"Today?" Makenna's face lights up.

"Could be." I feel bad to be the one to divert her from her 'Billy' high, but she's my responsibility and I can't help but feel she was lured away by this woman. And that phone call she was supposed to have made? I don't believe it. Or am I just being jealous?

"I don't want to say this," says Liv quietly to Makenna and me, glancing at Billy who's gone off into his own world, "but every day counts with him. Turner won't mind waiting a day or two, Makenna, if it's to be with your long-lost grandfather."

"I'm done," says Billy and hands his glass to Makenna.

"Was it good, Grandfather?"

"It was, sugar. It was very good."

I am being jealous. Who am I to deny Makenna this time if she wants it? A respite for her, worlds away from everything that has weighed her down for the last week or so. And Liv, she's thoughtful, concerned. Maybe she's not who we thought, an Anna-Nicole-Smith-type marrying an old man for his money. Of course, she married an old man who has money and wouldn't let Olita visit him, but maybe she realizes she treated Olita poorly, just as I did.

"Honey," she says to Makenna. "Do you mind taking the glasses back into the house?" And the girl jumps up to do just that. After she's gone, Liv moves closer to me, whispers, "He's sick, Abbie. He has what's called Parkinson's with Lewy bodies. It causes dementia. He rambles on about your mother. He cared for her and even brought her here once, but Abbie, Olita wasn't her daughter."

233

Chapter 58
White Lies

I t's as if Liv has slapped me in the face. I don't know what to say, so I don't say anything.

She reaches out with those red-tipped fingers and pats my arm. "I know it seems as if there's a possibility, but it's just not true. I've hired a private investigator and he assures me it's something Olita's sister made up to keep her from claiming any of their mother's estate. Billy is her great-uncle, but not her grandfather."

"Then why haven't you told Makenna the truth?" I ask, unable to keep the impatience out of my voice.

"She just lost her mother and it looks as if Turner Bethune is the one who did it. I don't want to take away something that is helping her to cope. It would be cruel. I know she'll have to know sometime, but at least for now, a little white lie can't hurt."

A little white lie can't hurt. I've been telling myself the same thing. Can it be that this woman and I are both trying to protect Makenna until she's strong enough to find out the truth? In the distance I spy Ben ambling back along the dry creek bed. He catches me looking and waves.

"Beautiful place you have here," Ben shouts, coming toward us, and Liv straightens, twists around to see him. I wonder what he's thinking seeing the two of us sitting here whispering like conspirators?

"Liv," he says, as he climbs the steps. "I was wondering who's producing your EP?"

I try to catch his eye, but he's focused on Liv. I stand as Makenna opens the screen door and joins us. "Makenna, can we talk? Is that all right with you, Liv?"

"Of course it is." She meets my eye, and nods, and I think she's telling me that if I want to tell Makenna the truth, she'll be happy to let me.

"What is it?" asks Makenna.

"Privately, please."

She rolls her eyes.

I move fast down the porch, heading toward the dry creek path. She trots after me. We go around a bend and I say, "So you've met Billy."

"I have."

"And Liv? What do you think of her?"

"I don't know. She's nice."

"Did she dye her hair?"

"You brought me over here to ask that?"

"No, but she had brown hair when we saw her in Indian Wells."

"So what? People dye their hair all the time."

"It's just that for a minute, when we first got here, I thought she was – oh, never mind."

"She looks like your mother?"

"Yes. What kind of game is she playing?"

"She does that for Billy. She says he's more himself when she has red hair."

"Really?"

"Is that it? All you wanted to talk about?"

"No it's not. Why didn't you wake me up when you left?"

"You wouldn't have let me to go. Liv said they were leaving to come up here and if I drove to the desert right away, I could ride in the limo. I wanted to do it, so I did."

"If something had happened to you..."

"Nothing did happen, did it? Look, Liv is nice and Billy's sweet, and she says he has good days and bad days and this hasn't been a good one, so I want to stay."

"Makenna, I can't just leave you here."

"A day or two? Please, Abbie."

We're standing under a tree and a light breeze rustles the leaves overhead. Liv has proof that Virginia Gifford wasn't Olita's mother and yet, she wants to do this kind thing for Makenna. The girl's dark expectant eyes are pinned on my face, and I can't bring myself to say no.

"A day or two maybe, but before I say yes, I need to hear you tell me no one is making you stay."

"That's crazy. No one's making me do anything, Abbie, except you. Liv made this nice offer, and I took it, and it's turned out perfectly. If Turner gets out, then you can come get me or he can. Besides, Abbie, it'll be good for you too. I know you want to be alone. You never wanted all this – you didn't really want me."

Tears come and I throw my arms around her. She hugs me back. She feels like a daughter, warm and soft, smelling of shampoo. "Don't think that, Makenna. Ever."

Chapter 59
Cajoled

We drive east through hills on the winding road. We haven't passed the abandoned house yet, and I wonder if its eyes will glint as they did on our arrival.

Ben gives me a quick look. "You okay?"

"I'm just thinking." Letting Makenna stay with Liv and Billy seems right for her at this point, yet I already feel the ache of it. "Are you as exhausted as I am?"

"I'm okay."

"Do you mind taking me out to Indian Wells and fetching my car? If not, we could just go home and I'll get Craig to take me." The very thought makes me wince. I can hear my husband's parade of questions in my head as well as his reasons why I can't take care of myself. I could take a taxi.

"No, no. We're in this together."

"You don't have a gig tonight?"

"We'll be back in time."

The abandoned house is up ahead and in daylight, it appears more melancholy than sinister, a simple farmhouse with one of those bread-loaf mailboxes on the road and a tire swing hanging from an oak tree in the yard.

"You know, you really surprised me back there," says Ben.

"How did I surprise you?" I frown, thinking he's going to chastise me for my anger at Makenna when we first got there. That's what my father would do, that's what Craig would do.

"I never thought you'd leave her there. You didn't have to, you know."

"She's been through so much. I didn't want to deny her the one thing that would make her happy."

"You think she's safe there?"

"You think she's not?" Have I made a wrong decision?

"I don't know. When I walked around, I didn't find anything suspicious. No limo, but it could've been hired. It's probably okay."

"Probably? What are you getting at?"

"Well, what do you think of Liv?" he asks. We're almost through the tract of houses now, the freeway just beyond.

"You seemed to find her pretty interesting."

"Not me."

I mock him. "'I'm in a band. Who's producing your LP?'"

"It's EP not LP, and people don't always act like they feel. Sometimes you're nice so you can learn a thing or two, you know?"

"And what did you find out?"

"She's waiting for Billy to die."

The car shimmies as we turn onto the freeway. It's windy without the protection of the hills.

"How could I take her away? She's lost her mother, she may lose Turner. He's all she's got."

"She's got you, Abbie. Liv is going to use her to take care of him, you know. She's got her eye on a couple of days of kicking back in the country while Makenna does the dirty work."

"She won't mind. Anyway, she'll be safer there than with me if Turner Bethune gets out."

"So you think he killed Olita?"

I hesitate before answering, then, "The detective is convinced he's guilty. It doesn't make sense to me that he did it, but if he did, he's got everyone good and confused."

"Or someone has everyone good and confused. You think he tried to run Makenna down with a car?"

"It might've been an accident. I mean, we were racing through the parking lot, not paying attention, but honestly, it's too much of a coincidence." I tell him about our visit with the two old men on Makenna's street and the car one of them saw, something I'd left out last night. "It sounded like it was the same car from the Target parking lot."

We speed along, neither of us talking, the miles disappearing. After a while, I say, "You know something I noticed about Liv?"

"What's that?"

"When we first got there, she and Makenna were on the porch, and for a moment, I thought she was my mother."

"Your mother?"

"I knew it wasn't her, but it was a strange feeling. Makenna says Liv dyes her hair red because it makes Billy more comfortable. The woman knows all about Virginia."

"Your mother had red hair?"

"Yes, maybe a little more strawberry blond."

"Makenna probably filled her in on the relationship."

"But it sounded like she's been dyeing her hair for a while before Makenna showed up."

"She was blond on Conan O'Brien. Maybe it's as simple as Billy told her he liked redheads because Virginia was a redhead."

"He told her about some ancient love affair? Is that what you would do?" This question reminds me of Ben's kiss last night and I feel my face go hot.

He smiles. "It depends."

"You know, another reason I left her up there?"

"What?"

"Liv says Olita isn't my mother's daughter. Don't interrupt. There's more. I have Olita's birth certificate and it clearly states that Billy's sister and brother-in-law are her real parents. He and my mother had an affair, but not a baby."

"Come on. Everything you said last night made me think you believed your mother was Olita's mother. The freckles, how much Makenna reminds you of your daughter,

I believe it. What changed your mind?"

"Liv said she hired a private detective to investigate and he claims that Olita's sister made it all up. I've talked to the woman, and she seems capable of doing just that."

"Did Liv tell Makenna this?"

"No. She says she doesn't want to take something that makes her happy away. At least, not yet."

"That's pretty decent of her."

"Yeah, it is, and if I made Makenna leave and he died without them spending time together, I'd feel terrible."

Chapter 60
Dr. Gaines

We spend the rest of the drive in silence, both of us tired, but when we get to the McDonalds parking lot near Indian Wells where Makenna left the Suburban, I suddenly feel the awkwardness of our situation. Two almost strangers have spent twenty-four hours plus in each other's company which would be all right – except for that kiss. It still warms me to think of it.

Ben parks next to the Suburban. It hasn't been towed and there's no ticket. Lucky me.

He starts to say something, but I cut him off. "Thank you so much for everything, Ben. I owe you big. Go to your gig. I don't want you to miss it." I quickly pat his hand and scramble out of the car.

"Abbie."

But I don't turn around. I feel prickly, smelly, stiff, and old as I slam the door and limp to the driver's side of my car. I climb in and turn to wave at Ben, thinking we'll caravan back, but when I look around, he's no longer there.

The air inside my apartment at the Tiki Palms is stale and reminds me of the bars my father used to hang out in. Childhood memories ambush me with martial regularity these days. Those bars. How could I have forgotten the smell? He'd plop me at a table in a corner, handing me a Shirley Temple and a deck of cards. Hula girls on the back, four different poses, four different flower leis, four colors of grass skirts. I'm an expert at solitaire because of it. I wish I had a deck now. And a good stiff drink. I could use one, but there's nothing alcoholic here.

The faded walls, a rug like mud, it all depresses me. Hot and exhausted from — what — days of emotional and physical depletion, uncertainty, and most of all, doubt about everything I thought was true and what it means, my stomach churns, my brain nothing but muck. Along my skin, nerve endings tingle on the outside as well as on the inside. I got my wish. I'm alone on my own private island.

I strip off my clothes and wander into the bathroom. I take the bottle of Ativan out of the drawer, take a pill or two.

•◇•

The phone rings at least a dozen times before it registers as noise outside my head. When I figure this much out, I answer it, my arm leaden, numb. Beyond the windows, the evening is just turning charcoal. "Hullo."

"Is this Abbie Palmer, the woman who called looking for Dr. Archibald Gaines?"

"Yes? Yes. Is this his daughter?"

"Daughter-in-law. Did I wake you up? It's only 10:00 P.M. here. I thought I'd try and catch you. We just got back from vacation and your message sounded urgent."

"That's all right. I'm glad you called." I stretch and yawn, rub my eyes to wake up.

"I wanted you to know that I'm sorry, but Dr. Archie passed over ten years ago."

"Oh, I'm sorry." Is this good news or bad? I wish I didn't feel so groggy. "Thank you for calling me back."

"I do have an answer to your question for what it's worth," the woman says.

"Yes, please. That would help. Thank you." Who she is settles into place, where she fits in this jigsaw puzzle of half-sisters and teenage girls. "My husband said to tell you that whatever his dad put on that birth certificate has to be correct. Doc Archie was beyond reproach."

"But, wait," I say, "what I – what if lying on a birth certificate would help someone out, someone he knew and respected? Would he do it then?" I'm almost fully awake now.

"I don't think so. You see, he wasn't the kind of man to lie for any reason." Then she adds, "It doesn't sound as if this is the answer you wanted."

"I don't think it is," I say.

"It's none of my business, but if it's a case of parentage, why don't you have the people involved swabbed?"

"Swabbed?"

"You know, DNA?"

Now I'm awake.

Shocked by the simplicity and obviousness of this idea, I thank her and hang up. And dash to boot up the computer. Detective Tellez had mentioned DNA during our meeting, but I'd forgotten. I guess after a while, it seemed to be something to think about later. I sit back from the keyboard for a minute. Yes, I want to know for sure. I told Makenna the other day I wanted to know everything. I'm finally tired of this see-saw I've been on with Makenna – we're related, we're not related – I want definitive proof.

Google gets me to several DNA paternity websites in a matter of seconds. The one that catches my eye is the one that says, "Start your test today."

It seems simple enough. Swab the inside of the cheek of each person to be tested and mail it away, all for a handsome fee. I'll do Makenna and Billy and me. Will Liv allow me to swab him?

I print up the do-it-yourself instructions and not allowing myself much time to think, I shower, wash my hair, and pull it back in a ponytail like Makenna wears hers when she doesn't have time to flat iron it. I tilt my head and frown. Makenna looks like Christie. She looks like me, for God's sake, and there is a cord between us, connecting us like tiny pearls. Well, science will tell us one way or the other.

Then I remember what time it is. I don't want to drive up to Val Verde and have to spend another night in the county park, so I force myself to lie down, sleeping fitfully, drifting through images of strawberry blonds in hula skirts, Q-tips filling the bathroom sink, the toilet, the floor, me always driving and driving and driving on a never-ending ribbon of asphalt.

Chapter 61
Probing Deeper

Thursday, May 30, 2002

I head for Thrifty's on Fair Oaks as soon as I brush my teeth, and wait by the door until they open. Inside I buy six two-packs of sterile cotton swabs, just to make sure, a box of gallon-sized plastic bags, the kind that seal together with some invisible zipper, and a box of paper envelopes, business size. I double-check my list printed from the Internet. That should do it. Now all I have to do is get Makenna's and Billy's DNA and my own.

I'm climbing into the Suburban, thinking about which route to take, when it hits me. Last night we went directly from Val Verde to Indian Wells to fetch my car, driving right through Pasadena on the 210 Freeway. Why couldn't Liv and Billy pick Makenna up outside the Tiki Palms on their way to Val Verde – instead of Liv asking the girl to drive all the way out to the desert first?

Makenna said something to me about how their trouble started with me. Maybe she hit on something. How did she say it, once Olita met me, she died? But before she met me, she met Liv.

I'm heading north and west through flat morning light when another thought smacks me. The cops came to Cascades because Makenna tripped the alarm climbing over the wall. If she'd been invited, the guard at the gate would've been told. Why sneak in? Maybe Makenna never called Liv? Or if she did, Liv rebuffed her the same way she rebuffed Olita, and Makenna decided to go anyway? And once she was over the wall, she went to see Billy – she had the address – and Liv decided to welcome her, sending the cops away.

So why lie? Why would Liv agree to say she invited Makenna? So the girl wouldn't be hauled off to jail? So she wouldn't be in trouble with me? Me? What does Liv expect to gain?

I want to talk to Ben. Where's my cell? Of course. I bang the steering wheel with the palm of my hand. It's at home, charging.

Let me think. If Liv lied about inviting Makenna, has she lied about anything else? Or wait. The bigger question is why did she marry Billy in the first place? Obviously, connections to the entertainment industry and/or money? I picture the gate to the exclusive Cascades with its guard, the expensive Jaguar, Liv's sleek celebrity body, her designer yoga outfit.

Then Liv's nightmare. Olita shows up claiming to be Billy's daughter. Liv shuts her out and Olita is upset. Liv keeps father and daughter apart because Olita is in the will. Billy wouldn't know what was going on so Liv forges a new will, and has Olita killed. But with a fire-bomb?

The idea that Liv Amaral Eastlake, rising singing star, might actually commit murder in such a bizarre way doesn't make sense. It's too far-fetched. Or is it? She'd need help. An accomplice. Turner Bethune? Liv and Turner? As a power couple they'd look right, but, no, never. Never.

It takes me less than an hour driving with a heavy foot to get to the Hasley Canyon off-ramp. Past the farmhouse, its window eyes vacant. Through the "suburbs" and up the steep hill again. I stop at the crest. This is not like the song, *Down in the Valley*, with its meandering stream along mossy banks, ponies prancing across a meadow, the requisite red barn. No. Val Verde is more of a jumble. Small hills bump together in this basin, scrub covering the tops, little houses crowding the cuts. In the distance, larger hills, almost mountains, rise up.

My mother was here two lifetimes ago, hers and mine, and though Liv says Olita wasn't her child, I want to hear it from Billy himself, who he was, who Virginia was, how they met, how they fell in love, how they lost each other. A car honks behind me, and I roll down the grade into the small town.

I have no problem finding the canyon road and head straight to Billy's house and pull the Suburban onto the verge. I grab the plastic Thrifty's bag with the once-and-for-all DNA test kit inside and get out of the car.

A padlock hangs on the front gate where yesterday there was no padlock. It's rusted and old, but when I yank on it, it holds. I holler through the six-foot hurricane fence, "Makenna!"

Nothing.

"Hey, Makenna! It's Abbie."

The front door doesn't open. No one peeks through the window. "Shit!" Where did they go? I look around the dusty cul-de-sac. There's a woman in a yard a short distance away, so I hurry over. She's small and wiry, her black hair streaked with gray, her hands rough with calluses.

"You just missed her," she says.

"Who? Makenna? The girl?" I ask.

"No, the lady, the Mrs. Billy Eastlake. A car came and took her away."

"What about Billy and the girl?"

"I don't know any girl, but Mr. Billy wasn't with her. I saw her lock the gate and get into the car. She was alone."

"What kind of car?"

"A limousine. She always comes in a limousine."

"You didn't see Billy?"

"No. He probably went somewhere earlier, you know, but I didn't see. She locked the gate. Catalina can't go in so he can't be there."

"Who's Catalina?"

"She takes care of Mr. Billy when that lady leaves him here, but she went to Valencia to see her daughter. They didn't need her this time. No one's home. Sorry."

"Thank you. And you didn't see an African-American girl?"

"No girl."

"Thanks."

I unlock my car and get in, but I don't start the engine. I have to think.

I stare at the house for a minute or two. I glance over my shoulder at the yard up the road. The woman has disappeared.

This time when I get out and close my car door, I do it quietly.

Chapter 62
Rotten Eggs

I haven't climbed many fences lately, and this one sways under my weight. It's high, and when my sweatpants snag on the wire, I have a moment of panic, but I make it over. I hurry down the broken cement path, cross over the bridge, and knock on the door. I don't knock hard because I'm afraid the woman down the street will come running after me and tell me to get the hell out of here. I try the door. Like the gate, it's locked. I knock louder. Silence except for the whinny of a neighbor's horse.

Peering into a window, I see only darkness until I realize I'm staring at a drawn curtain. This agitates me more than the fence.

I jog to the back of the house where there's a small patio paved in cracked concrete. A breeze washes over me, and I catch the faintest whiff of something. Somebody cooking? Scrambling eggs? Bad eggs. What is that odor?

I tap on the glass in the kitchen door. Try the knob. I press my face into one of the panes, hands on either side. There's a curtain here too, but it's gauzy and I can see something on the kitchen floor. Then I hear a cough. Makenna? Billy?

A buried memory unwinds in a flash. Me in someone's arms, rushing through another kitchen, my mother stooping in front of the stove, reaching into the oven. Was she baking cookies? Oh my God. Gas!

"Makenna!" I rattle the door handle. Twist around, scan for something, anything I can use to break the door glass. Table. Pot. Lawn chair. I grab a terracotta pot filled with dirt and smash it against the window in the door. It splinters wood and glass, the smell of rotten eggs rocking me back, and I stumble, then lurch two or three feet away, gasping for air. One deep breath, two, then back to the damaged window. Stick my arm through jagged glass and turn the door handle. It snaps unlocked. I pull my arm back through, scraping skin on broken shards. Twist the knob, but the door doesn't open. Dead bolt. I shake off rising panic, dizziness. Stumble to the edge of the patio.

Another breath, thinking no phone here, no phone. No deadbolt key. Please make it a knob. I suck in air so I can shout for help, but cough instead, teeter and gasp, "Help. Help." Then one loud scream, "He-e-l-l-l-p!"

My hand is slick with blood. I take off my t-shirt, reach through the smashed window space and find the deadbolt knob. "Thank you." It clicks and shoulder to the door, I fall into the kitchen.

Dark in here, disorienting. My eyes water. The stove, refrigerator, counter seem to shimmer. Strong smell of sulphur. On the floor next to the sink. Makenna. I can't hold my breath. Breathe in gas. Sink down next to her. "Makenna. Wake up. Can you hear me?" She coughs, groans. I pull myself onto my knees. My head pounds. Heart pounds. Breathe in gas, fight to stand, lean over to grab her ankles. She's heavy, too heavy, but I have to get her, pull her out. Grab her ankles, hands slip, I tumble back, hitting my tailbone on the floor. The pain reverberates and I gulp for air, what happened to my lungs?

Door is open. Air must be coming in. I scoot on my butt toward the girl. Have to do this. No one coming. I'm in this alone. I grip her ankles again and use my legs to back along the floor, grumbling like an overloaded earthmover, then I tug her up to me as close as I can, and do it again until the threshold of the door hits my butt. I climb up the door jamb, hand over hand, and once I have my feet under me, lean down, my head churning inside my skull, and yank the girl with me, again falling backward to the ground.

We're half in and half out of the kitchen door, Makenna on top of me. I struggle to pull myself from underneath, trip over her to get back inside, and on my hands and knees, I lift her up and with my shoulder, shove her onto the patio. She flops back into my rubbery arms, forcing me to use my whole body, my legs slipping on the linoleum to get her head past the doorway where she finally flops sideways onto the cement. She's out of the house and into the air, and remembering Billy, I turn into the kitchen, and my swamp is a spinning whirlpool, the glass shards in the door glittering like teeth, and I faint.

Someone drags me out into the air and leaves me in soft warm dirt. Pain splits my chest with every breath. My eyes open and close. Then open again. I don't know who is here, but I say, "Makenna, Billy."

A man's voice answers, "You're all right now." Somewhere in the distance, I hear a siren. We're rescued, and I close my eyes again.

I wake up with an oxygen mask covering my face. We're moving, rocking along, a siren wailing in my ear so I know I'm in an ambulance. A paramedic hovers over someone next to me. I turn my head, but I can't see who it is. I reach up for the oxygen mask and struggle to get it off. My voice comes out as an unintelligible croak. The paramedic turns toward me. His eyes are dark. Behind him, Makenna with her own oxygen mask.

Another croak from me and he says, "Just rest."

I brace myself and try to hoist up my elbows. "Is she okay?"

"It's too early to say."

Chapter 63
Abbie

I'm drowning in murky water, struggling to get my arms to move, my legs to kick, yet there is some kind of vortex sucking me backward, and I'm holding a baseball bat, and I try to let go of it but I can't, no matter how much I try. My other arm is doing all the work, struggling to pull me through the water, hand cupped in an effort to propel me forward, all this in spite of the streamers of blood and torn flesh undulating around me like jellyfish.

"Abbie."

A voice from the surface, an echo of hope. I glance behind me, panicked. The mouth that's sucking me back is so close I see its rim of teeth glittering in the goo.

"Abbie."

The bat is tugged from my hand, spins past my face, and I realize it's a human leg, a woman's leg. I open my eyes, turn my head, and there's Craig standing next to my hospital bed, his face pale and lined.

He leans close, whispers. "You're okay. You're fine."

The nightmare clings to me; my heart pounds.

Then I remember. "What about Makenna?" My voice is rasping.

He strokes my face, says, "You don't seem to have those fingernail scratches on your forehead."

"Makenna?"

"Don't worry. Just rest."

"What do the doctors say?"

"Not now, Abbie."

"Now, Craig, please. Just tell me."

He looks around and pulls up a chair. Sits down. "They're worried about brain damage, if any and how much. Apparently breathing in gas deprives the brain of oxygen, but since you found her on the kitchen floor and since natural gas is lighter than air, they're hoping she was able to get enough oxygen to prevent permanent damage. She's alive, thanks to you."

"When will they know?"

"Soon."

"Soon. And Billy? Was he in the house? I never saw him."

"You want to know all of this right now?"

"Yes. Please."

He lowers his eyes. "I'm sorry, Abbie."

"No." The loss takes my breath.

After a moment, I manage to say, "Where was he?"

"They found him on his bed. The gas leak was in the dryer line, and the laundry room is between the bedroom and kitchen. They said he probably wasn't aware of what was happening."

Tears come. I roll away from Craig. I want to sink back into my dream. The nightmare. The glittery teeth.

"Abbie?" asks Craig.

"What?"

"Are you okay?"

"No, yes. Do you know who carried me out?"

"A local man. His name is Louis, I think."

"Luis, the storekeeper." For some reason, I thought maybe it was Ben, but how could it be? I wonder if anyone has thought to tell him what's happened. "How did Luis happen to be there? I need to thank him."

"A neighbor. She heard you yelling for help. Apparently she called him and the police. He got there first."

"Thank you, Craig, for being here."

"Where else would I be? Say, are you interested in a visitor?"

"I don't think so. Not yet."

"Don't you want to know who it is?"

"Not now."

"She drove like a maniac to get here."

I glance up at the door. And there she is, my daughter, Christie. And a second later, she's in my arms, warm and sweet, and I cling to her.

•◊•

Later, when the telephone rings next to my bed, it startles me awake. I fumble for it in the growing darkness of the hospital room and mumble a groggy hello. It's Laura Tellez who asks, "How are you doing?"

"Better."

"And Makenna?"

"I – I don't know. I've been napping, but I told them to call me when she wakes up. We should know more about her condition soon. They don't say it's a coma, but I'm still worried."

"She'll be okay. She's young and strong. So they're keeping you overnight?"

"Doctors, you know, they want to be sure."

"I'm sorry about Billy Eastlake, for his own sake as well as for the girl's and yours."

My throat clogs up.

After a moment, she says, "I've read the Sheriff's report, the one you gave him."

"You got that fast."

"He faxed it to me as soon as he got back to his office. You saved Makenna's life. Again."

"Adrenaline," I say. "Mothers-lifting-cars-off-of-babies stuff."

"And you were there to do it. That's what blows me away. How did you know to go back up there?"

"I don't know. You read my statement. It came to me in flashes."

"Is what I've read in the sheriff's report really what you think happened?"

254

"Exactly that. Liv killed Billy and she killed Olita," I say.

"As far as I can see," says Laura Tellez. "Liv and Olita never had any contact."

"But they did. Olita went out to their house and Liv wouldn't let her visit Billy, and I don't think she ever told Billy his daughter was trying to see him."

"Okay, but what does that prove?"

"That she didn't want him to know Olita was looking for him. Liv married Billy for his money and Olita stood in her way. Makenna stands in her way too."

"Abbie, you've been through a terrible experience. It's normal to want to blame someone."

"Check Billy's will," I say. "I bet you anything Olita's the primary benefactor with any of her children inheriting if something happens to her. And it did, Laura. Olita's dead. Billy's dead. And Makenna —"

"I'm not sure about this. When are you coming home?"

"I'm staying here until I can bring Makenna with me. My husband and daughter are at a hotel."

"Then I'll have to come to you. I have some things to do tomorrow morning, but I'll be up in the afternoon."

"Check the will, Laura. Please."

"Abbie, I don't know if that's actually something I can do."

Chapter 64
Evidence

Friday, May 31, 2002

Christie brought clothes to me at the hospital, fresh jeans and a t-shirt from the local Target while Craig took care of my release, and now they've gone back to the Embassy Suites to give me time alone with the detective. I don't want to leave until I have a chance to talk to Makenna's doctors so I wait for Laura Tellez in the family waiting room. It's pleasant enough with a small chapel on one side and garden patio on the other.

The detective thinks I have it all wrong about Liv being responsible for everything that's happened, but I know I'm right.

Laura Tellez rushes in through the door, a little out of breath, and sits down across from me on the little sofa.

"Any word on Makenna?" she asks, leaning forward, concern on her face.

"Not yet."

"And how are you?"

"I'm fine, but worried about what's going on in the case."

"The case?" She smiles. "Have you thought about a career in law enforcement?"

I try not to take offense. Smile back. "Were you able to check the will?"

"You like to get right to it. Okay. Billy's estate goes to Liv. No pre-nuptial agreement. Therefore, she had no motive to kill Billy. He was ill, and all she had to do was wait."

"Then she forged it. She must have."

"I'd never heard of Liv Amaral until you decided to

become a crime fighter. Nothing anywhere points to her in this case."

"That's exactly how she planned it. She's Turner's lady-in-distress, the one he met the night of the firebombing. Think about it. Who better to set up for murder than Turner? You said yourself the first person the cops suspect is the spouse or lover. Don't you see? She lures him home from Austin with some pretext and then she disappears. I bet the man who overdosed was her accomplice. I bet she killed him too."

Laura Tellez takes a deep breath. "Abbie, I don't know what to say. That man was a junky. There is no record that Turner's woman exists. We've talked to Liv Eastlake. You say the gate was padlocked. She says there was a padlock on the gate, but it wasn't locked. You assumed because it looked locked, it was locked."

"The gate was padlocked. You think I'd climb over a six-foot fence if I could go through a gate? She was there, waiting. She wanted to make sure the gas did its job. She pretended to go off in the limo and was hiding in the trees or behind the garage, and then when I showed up, she unlocked the gate after I went over the fence. Don't you see?"

She sits back and studies me, and for a moment I remember what it was like to be in that interrogation room with her, but I keep going. "Think about it. She's twenty-eight years old and she marries a man more than twice her age. He's sick with Parkinson's, he's becoming senile because of some variation called Lewy bodies, and he had no one around to warn him about her. And," I suddenly remember another point, "Makenna said Liv dyed her hair to make him think she was my mother."

"Do you know how crazy this sounds?" says Tellez calmly, no accusation in her voice.

"I don't understand you, Laura. You've made up your mind Turner Bethune is behind this, and you won't listen to obvious facts."

"I'm listening to you, aren't I? I drove all the way up to hear what you had to say. Don't you think I've got people checking these things? So far nothing has changed my mind about Bethune. Fingerprints put him at the scene of the crime in the San Dimas case. He was in that apartment."

"Of course he was. He's said from the beginning he went there the night of the firebombing. What did he tell you about the woman he met?"

She shakes her head. "She needed him to intercede with the warden on behalf of her brother, some gang on the inside was threatening him, but he never did it. And there's no prisoner with the name she gave him in any prison in California. If Turner Bethune was there at that apartment, and it looks like he was, it wasn't to meet some woman who doesn't exist. Don't you see, the more we dig, the more we find evidence that he's guilty?"

"I don't believe it. I don't."

"It gets worse. The junkie who OD'd, the one who said he didn't know anything about a woman? It was his car that was seen cruising Olita's street on the night of the pipe bombing, and we found a $10,000 check deposited to his account signed by Bethune." Detective Tellez leans back in her chair.

This rattles me. A check signed by Turner? Could he have paid this person to kill Olita and then run down Makenna? No.

"Can you show a picture of Liv Amaral to Turner?" I ask.

"Just stop."

"I can't. I won't. Please do this one last thing. Please."

"What good will it do?"

"If Liv Amaral is the woman who met with him about her brother, everything falls into place."

"Okay. I'll crosscheck Liv Amaral with the man who OD'd and see if anything pops. And yes, I'll show the picture to Bethune."

"And you have someone keeping an eye on her?"

She stands up. "She's not going anywhere, Abbie. She has a lot of money to collect. Now I'm going to go talk to Luis Hernandez and the neighbor who called him when she heard you screaming. Your job is to stop worrying about this. You saved Makenna's life. Twice. You can rest now."

Chapter 65
Handcuffs

I wander out onto the little patio off the family waiting room. The late afternoon sun feels good on my face. I take in a deep breath and try to get myself to relax. I know I'm right about Liv, but I don't know how to prove it.

"Are you Mrs. Palmer?" A candy-striper pokes her head out the sliding glass door. "You have a phone call."

"Who?"

"Your husband." She points to a extension on the outside wall. "Line 2."

I tell Craig about my conversation with Tellez and he says, "Maybe she knows more about the case than she can tell you. You have to trust that she knows what she's doing. Want me to pick you up and we can grab a bite to eat?"

"The hotel's a couple of blocks? I can walk."

"You sure?"

"I need the exercise. I'll check to see if there's any news about Makenna and head over. Can I take a shower?"

"Go ahead. They have complimentary happy hour here so we'll be down at the bar. Just come whenever you're ready. You have the key I gave you?"

I ask the family waiting room receptionist about Makenna and she checks. Nothing yet. I tell her to call the hotel if there's any news.

Moving my limbs feels good, breathing outdoor air. I've only been here a short while, but it feels like weeks. Hospitals are like that.

By the time I walk up the steps to our "suite" I'm feeling more myself, more optimistic about Makenna so when I find Target bags sitting on the sofa in the front part of the suite, I dig for another shirt, clean underwear, and head toward the bathroom.

A knock followed by an exuberant "It's Christie," gets me over to the door to the suite, swinging it open, but it's not Christie. It's Liv. She shoves her way into the room, and as I stumble and twist away, she slams the door behind her.

"Don't," she says in a weary, annoyed voice. She's back to blond hair again, but the thing in her hand is what gets my attention. A gun with a tube screwed into the muzzle. A silencer?

"What — what do you want?" I can barely get out the words.

"I heard you talking at the hospital with the detective." At my look of surprise, she shrugs. "The chapel is right there. It's dark. It's quiet. Voices travel."

"But then you heard she doesn't believe me."

"She's starting to believe, so you've forced me to take a risk here, and I'm not too happy about that. If you play along, I won't hurt your husband or your daughter. If you co-operate, I'll let Makenna live too. I'll take her under my wing and we'll be best friends. Do as you're told, make a small sacrifice, and your family, including your precious little bastard niece, will survive all this. Let's start by going into the bedroom."

"I don't understand."

She wags the gun. "Oh come on, Abbie. Just do what you're told or we'll sit and wait for your family to come back and see what happens then."

She walks toward me and I consider going for the gun, but she says, "You want your daughter to walk in and see your brains scattered all over the wall?"

I give in, back into the bedroom.

She says, "Sit on the bed."

I do it.

She slouches a strap of her designer handbag off her shoulder and when it falls open, she takes out a pair of handcuffs. Throws them at me. "Put those on your feet."

She gives me that thin smile of hers, and I decide to do

what she says. She doesn't want to shoot me or she would have already. She won't risk it because, as Tellez said, she has a lot of money to collect.

Another pair of handcuffs comes out of her purse. "Now your wrists."

I hesitate, my body trilling with adrenaline, thinking moms and babies and cars, if I move fast enough, but my feet are shackled. Why didn't I take the chance when I could?

The gun is cold against my temple. "Cuff your wrists. If you don't, you'll start a chain reaction that will devastate your son when he gets back from Brazil."

She knows everything.

I grapple with the handcuffs hoping they're too small but, of course, they fit. I glance around the room, looking for help, some idea, some weapon. Her purse is on the floor spread open, but no second gun in there, no knife, nothing. Anyway, I just handcuffed myself. I'm going to die.

The telephone rings. She shakes her head. Says, "We'd better hurry."

If only someone would show up. I stop myself there. She's made it clear anyone coming into this hotel room will die.

"Don't lie down," she says. "Not yet."

I didn't realize I was falling back. The only comfort I can glean is when they find me dead, they'll know she did it. And she'll have to flee. Or maybe not. Maybe she's got that figured out too.

In this suite hotel, the sink is near the bathroom, but not in it. She walks over, grabs a glass, fills it with water, and brings it back to me. "Take it."

I take it, and she takes it right back, holding onto its rim. For the first time, I notice she's wearing gloves, the kind surgeons wear. She sets the glass on the nightstand and from her handbag, she pulls a prescription bottle. Shakes it at me. The thought that comes to me is that this woman loves an

262

elaborate plan.

She snaps an easy-open lid and dumps the contents on the top of the nightstand next to the glass. Holds a pill toward me. "A little stronger dose than you're used to. Open wide."

Chapter 66
Pills

I'm waiting for my life to flash, but all I can see is Liv Amaral's smug face. I tighten my lips. She aims the gun at my stomach. She says, "There is only one win for you here."

I open my mouth and she pops in a pill. I tongue it between my cheek and teeth. She brings up another. I do the same with it as I did the first, pretending to swallow, but realize the first one is already softening.

"And one more."

When she puts the glass to my mouth, I gulp the water fast, hoping none of the pills will slip from their place.

"You can lie down now."

I do it.

"You know how Ativan works, don't you? Let's wait just a minute." Now that I'm on the way to being sedated, she gently drops her gun onto her open purse on the floor and goes about arranging the glass, the prescription bottle, and scattering the pills, sprinkling a few on the ground.

I turn my head away while she is doing this, trying to spit what's left of the Ativan out of my mouth. Three isn't enough to kill me, even at a large dosage level. Maybe she just wants me quiet. Maybe she isn't going to kill me after all.

"There," she says, satisfied with her work.

She reaches into her handbag again and catches me watching her. "It's a beautiful piece of leather, isn't it?" She runs her red-tipped finger around the monogram, then reaches in and brings out a hypodermic needle. "This will be more efficient than force-feeding you pills you hide under your tongue. Just a little pinch between your toes."

The gun scared me; the needle is worse because I

suddenly know her scheme. She'll take the handcuffs off before she leaves, and Craig and Christie will come back to the hotel and find me. They will believe I killed myself, and I will have done to my family, my daughter, what my mother did to me.

I have to act, and now.

She advances – so damned pleased with herself – I do the only thing I can do in a bed with my hands and feet restrained. I tighten my body like a spring and roll. I can't control speed so I count on surprise. She sees it coming and leaps back. Grinning as if this was a joke.

I crash onto the floor, bones jarring. Keep rolling. She leans down, laughing, flourishing the hypodermic.

I knock into her. She stumbles, her foot landing in her purse. Panic flashes across her face. Her toe catches on the strap, and she tumbles forward, smack onto her knees, the needle hurtling out of her hand, bouncing and spinning away.

Like a worm, I scoot back to the bed, press my shoulder against it, and pivot so I can arch my back, and get my feet underneath my body, cuffs at wrist and ankle digging into flesh.

She stretches out on the carpet, grasping for the hypodermic.

Crouching on my feet, balancing against the mattress, I launch at her. She turns just as I bang into her and she topples over, both now flat on our backs.

Her gun gleams inside her purse not two inches from her hand. She grabs for it, turns toward me, but I'm holding my cuffed legs together like a mallet, I swing them around and land a blow hard on her chin. She shrieks and falls.

I scramble on top of her, press the handcuff chain at her neck.

Thank you, maple-syrup pancake diet. My weight is a weapon, keeping me on top and in control. I can't get to the gun, but neither can she.

"I can't breathe," she chokes out and squirms, but I hold firm. We're at an impasse, and I don't know what to do next. Wait for Craig and Christie? No. All I hope is adrenaline can counter the Ativan in my system and maybe holler for help. I open my mouth to scream, and she twists and squirms underneath me.

On the carpet is the spray of pills Liv used to stage my "suicide." My right hand can't quite reach them. I shift my body. The chain loosens at Liv's neck, and she elbows me, fighting back, but when I press her neck with my forearm, she quiets. I stretch for the pills again and use my fingers to scrape them closer. Liv squirms beneath me but I'm able to squeeze the tablets between thumb and index finger and drop them into my palm.

I say, "Time for you to take your medicine." She tries to turn her head, but I use my nails to claw open her mouth and smash two pills against her teeth, shouting as loud as I can.

There's a ruckus at the door, but I don't move a muscle. I don't trust Liv not to go for her gun the minute I remove the pressure. I hear people rushing into the suite and then into the bedroom, and there's Detective Tellez, talking on her phone; and once again I'm hearing sirens.

Chapter 67
Water and Sun

Saturday, June 1, 2002

Yesterday, Detective Tellez took Liv Amaral into custody with the help of the local cops. The detective had come to the hotel on her way back home to tell me that she'd faxed Liv's picture to Turner in jail. She wanted me to know that he'd said the picture wasn't Marlene, the woman he met with, and therefore Liv was off the suspect's list. I would've told her Liv was a mistress of disguise, but I guess she figured that out when she arrived at the hotel and found a gun, a hypodermic, and me in handcuffs holding her down.

After the detective got everything under control, Craig, Christie, and I went back to the hospital to check on Makenna. There was no change in her status, so we spent another night at the Embassy Suites, but in a different room from my "take-down" of Liv, the criminal mastermind, Craig and I on the queen in the bedroom, Christie on the pull-out in the front room. Craig wanted to talk about everything that's happened and what it might mean, but since I haven't sorted anything out for myself yet, I pretended to be asleep.

This morning, we all woke groggy, exhausted, yet relieved, knowing that Liv Amaral was being grilled in some sterile interrogation room by Detective Tellez and her cohorts, and now, while Craig and Christie eat the complimentary breakfast, I take one of their cell phones out to the pool to call and find out how it's going.

When the detective answers, and I tell her who it is, she says, "Abbie Palmer. Who knew?"

"What's that supposed to mean?"

"Well, your assumptions about Liv seem to be right on the money. I don't have the full story yet, but she's the one. Turner's being brought over to the station to take a look at Liv. He'll give a statement, and then he'll be released. He's heading up to the hospital as soon as that's done. How's she doing?"

"The same."

"Sorry to hear that, but I'm sure she'll be okay. I'll be heading back up once I get things squared away down here. We got some results from Makenna's blood. The technicians up at the hospital discovered the date-rape drug, Rohypnol, in her system. Evidence, as I see it, that someone drugged her just before the gas leak occurred."

"That's so – I don't know – fiendish."

"That's a good word for it."

"So what's Liv saying?"

"Not much. She has a lawyer, but once we have all the evidence compiled, we'll see what the D.A. can do. And Abbie, I found a connection between the junkie, Julian Denzer, the guy who was renting that apartment in San Dimas, and Liv. They went to middle school together. Oh, and just one more thing. You need to call your friend Ben."

After we hang up, I waver about calling Ben. It's not just the kiss between us, but the awkwardness the last time we saw each other. The kiss meant something to me. The intimacy with someone other than Craig was thrilling. The feeling lingers, and I don't want to lose it. I sit back in my chair, empty my mind, and let the morning sun warm me. After a while – I don't know how long – I sit up and call information for Ben's phone number since I'm not using my own cell. And where is that cell?

"Hullo." His voice is low and husky.

"It's Abbie."

"Oh, jees, Abbie, finally. What's going on? I've been so worried I called your Detective Tellez."

"I know. Sorry it's taken so long to call you back. I've

been busy."

"She said you had some trouble up there, but you're both okay. What's happened? I haven't seen anything on the TV or radio."

"I'm surprised. It's kind of big." Then I tell him a condensed version of everything that's happened, ending with the grueling wait for Makenna to wake up.

When I'm done, he says, "Jees. You should have gotten me to go up with you. I would've gone."

"I thought about it, but it was early and I knew you'd been working. I was going up there to get DNA samples, that was all. I didn't really figure out that Liv might be the bad guy until I was on the road."

"Still, I would've been glad to go with you."

Silence between us for a moment, then I say, "Craig and Christie are up here with me."

"They are? Good. Of course."

"I don't have Makenna's version of events yet, but I'll tell you the story when I get home." I won't let myself think, if she wakes up. And where is home?

"Good. I hope she and Billy had time to talk."

"Me too."

When I hang up, I notice Christie is walking toward me, waving to get my attention. I can't tell if she's upset or not, so I hurry over.

Chapter 68
Awake

Makenna's face is ashen, her hair curling against the pillow. She's sitting up, sipping water through a straw when we crowd in. The doctor has given her the okay for visitors.

"Abbie," she tries to shout when she sees me and starts to sob. I cry too, rushing to hug her.

Behind me, I hear Craig pulling Christie out of the room.

After a moment, I say, "You're okay."

She nods. Swipes her hand across her eyes. "What's going on? Nobody's told me anything. How's Billy? Have you talked to Turner?"

So it falls to me to tell her the story and to break the news about her grandfather. These are the things I have to do if I'm going to be a continent instead of an island.

I tell her everything I can think of, from deciding to go back to Val Verde to finding her on the kitchen floor and dragging her out, from feeling overwhelmed in the waiting room to taking down – that's the phrase I use – Liv Amaral. I want to ask her what happened after Ben and I left the house in Val Verde, but it can wait. I tell her that's enough for now, and she should rest.

"What about Turner?" she asks.

"I think they have to let him go."

A big grin cracks her face. I tell her I'll wait until she's asleep before I leave. She's snoring sweetly before ten minutes pass.

•◊•

In the afternoon, we go back to see Makenna. She looks

rested and happy to see us. One of the nurses has brought chairs from other rooms so Craig, Christie, and I all have seats. I want them to hear about Makenna's visit with Liv and Billy so they can feel included. Plus I want them to know her, appreciate her, and love her as I do.

"Okay, Makenna, you heard what happened to me, now I'm anxious to find out what happened to you, everything, the whole story, and start with Liv. Did she really invite you to drive to Indian Wells?"

Makenna looks sheepish. "No, she didn't. You hadn't called her back, so I did it for you. I got her number off the answering machine. She said she couldn't talk because they were going on vacation the next day, so I decided to go up that night." She hesitates.

"Go on," I encourage her.

"She was so nice when the police came. She told them I was Billy's granddaughter, and I was supposed to stop at the gate, and I was afraid since it was the same guard we'd seen before, the one who wouldn't let us in. It was a total lie, but since the cops bought it, I didn't care."

"She lied to you about calling me too."

"She promised she would and said she'd tell you she'd invited me to join them and that she'd also invite you to come up to Val Verde too. When you showed up, I thought that's what she did. Then you acted kind of weird about everything."

"I never got that phone call."

"I know that now, but you never check your cell, so I thought that's what happened."

"So how was she with you? And with Billy?"

"Actually, she was great. I think that's really all I paid attention to for a while, that she was patient and kind to him. And she was nice to me. I helped her pack for the trip to Val Verde, and she gave me a suitcase too, a Louis Vuitton. I got to look through her dresses and she gave me that sundress I was wearing and some sandals, though they were

271

a little tight."

"So any suspicions you had about her being a gold-digger just went away?"

Makenna rolls her eyes. "Maybe, a little bit, but Abbie, she seemed to care about me and about Billy, until after you and Ben left. Then she seemed different, more impatient."

At the mention of Ben, I glance at Craig because I'd left him out of my own narrative. Never used the word "we." I say now, "Ben's the apartment manager who was nice enough to drive me up there when Makenna stole my car."

"I didn't steal it. You let me drive it all the time."

"Okay," I say. "You borrowed it. Go on with your story. What happened after we left?" I don't look over at Craig this time. This is a topic for later. No, this isn't even a topic.

"I hung out with Billy – I have some stuff to tell you about – he definitely remembers Virginia Gifford."

She directs a sly smile at me, and I shiver. "Go on."

"After you left, Liv said she had things to do, call her producer, arrange another session, something like that, and went into their bedroom. Then Billy took a nap, and Catalina – she cleans and cooks for them when they come – came over to cook us dinner, and Liv played some of her music."

"So nothing suspicious happened?" this from Craig. Sitting forward in his chair, arms on his knees, he seems as fascinated as I am.

"No, and not in the morning either. We had breakfast and then Liv said she had to go down to L.A. and would I mind staying with Billy and I said I'd love to, and then – and then that's all I remember until I woke up here."

We all sit back in our chairs. We all know what happened next.

After a moment, I ask, "So, Makenna, are you tired or can you tell us what Billy said about my mother?"

272

Chapter 69
Stories

This is the moment I've been waiting for, to hear what Billy might remember about my mother. I stretch forward now, waiting while Makenna changes her position, blows her nose, sips water, her eyes sparkling at me.

Finally, she says, "Sometimes, Billy had trouble remembering who I was and even Liv – I think maybe she was fooling with his medications – and when I asked him about Virginia, he didn't really respond, then I remembered the old guy at the country home said they called her 'Gin,' so I asked about Gin. And he got this slow little grin on his face, and said something like, 'Gin, Gin, Gin. She was my girl.'"

My arms are tightly crossed in front of me, me listening with my whole body.

"They met in Palm Springs, Abbie, when that picture was taken of her for the cover of *Life* magazine. He actually knocked her into the swimming pool. That's how she got that whole wet-water look. The photographer snapped the picture at the moment she climbed up the ladder. Billy said she was magnificent, but some guy called him out because he was black and had disrespected her by pushing her into the pool. But she moved right in between them, stopped the fight. He said for him, it was love at first sight."

"He remembered all that?"

"It was so amazing. Liv was, I don't know, somewhere else, maybe on the phone, and we were on the porch, and for a while, it was like he wasn't sick at all. He brought her up there to Val Verde, you know, for the Fourth of July. Everybody in Val Verde would meet at the park and Billy would get up on stage and do his routine, and then they had fireworks. But something happened to Virginia there, and he had to take her home. Someone got after her for being white. Told her to leave Billy alone. You know this used to be where black people from L.A. came for vacation. Everybody was black."

"Oh," is all I can say.

"Well, she found out she was pregnant not too long after that. She didn't know what to do, so Billy took her on a train to Louisiana, but they couldn't travel together on the train. He borrowed a porter's — I think it was a porter's — uniform and was able to sneak in to visit her. He said even though he was in pictures, white people never recognized him. It was like he was invisible. Anyway, they got to Beauport and his sister, who I thought was my grandmother Miriam, took Gin in and she had my mother there."

I let out a long low breath. Makenna is watching me expectantly, and I meet her eyes, and nod because, of course, my mother was Olita's mother. I think somewhere deep inside me, I knew it all along.

"She left the baby," Makenna goes on. "She told Billy there was no other way, and they came back to California. Abbie, this is where it gets really sad. Billy thought they'd stay together, get a little apartment somewhere like Long Beach or Redondo Beach, and see each other as much as they could, even visit their baby a couple of times a year, but Gin said she couldn't do it, and it wasn't because she didn't love him or because she was worried about her career. She was depressed. Billy said she was broken."

"Broken," I say out loud. I'm crying, Makenna's crying. Christie gets up and hugs Makenna, then she comes over and hugs me.

"What's going on in here?" the voice booms somewhere behind me and I turn to see Turner Bethune. Makenna whoops and tries to get out of bed, but he's at her side folding her into his big arms. Craig comes up behind me, puts his hand on my shoulder and squeezes.

Turner holds Makenna at arm's length and says,

"You're looking pretty good. How you feeling?"

"Totally great," she says.

I get up and say, "We'll let you two have some time together."

"No, stay, please," says Turner.

"Stay," agrees Makenna. "I want him to tell us about the woman."

"What woman?" asks Christie. "There's more?"

"What I want to know," I say, "is why in the world did you write a $10,000 check to Julian Denzer?"

Craig indicates his chair, and Turner nods, and sits. "I gave that check to Marlene, the woman I flew back from Austin to help, the one who now turns out to be Liv Amaral. She told me Denzer was a lawyer who could get her brother out of the general population in prison, but they had to move fast because he was being harrassed. I won't go into the details, but it was a loan. I met her through my death penalty work. We'd talked on some project before, and she'd been worried then her brother was going to kill himself or get killed. I gave her my card in case I could help, and she called and said she'd talked to this lawyer, and she needed money. She was pretty messed up herself."

"You came back to LA to help her, but didn't go home?" I ask.

"She wanted to talk, and so that's what we did. Now I know it was all a set-up." He shakes his head. "Thank you, Abbie, and you too, Makenna, for believing in my innocence." Turner stands and I stand as he turns his burly body on me. He whispers, "I only wish Olita could be here with us."

"Me, too. You don't know how much I mean that either." I let go of him and add, "We're going. Come on, Craig, Christie, let's give these two time alone." I kiss Makenna's forehead; we say our good-byes, then stumble around chairs and out the door leaving Turner and the girl to talk about everything they've been through.

Chapter 70
Old Spice and Whiskey

I come home from my Saturday morning class. Not one I'm teaching, but one I'm taking at Art Center. Painting for Beginners. I've been through two funerals — Olita's, Billy's — and Turner and Makenna have moved to a large townhouse not far away. I pull into the carport at the Tiki Palms, and Ben's two girls race over as soon as I climb out of the car. He's got them for the summer to help make up for the fact they've moved to another state. He's in heaven. Sometimes I baby-sit. The girls come over and sleep in my bed, and remind me of Makenna and how she looked like an angel against the white sheets.

"Hey, Blanca. Dee. What's up?" I ask.

"You've got company," Delia says, pulling on my hand, dragging me toward the courtyard.

"I do? Who?"

As we come around the gnarly old agave, palm tree, bird-of-paradise plant conglomerate at the corner of my apartment, I spot an old man sitting on the top step of my little porch. He's African-American with grizzled hair, grizzled beard, wearing a tan windbreaker. When he sees us, he grabs the cane that's laying next to him and pulls himself up.

"Hi there," I say, wondering who this guy could be. A friend of Makenna's? Turner's?

"Hi there back. I am happy to meet you," he says. "You're Gin's little girl, for positive. You have the look of her, Abbie. Jack told me you did. My, my, do I miss your mother."

I stare at him, unsure that I've heard him right. "Gin?"

"Virginia. I called her Gin. Name's Ambrose Lipscomb, Ambie to my friends." He holds out his hand and I take it.

It's cool and rough and strong. His smile takes me in.

The girls hang on my arms and stare up at this old guy, wondering what's going on. My heart is racing. What have I done to deserve this?

Ben comes out of his place. He waves at us and I wave back. Our eyes meet and there's a close, warm feeling to it. I'm glad things aren't awkward between us. We've talked and agreed we can be friends, special friends with a bond of knowing that in another time, in a different circumstance, we could have been more. Just this is enough for me.

I invite Ambie into my apartment. I've kept it for the summer as a studio. It's my island. I've moved back to Woodbine Street and things are better between Craig and me. We're going to counseling.

When Ambie walks into my place, no tidier than it's ever been, he leans with two hands on his cane and looks around.

"Hm-hm-hm," he says. "This puts me to mind of my own place in the fifties. I think mine was a little more organized." He glances at me to see if I smile, which I do.

"Can I get you something? A diet Coke, water?" I ask.

"You got any whiskey?"

I hold up my hands, shake my head because I don't. He laughs. "Never mind. I brought my own," and he pulls out one of those small silver flasks that fit neatly in a hip pocket. "Billy gave me this a long time ago. He was a good man, Billy was. I'm sorry I couldn't make it to the funeral. I was undergoing some treatments for my cancer. Now I'm on the mend."

"Good. I'm glad. Please sit here." I pull out the rocker.

He eases himself into the seat and rocks back and forth, then says, "Those two, your mother and Billy, they was crazy about each other, but honey, it just wasn't meant to be. The times were all wrong. Jack and I were lucky, we could do a workaround, but I don't think your mama was a lucky woman. Things just never seemed to work out for her, except maybe when she had you. That was the first time I saw her smile since she told me she was pregnant with Billy's child."

I soak this in, my mother's smile just for me.

"You were such a lively child, so full of life, so curious about everything. You asked me a million questions. You remember me at all?"

I study his face. I like it. Different from Billy's, rounder, softer, his eyes alert and warm. Do I remember him? Something nibbles at the corner of my brain. I say, "I think I do."

"Well, you were four years old when I last saw you so I guess you might not remember. Abbie my girl, I've brought you something special."

He stares at me for long moment. I wonder what could make me happier than just sitting here listening to him talk. I can see the moisture in his eyes.

"Hold on," he says and reaches inside his jacket and pulls out a stack of letters tied with twine. "These aren't love letters or anything romantic. These are the letters your mother wrote to me after she married your father. I was kind of her confessor. I think you should have them now."

I take them from him and feel their weight. My heart is lifting. "Thank you, Ambie. This is more than I could ever hope for."

I study his face, and the nibble in my brain blooms into a memory. Someone coming into my room, scooping me out of my bed, and carrying me through the kitchen where I thought my mother was baking cookies. It was Ambie who saved me on the day my mother died.

I lean down to hug him – he smells of Old Spice and whiskey – and whisper, "I remember you now, and my mother. You made her laugh."

Author's Note

My writing journey began at eleven when I scribbled my first (incomplete) novel in purple ink about the Twellingtons Twins. I felt launched when, at eighteen, I won second place in the *Atlantic Monthly* High School Creative Writing contest, but very quickly found myself on a kind of writing waiting list. Waiting to learn, waiting for advice, waiting for time, waiting for encouragement, waiting for confidence, it was a list I stayed on for years because I was too busy living and too afraid to give up "real life" for something I felt was basically selfish. To be any good, I would have to spend more time than seemed fair to those around me, and underlying that, was my belief that all I would achieve by writing was to embarrass myself. However, the desire to put words on paper never went away and sometime in the late 1980s, I began to add writing time into my life.

Over the years, I've garnered information for *What Came Before* from so many sources it's hard to pin down, drawing on my own half century of reading, including African-American history. However, any time I've been in doubt about a fact, I've searched the internet for answers. To list every place I've visited is impossible, but I've spent much time on Wikipedia to find out about the chitlin' circuit and the comedians and performers who serve as inspiration for my characters as well as reading about historical events to gain a sense of the 1940s and '50s. I've created a bulletin board in my writing room so that I have a sense of all my characters' lives and have included pictures of Joan Bennett, Marilyn Monroe, Nipsy Russell, Redd Foxx, Jack Benny, and Sammy Davis Jr, Tavis Smiley, Malcom X, Bill Cosby, and Julianne Moore, my model for Abbie. None of the persons in this novel are real. Any similarity to persons real or imagined is completely coincidental and unintentional.

The places are based on real places. However, liberties have been taken in their descriptions, and there is no Marion Drive in Pasadena, no Tiki Palms or Woodbine Street in South Pasadena, no Beauport in Louisiana, no Cascades in Indian Wells. Val Verde does exist and there may be a grocery store there, but the one in this story is made up.

What Came Before has taken me twelve years to complete, writing in fits and starts, never quite abandoning it, clinging to it as something I had to finish if only to prove to myself I could. It's traveled with me to writing workshops in Iowa, Oregon, Vermont, and Banff. It's lost many first chapter contests, been read and critiqued by at least three separate writing groups, and declined by mentors. It's been told in first person and third and then back to first, in present-tense and past-tense, and back to present. It's contained two narrators, one in present day and one who remembered the past, but the past was eventually jettisoned. It's benefited from my experience in writing screenplays and flash fiction. It's not a deep book, it's not the most literary of novels, but I hope it is entertaining and somewhat thought-provoking.

Research & Acknowledgments

I owe the completion of this book to a great many people who have given me encouragement and advice over the years including Tim Degani, Nicholas Degani, Hillary Degani, Doris Degani, Jane Aegerter Marshall, Claire Belanger, Gale Inadomi, Larry Inadomi, Estelle Underwood, Trish Heckman, Cyndie Nathanson, Ken Nathanson, Joan Clark, Camille Gooderham Campbell, K.C. Ball, Betsy Weigandt, Rhea Wooten, Bev Callister, Sharon Trotter-Martin, Emily Choate, Diana James, Judith Carter, Louisa Nelson, and Judy Taylor. Some have been there for me throughout the process or showed up just at the moment I needed the most encouragement. To all of you, thank you.

I also want to thank the writers who were willing to read the novel before the final draft was completed and offered wonderful comments on the story and the writing, including Kathy Fish, Clifford Garstang, Christopher Allen, Bonnie ZoBell, Susan Tepper, RK Biswas, Tara Laskowski, Stefanie Freele, Robert Swartwood, and K.C. Ball.

Some books I've purchased to read, or that I've referred to about Hollywood's past, are:

The Century of Change
edited by Richard B. Stolley

Hollywood Then and Now
by Rosemary Lord

Inside Hollywood
by John Morgan Wilson

Los Angeles A to Z
by Leonard Pitt and Dale Pitt

Los Angeles Then and Now
by Rosemary Lord

Palm Springs Babylon
by Ray Mungo

Palm Springs, The Landscape, The History, The Lore
by Mary Jo Churchwell

The Fabulous Century, 1940-1950, Volume V
Editors of Time-Life Books

The Fabulous Century, 1950-1960, Volume VI
Editors of Time-Life Books

The Fifties
by David Halberstam

The Good Old Days, America in the '40s and '50s
Editors of Time-Life Books

About the Author

G ay Degani lives with her husband in a Victorian house in southern California where flocks of parrots congregate at dusk in the surrounding oak and camphor trees.

Three of her flash pieces have been nominated for a Pushcart Prize, *Something about L.A.* won the 11th Annual Glass Woman Prize, and several of her other stories have either placed or been short-listed in various contests.

Pure Slush Books released her collection of stories, *Rattle of Want*, (November 2015) and a short collection, *Pomegranate*, featuring eight stories around the theme of mothers and daughters, was self-published in 2009. She blogs at *Words in Place* where a list of her published work can be found.

Other books from
Truth Serum Press

Luck and Other Truths
ISBN: 978-1-925101-77-5

Rain Check
ISBN: 978-1-925536-09-6

happyme@t.us
ISBN: 978-1-925536-07-2

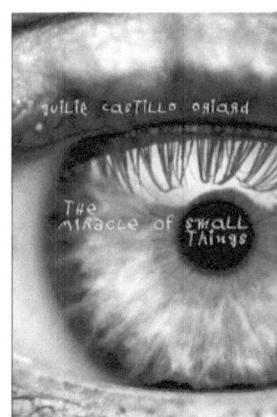

Miracle of Small Things
ISBN: 978-1-925101-73-7

La Ronde
ISBN: 978-1-925101-64-5

Based on True Stories
ISBN: 978-1-925101-75-1

Find all Truth Serum Press paperbacks and eBooks at
https://truthserumpress.net/catalogue/